"The Old Writer has come to the end of words..."
(W. S. Burroughs – "The Western Lands")

For
SUE

And for
ALISTAIR FRUISH
(For holding the gun to my head)

"Book Thirteen"

A. William James

Copyright © A. William James 2012

A. William James has asserted his right to be identified as the author of this work in accordance with the Copyright, Designs and Patents act 1988

Page 54: "Daybreak on the land..." quoted from "Playing in the Band" copyright ©1971: Grateful Dead, Robert Hunter, Warner Bros.

First publication
LEPUS BOOKS
2012

ISBN: 978 0 9572535 0 6

This novel is entirely a work of fiction. Names, characters and incidents portrayed are the work of the author's imagination. Any perceived resemblance to actual events, localities, or persons living or dead, is significant of paranoia.

All rights reserved. No part of this publication may be reproduced, stored in a retrieval system, or transmitted in any form, or by any means, without the prior permission of the publisher. Wanton disregard of this injunction may attract considerable bad karma.

LEPUS BOOKS

www.lepusbooks.co.uk

one

Sullen, he walked an hour despoiling virgin snow. A high cold cry disrupted the analgesic rhythm of his footfall. He looked up. Buzzards circled overhead.

A cartoon omen like that could spook a psyche sensitised to dread by a crafty toke of filthy GM skunk, but The Old Writer had practice dodging paranoia. He ducked from the path into the dead cover of the wood. The damp chill caught on his chest. He coughed. Somewhere through the pillared trees a mocking deer coughed back.

When he was a child without a thought of being old, and words were just breadcrumbs to be followed to The End, buzzards had been exotic birds, border guards to the wild highlands where anything might happen. Now these raptors were commonplace. They no more provoked the imaginations of the bored grandchildren to whom he routinely pointed them out than did the ragged proletariat of starlings that flocked the aerials and eaves of their domestic 'Gormenghast'.

The cult of Leepus had secured their family seat. A dozen books in half as many years of furious creativity. A *tsunami* of cash. The Old Writer had wanted to buy an island, preferably with lighthouse, but Helen hated boats. They had bought the big old house instead. It had numberless thick-walled rooms in which to muffle small children and their interminable distress, with an acre of garden to encourage physical competence and sustain the organic diversity essential to thriving growth.

It had the Tower of Babble, too. That had swung the deal for him.

The tower, a local grandee's architectural pretension, jutted ornate above a clumsy geometry of gables and moss-clumped roofs. Up there in his aloof turret a scribbler could think and smoke, smoke and write, and for occasional relaxation stare baleful over the mundane world beyond its ivied windows while he rolled another smoke.

Backed against the ancient wildwood edge by six lanes of constant traffic, The Village of Idiots skulked at bay in a foggy depression. Their house was its eastern outpost. The trees began one field from their paddock boundary and spread to the ring road that encircled the exhausted industrial town of Dismal, an indifferent reality into which The Old Writer had, sixty years before, slipped from Dead Doris's cosy womb.

In his childhood memory the forest was a damp entanglement of briars, where dead dark plantations of larch concealed sporadic grotesque oaks. There were makeshift car parks – the decayed concrete foundations of wartime ammunition dumps – where damp titty-books covered turd piles and occasional suicides choked in fume-filled cars, or kicked their last fandangos dangled by their braces from low branches where no bird had ever sung. There were rumours of a feral bull, witch covens and naked rites, an IRA arms-cache unearthed. Now this unwholesome territory was gentrified, opened to the light and paved with wheelchair friendly paths: an exercise yard for the urban rookeries of debt slaves.

Evading the buzzards' surveillance, he had followed the trail of a foraging pheasant through a snowy hazel coppice. Now a simultaneous awareness of the other's presence froze both The Old Writer and the fowl in suspended animation. He anticipated the inevitable clap of panic – the prey bird lurching upward, clattering through thin branches for the safety of the sky – but, though the pheasant crouched and tensed, takeoff was aborted.

A tiny whip of ginger violence lashed from ambush. A beak gaped, croaked once. Wings drummed. An eye rolled in its field of red and, redder yet, a thin jet of throat blood squirted, pumped by the bird's failing heart. Once; twice; three times. Dead.

The Old Writer acknowledged this perfect savagery with a tiny gasp of awe. Rearing erect a full six inches, a furry prick rigid with bloodlust, the weasel challenged him. No fear. Just scorn: its tiny black stare withering.

The Old Writer blinked and looked away. A patrolling helicopter throbbed above the motorway's tidal drone. A dog barked. A distant chainsaw chewed the frozen air. Calmed by these remote sounds of life continuing, he looked back. Assassin and victim were gone from the killing ground; only a cold-blooded epitaph remained, splashed scarlet on a snow-white shroud.

Grey sky shed shaved-ice dandruff. Done now with wildness and cold, The Old Writer stepped lighter on a path for home. The pheasant had taken his bullet. The buzzards could forget him now.

two

'It's no good getting arsey about it.'
Helen dabbed at the stinging cut above his eye.
'You built the bloody thing for him.'
'All the more reason he should've picked another target. Why not Cracked Jack—or better still the vile mother that spawned the little terrorist, or her fucked up girlfriend?'
His wife splashed iodine vindictive.
'Don't call our daughter vile. And if the lad had hit your dad on the head he'd have killed the poor old sod.'
'The downside escapes me.'
'It's clean.'
Helen reached for a towel, dried her hands.

'Stick a plaster on it. Then find young Cormac and tell him you were joking about 'spiking his sick little head on a pole to warn off other feral-child assassins'.'

'That would be a lie.'

'Tell him anyway.'

'Okay—but only if you accept the ultimate responsibility is yours.'

'What?'

'You grew that inedible fucking peasant food. A compost heap littered with half-frozen turnips is an obvious stash of trebuchet ammunition. What psychopathic ten-year-old could resist?'

Helen – The Unseen Hand, as The Old Writer characterised his wife with affectionate but sincere resentment – disdained his bait. Seconds later, the siren howl of the vacuum cleaner tormented him from a nearby room. He got up, reached instinctive for the coffeepot, and then – remembering the misery evoked by caffeine in an invalid bowel – for the canister of gentler *maté* instead. He poured boiled water onto the insipid substitute aware of a sullen presence in the kitchen door, turned to the stick-thin puckish boy shifting uncomfortably there and raised a throbbing eyebrow.

'Sorry, Granddad.'

'You should be you little savage. Could have caved-in my skull, made me a drooling cabbage.'

Cormac grinned, unconvinced by his victim's 'face of unforgiving wrath'.

'Wicked shot though, weren't it?'

'Wasn't it, you ignorant chav. But yeah—good job we didn't build the ballista, or I'd be nailed to the bloody wall.'

A moment's hesitation. The boy decided to push his luck.

'You said we could capture Carthage next time I was over.'

'I did. Let me do an hour's work, then come and find me in the tower. We should have time before your mother picks you up.'

'Right.'

A glint of anxiety troubled dark eyes.

'What?'

'Nothing—just Mum says they're going to chuck us out of our house 'cause Angie messed up with her ASBO thing again. So we might have to move into the caravan for a while.'

'Cool,' The Old Writer said, wing-shadow flickering in the periphery of awareness. 'Be good to have you all around.'

'Rome does not tolerate failure in her generals.'

The digital senate was excoriating. His grandson was not that chilled about it either.

'You dickhead.'

Cormac's thin lip curled.

'I told you to keep Scipio out of the fighting. He had seven stars. He was our faction heir. But no, Captain Wow gets him trashed by war elephants in a suicide attack, and the rest of our army routs.'

In defence, The Old Writer might have countered that their general had died leading a heroic cavalry decoy to draw the lethal elephants away from the vulnerable Cretan archers. All would be good if the fire arrows had not sent the terrible beasts amok. It was a gamble that went bad. On such tiny variables the tide of history turns, etceteras, etceteras.

But the boy was a black hole of betrayal. Silent contrition was the only response to his furious disappointment.

'It took years to build that army. Messana and Syracuse are rioting because we took their best units for the siege. Now Carthage'll never be our capital.'

The chair slammed back against the filing cabinet. The boy paused at the door. His face was white, clenched tight. His hand cut the air, a gladius drawn to strike.

'I hate—'

Head bowed, The Old Writer waited for the cruel blade to slip between his ribs, but his grandson spared him the killing stroke.

'I hate fucking elephants.'

The storm passed on, thundered down the tower's wooden stair.

The Old Writer took a breath. Cormac was an all-or-nothing kid: a joy when life rolled sweet, but in adversity – as had too often been the case in his short span – a demon of indiscriminate rage. The boy's character needed development. It would require a deft authorial hand to write him a survivable story arc, not to mention a chunk of luck.

He saved and quit the game, shut down the computer. His soul cried for a fat oily spliff but honour demanded denial. He did not officially smoke now. Vaping got him by. A periodic suck at his Chinese electronic ciggie maintained his nicotine addiction and kept his graveyard cough at bay. Maturity was the art of compromise.

The Old Writer compromised now. The cigarette's tip glowed LED-blue, cool in the gloom of the office. Its vapour was thin and tasted clinical.

'Will you hurry up and get down here. Everyone's waiting to eat,' called Helen from the foot of the stair.

She sounded tired. He pushed back his chair, braced for Pandemonium.

three

A house is a book; it needs characters to fill its pages and give its story life, an author to find meaning in the chaos of its days. The Old Writer claimed his was the controlling mastermind but deferred responsibility for the tedious plot-minutiae to Helen.

He watched his wife manage the table: one reluctant grandchild encouraged to eat its pasta with a word, another dissuaded with a glance from wiping sauce in her brother's hair, a wrist-slap for Obscene Irene who – covered by her daughter's distraction – extruded a licentious claw beneath the tabletop horizon in a sly grab for Cracked Jack's balls. Oblivious, the old man spooned vinegar through the toothless hole in his beard.

'Spoilsport,' said Obscene Irene and cackled.

Down the table, Helen rolled her eyes. The Old Writer winked. She smiled: a flash of the shy girl who still lived inside the matriarch, who had made him love her all those years ago, give her all those fucking babies.

'What are you gawping at you gormless twat?' spat Cracked Jack vinegary.

'Me?'

The Old Writer was unprepared for his father's sudden assault.

'No other twats here.'

'That's what you think, handsome.'

Irene grabbed the old man's hand, tugged it to her lap.

'Get off!' Jack squawked. 'Bloody old whore.'

'Granddad, please. Little ears hear every word.'

Vile Viola raised one stout bejewelled finger to red pursed lips. Her massive bosom quaked, flushed hot.

Christ, thought The Old Writer; how did his daughter ever grow so fucking huge?

'What's a twat?'

Cormac raised a curious eyebrow, feigned innocence for the wind-up.

'Twat, twat, twat,' the excited baby chanted, flung a fistful of tagliatelle into its grandfather's face.

He wiped off the mess with the dishcloth Helen tossed him. The laughter was general but Cracked Jack's mirth was raw with spite.

Trapped in genetic reflection, father and eldest son had spent their lives at war. Old Jack was always an angry man. Secret ambitions frustrated by domesticity, he begrudged his children the liberty he had never claimed. His eldest son struggled against paternal oppression throughout his pre-pubescent years, until the culture clash of a 'sixties adolescence rendered their worldviews irreconcilable. Violent rebellion established his inalienable right to read whatever 'stupid drivel' he chose, and they had coexisted, for the six or seven years he remained in his childhood home, in a state of armed neutrality.

Four decades of adult independence passed in mutual indifference, punctuated routinely at family events by their boorish clash of prejudice, hostilities moderated only by a shared consideration of frail Doris' craving for peace.

The gloves had come off when the death of his wife forced Jack – now officially demented – to suffer the humiliation of his son's cold charity. Weirdly, the vitriol his father now spewed uncensored provoked in The Old Writer only condescension, an exasperated love.

'It's none of my business, but you're a fucking mug, mate. If my old man talked that way to me I'd give the cunt a slap.'

ASBO Angie crumpled her empty lager can, drew sharp on a skinny roll-up.

The Old Writer had joined his daughter's girlfriend outside the kitchen door, seduced by the opportunity to cadge a drag on her after-dinner ciggie. He shivered now in the sharp night air, feeble beside the stocky woman in her sleeveless vest.

'He's my father, goddamnit—not some detainee in Bagram.'

'Fuckin' soft hippy.'

Angie's eye twitched. She exhaled smoke, condemned him with a sneer. He took her crumpled cigarette, sucked the last comfort from it.

Whatever other damage she inflicted, he thought, at least this most recent of his daughter's lovers would not leave her with another child. Perhaps that was the attraction. Four kids in ten years, abandoned by three deadbeat dads – a junkie, a compulsive gambler, a halfwit fuck-up musician – Vile Viola was unlucky in love, to say the least. It remained to be seen if a volatile ex-Military Policewoman, with two Afghan tours, a medical discharge and drink-related antisocial tendencies, had the potential to break the pattern.

'So, Cormac tells me you're having problems with the council.'

'Yeah, sorta. Fuckin' hick neighbours start on the kids with their homophobic crap again. So I torch their fuckin' car to modernise their attitude.'

'Jesus, Angie.'

'I know—I'm a stupid bitch. They can't prove shit but they go crying to the council anyway. Claim I've threatened to hang one of their idiot spawn at random from a lamppost the next time anyone says 'dyke'.'

'Have you?'

'Yeah—and now we're getting evicted.'

She shrugged, defied disapprobation.

'Fuck 'em. Serve 'em right if a tribe of pikey scum moves in when we go.'

The Old Writer failed to suppress a chuckle of admiration. He should have been appalled. The woman was a psychopath uncompromised by political correctness, but she had a certain violent charm that he found peculiarly attractive.

four

The kitchen was chilly and grey, a freezing fog outside. The Old Writer watched the kettle for a full five thoughtless minutes before he remembered to switch it on. His head ached and his stomach churned: the dyspeptic aftermath of restless sleep.

He had woken in a breathless tangle of duvet. Helen was long-since departed from the bed so he lay for a while, regained equilibrium.
Once, he had relished dreams, welcomed their rich imagery: the exotic landscapes that delighted his nocturnal mind and catalysed creativity. Now they were just a monotonous struggle with incoherence. He was typecast in a repetitious passion play,

condemned to perform interminable variations on a dreary theme.

He called it 'Narcopolis', that vast mayhem of ambiguous urban threat through which he must marshal successive gaggles of incompetent dependents in pursuit of some arbitrarily vital goal. Whether his wayward charges were family, old lovers or friends was immaterial to the outcome of the enterprise: invariably failure, frustration, the poignant shame of inadequacy exposed.

He rationalised these episodes as writers' dreams, expressions of a scribbler's guilty neglect of his duty of care to character and plot; this insight made them no less anxiously exhausting.

The need to piss had eventually hauled him from the bed, sent him stumbling bleary to the bathroom. He was standing over the toilet bowl, conscious of nothing but the need to direct the impending unruly flow, when Obscene Irene ambushed him from behind.

'I'll hold the old fella for you if you like. Then you can soap my titties.'

His twitch of surprise cracked an involuntary whip of urine across the floor. He had turned to find his mother-in-law, lewd in scrawny nakedness, smirking from the tub.

'Damnit, Irene—some privacy would be nice. You've got your own bloody *en suite* in the granny flat,' he had said and fled in disarray.

The Old Writer drank his tea and read the note Helen had left on the kitchen table.

Couldn't wake you. Taken your dad to his memory clinic. Keep your eye on Mum. H.

Her handwriting was spiky, a reflection of her mood. He sighed, stuffed the toaster with ragged slabs of bread, keyed the radio on.

An excited girl chirped local news in counterpoint to an over-urgent beat: *'Council blasted as big freeze turns roads to ice rinks...*

Pet snake blamed for neighbour's missing dog... No evidence to link church hall arson to Islamists, claim police...'

The phone rang. He choked down a mouthful of dry toast, silenced the radio, moved to answer the call.

'Hi, privileged winner,' a robot voice smarmed. 'You have been selected to receive a valuable reward. Stay on the line to hear details of your fabulous Caribbean crui—'

'Fuck off and die!'

He discarded the handset with vigour.

'I only came to apologise,' said a querulous voice behind him. 'Sometimes a devil gets into me.'

He shivered, glimpsed Helen's future decrepitude foreshadowed in her mother's anxious features.

'I know, Irene. No harm done. You just gave me a bit of a fright.'

The Old Writer rested a sympathetic hand on the old woman's frail shoulder, steered her to her TV chair.

'Sit yourself down and I'll put Trisha on.'

Disarmed by her vulnerability, he was reaching for the controller when the crone pounced, snagged his arm with a cruel claw and winked her evil eye.

'It's just our dirty little secret, right? No need to blab to wifey.'

The Old Writer hovered the cursor over the icon marked "Leepus—Bk13" but did not double-click. His uneasy dream still hung over him. A headache aborted foetal creativity. Cormac and his bloody turnip could take the blame for indolence today.

There were thirty-three unread emails in his inbox. Deleting the obvious spam left three. The first was a *pro forma* request for an autographed photo, the receipt of which was guaranteed to 'light up the day' of brave twelve-year-old cancer-victim Jody from Saskatchewan, 'your greatest Canadian fan'.

The next invited him to attend a forthcoming 'Celebration of Mystery Writing' at the University of The Midlands, wherever the fuck that was. It hinted that Leepus might snag another award. He saved it for consideration.

The last was from *passion8one@freemail.com*. He recognised the address but a morbid curiosity made him open it anyway.

Crystal was a fucked up kid. Her first email had arrived about eighteen months before. "Leepus: The Jesus Girl" had struck a chord in her imagination, moved her to confide her undying love for its omniscient creator.

Reading between her unpunctuated lines, The Old Writer had glimpsed a lonely child of hippy communards stranded by young adulthood in a bleak provincial bedsit. Mental health was definitely an issue. There were hints of abusive boyfriends and drug confusion, of suicide considered.

The Old Writer had hesitated but felt obliged to craft a considered reply. He pitched it avuncular but hip, diverted her inappropriate affections with humorous self-deprecation, offered discreet lifestyle guidance while affirming his respect for the primacy of free will.

Once a month since, or thereabouts, The Old Writer had found a fresh deposit of emotional turmoil uploaded to his mailbox. He had patiently deconstructed Crystal's paranoid delusion that a TV weatherman's forecasts nightly ordained her fate. A stern paternal tone contradicted the wisdom of her announced intent to share her bed with a 'professional thief' and adopt his Temazepam habit. He had encouraged her doomed pursuit of an NVQ in horticulture, shared her eager dread at the prospect of maternal reconciliation, offered rational commiseration when this embittered encounter disappointed; but consistent rebuff of flattery failed to deflect her fanatic arrows of love and his patience had eroded.

His last email – a terse acknowledgment of Crystal's detailed recollection of her lurid dream in which The Old Writer had fulfilled a succession of unrealistic but biologically precise sexual expectations – had been sent over two months before. The lack of a prompt reply encouraged the hope that his admirer's unhealthy heat had finally been quenched, preferably without resort to lethal overdose. The opened mail that now filled his screen made it clear this was not the case.

The Old Writer had imagined her older.

A chubby kid, his seductress had draped her shabby boudoir with exotic Indian cloth. A romantic constellation of candles illuminated the heap of grubby cushions on which she knelt, posed naked but for the T-shirt pulled up to reveal plump asymmetrical breasts. Her belly button winked shy from a cushion of puppy fat creased above her sparse-shadowed groin. On one pneumatic inner thigh: a tattoo-butterfly fluttering poignant. Bruises on the other recalled a cruder touch. But it was Crystal's eyes – glittering dark and nervous over the veil of her lifted shirt-hem – that disturbed him most profoundly. They reminded him of his daughter's, how she would peep over the bed-sheet at him as he read her a bedtime story all those distant years ago, before she got fat and fecund and learned to peep at men.

A crow rasped harsh outside in the sullen air. The Old Writer was suddenly despondent. His hand trembled as he exorcised the sordid image. It vanished instantly from the screen but would haunt his mental hard drive much longer, he suspected.

He had stared out of the high window at least an hour, lulled into a sepia world that blurred and resolved with the ebb and flow of the fog. He might have stared an hour more if Obscene Irene had not shrieked raucous from below.

The shriek repeated insistent – an infant pterodactyl in demand of meat – as The Old Writer clattered stiff-jointed down the wooden stair. He had time to imagine the full horror show of catastrophe that might have befallen the harridan, but frankly he preferred not to.

The Old Writer found Obscene Irene perched rigid on the edge of her TV chair: jazz hands fluttering spastic, head craned on tortoise-neck, jaundiced eyes averted from the unpleasantness in her lap.

'Get the filthy thing off of me,' she squawked.

Relieved not to find her in flames, he indulged a mild urge for payback.

'Hold still then. Don't want it to bite.'

Irene shuddered as he plucked the dusty conglomeration of feather, bone and plastic from its withered crash-site.

'Is it dead?'

He smiled.

'Has been for twenty years.'

'Where the devil did it come from? I nearly wet myself.'

'Nearly is good.'

The Old Writer remembered his son reaching with drawing pins and fishing line, tiptoed precarious on a stool.

'John hung it up there. Must have been about eight or nine when he made it. It's the fuselage of a B52 with a barn owl's head and wings. Called it "Nature of Death" as I recall. Precocious little sod.'

'Well it could have been the death of me. I was just having a little beauty sleep waiting for the snooker to come on. Next thing there's an animal burrowing at my fanny.'

'Teach you to be more careful what you wish for.'

He turned away, mutant corpse cradled.

'Just relax and get your breath back. I'll put the kettle on.'

'It's beyond me why any child would make such a disgusting thing.'

Her voice followed him to the kitchen.

'Unless he was disturbed.'

'He's an artist, Irene,' he called back defensive. 'That's what artists do. And these days he gets money for it, too.'

'Well it's creepy. No wonder that nice little girl upped and left the mucky bugger on his own.'

The Old Writer suspected there was a degree of truth in Irene's observation.

Jilted John was a sweet kid but weird. His chosen medium for the artistic expression of his preoccupation with life's darker aspects – the creation of nightmare tableaux of disturbingly mutated taxidermy specimens – would certainly inhibit traditional domestic bliss. His compulsion to fill both studio and home with junk-shop scavenged stuffed animal cadavers, collected as raw material for his monstrous creations, would be hard to live with too.

But the love of his life, Shy Skye, had idiosyncrasies of her own and, for seven seeming-contented years, she had been John's patient muse and loyal emissary to the world of humans. News of her delirious betrayal – born again in the passionate arms of both Christ and the rabid evangelist who had subverted her – had left The Old Writer and Helen concerned for the mental welfare of their eldest son.

John's connection to hearth and home had always been tenuous; the shock of his lover's departure had rendered him near invisible. Helen's distress – maternal compassion unrequited by monosyllabic phone calls – had eventually embarked her squeamish husband on a mission to confront their son's depression man to man.

The shabby backstreet undertakers' parlour had been bought from its bankrupt family owners with a parental loan and converted for use as a studio cum living space.

'Just thought I'd check you were still alive,' The Old Writer said as John admitted him hesitant over the threshold.

'I'm clinging on.'

His son's demeanour raised no immediate suspicion of extremity. The boy looked clean enough: dreadlocks neatly trapped by headband, beard carefully braided and adorned with ethnic beads, smile customarily self-effacing.

They danced awkward, negotiated the mountain bike propped in the narrow passage, ducked into the sitting room. It was oven hot, the window of the pot-bellied stove incandescent, orange-white.

The acid pungency of baked taxidermy flared The Old Writer's nostrils. A score or more stuffed birds sweltered in glass cases, posed stiff on truncated branches against painted habitats. Blind bead-eyes glittered in cruel mockery of life.

'Fuck. Nice and cosy in here, mate.'

'I don't like to be cold.'

The Old Writer groped for eloquence, came up dry.

'So—been working much?'

John shrugged.

'Not much. How's that Leepus book going?'

'Yeah, getting there,' The Old Writer lied.

'Coffee?' asked his son.

'Cool.'

John drifted off to the kitchen, left his father to sweat.

Desperate for relief from the boxed sun in the corner, The Old Writer moved to the sofa by the window across the room. His skin prickled. The seared air rasped his throat. He knelt on the grimy sofa arm, reached for the window catch, found it seized shut. He peered at the small yard, dull through streaked glass. Its centrepiece was a totem pole of carved grotesques, studded with bleached bird-skulls and fluttering with feathers. A rusted brazier overflowed with ashes: paper mostly, and the part-burned lattice of a wicker basket.

Cats. There had always been cats when he had visited before, three of them at least, that arched and stretched and scratched and sneered with sinister omnipresence.

The coffeepot death-rattled on the cooker. John watched it, sucked at a baggy spliff. The boy never could roll a decent joint.

The Old Writer flipped off the gas, scanned the tiny kitchen for cups. They were all in the sink, oiled seabirds mired in a greasy dishwater sea. He rinsed a couple under the cold tap, filled them with coffee black and thick as tar.

'Thanks.'

The loose cuff of his son's embroidered shirt slid back as he took the cup. The Old Writer glimpsed a weal, red raw on pale forearm skin.

'Playing with fire, boy?'

John stiffened, adjusted his sleeve to conceal the wound.

'Sort of.'

'Looks sore. You should put something on it.'

'It doesn't really hurt. Not in the wider scheme of things.'

Against his better judgement, The Old Writer accepted the reeking spliff, realised only as the harsh smoke ravaged his throat and lungs that the bastard had rolled it with pure weed.

His chest spasmed. He hacked, spluttered, practically coughed his eyeballs out. Tears liquefied his vision. It took a minute's extreme effort of will to restore normal respiration, by which time sly cold narcotic fingers had worked deep inside his brain.

'Fucking skunk! Toxic shit is evil. Why doesn't anyone smoke normal dope these days?'

'Jude would call you a lightweight.'

'Yeah. But your brother is an animal. His opinion doesn't count.'

'So how's Mum?' John asked to change the subject.

He had argued with his brother at The Old Writer's last birthday party. Rude Jude had got Shy Skye smashed on tequila shots and flattery, encouraged her to dance gauche on the table. Jude could be cruel sometimes; John could be over-sensitive.

'Mum's good. Worrying about everyone, running around doing good from dawn till dusk, as usual.'

'Give her my love.'

'Why not give it to her yourself?'

'I would, Dad—but her bottomless fucking compassion just makes it worse, you know?'

The skunk had darkened the periphery of The Old Writer's world. He focused on his son haloed by gloom, on the wet glint of his eye that he concealed turning away.

'I know, boy. It's okay. When you're feeling stronger.'

John twitched at his father's touch on his shoulder. Wary of emotional quicksand, The Old Writer backed off. A worktop pyramid of tinned cat-food suggested a less sentimental tack.

'I guess at least she had the grace to take her mangy moggies with her?'

He grinned, a forced bonhomie. John grinned back brittle in the gathering kitchen dusk.

'Guess again. Apparently her reverend new fuck is blessed with an allergy to felines. A sniff of cat sends the arsehole into anaphylactic rapture.'

Abrupt, John headed for the door.

'Shame all pussy doesn't have the same effect on the cunt.'

The uncharacteristically crude afterthought hung ugly as John plodded off up the stair. Restless, The Old Writer drifted down the short passage to the former mortuary room, now a chilly studio. He nudged open the door. The sound of his son's micturition trickled from above. Sympathetic rivulets writhed cold down his spine as he checked the work-in-progress laid out on the embalming slab in a pool of savage light.

Three charcoaled wooden crosses jutted stark atop a Calvary of bones. Crucified on each symbolic scaffold: a scorched and contorted cat-corpse snarling toothy in agonised rage.

The Old Writer retreated shocked. Cold insects crawled his skin as he waited in the infernal sitting room, his dark child's descending footfall on the stair. The boy needed a stern talking to, a rational perspective to clarify the black confusion of his plot. The Old Writer wrestled to phrase wise insight, script comfort and supportive love. In the event, and not for the first time, words failed him absolutely.

The twenty minutes more that his pastoral visit endured had passed in stilted and hopelessly diminished repartee. John was clearly not disappointed when, evening traffic avoidance his lame excuse, The Old Writer had embraced his son perfunctory, fled guilty into the night.

Ashamed of his feeble dereliction he had excised the ugly detail from his mealtime report to Helen. But his obvious lack of appetite and the anxiety palled around their table ensured the cruel subtext infected her with doubt.

They had passed a distracted evening numbed by white-noise TV, spent the night side-by-side in the dark silence of their bed, each singularly conscious of the other's sleepless breath.

'So who does a girl have to shag anyway to get a cup of tea round here?'

Obscene Irene's bony knuckle poked The Old Writer from his trance. He turned, met her inquisitive bird-eyes with the wateriness of his own.

'Sorry. Just thinking about stuff. Kids—they grow up but they never leave you, do they?'

'To state the bleeding obvious.'

Irene grimaced vague disdain.

'Think less and write more. That's this wise old woman's advice to the young.'

She scrabbled a balled tissue from the frayed sleeve of her cardy. A fleeting kindness dappled the wintry landscape of her face as she fumbled it into his palm with crooked fingers, scuttled back to her lair. 'Now pull yourself together, boy,' she called. 'And bring me my bloody tea.'

five

'If you'd just pop on your new glasses for me sir,' his Optical Advisor twinkled. 'And look directly at me so I can check the correct lens alignment.'

The Old Writer blinked into bright emerald eyes, grabbed a snapshot, caricatured the woman's life.

Like Leepus.

She was forty, childless, divorced maybe widowed, skinny from an excess of nervous energy and health food. Her job paid okay but she struggled with her mortgage, worried she might have to move downmarket, live alongside the common and uncouth.

Leepus would have held her gaze a little longer, sexed-up the mundane transaction, derailed her script with a charm of nuanced wit and pursued a deeper probing of her feminine mystique. The Old Writer was too old for that messy shit.

The bright fluorescence of the fitting room nagged the dull ache in his head; it picked out the flecks of dandruff on her tunic shoulders, the foundation adhering to the fine hairs of her sparse moustache.

'Perfect. I think they suit you very well, sir.'

The green eyes flickered, cancelled his examination.

'If you'd just pop them off for me again, I'll give them a final polish and pop them in a case.'

The Old Writer checked the nametag on her lapel. A discreet silver crucifix studded her buttonhole, provoked his sudden impatience.

'Thanks. I'll wear them, Alice. Just pop the old ones in the charity bin. Some African poppet might as well make use of them. Enhance their capacity for bible study, eh?'

'Of course, sir.'

Alice gathered documentation unruffled.

'And I'm pleased to confirm we can offer that service at no additional charge.'

She stood trim: shielding her breasts with sheaved paper, cocking her elfin head.

'Please follow me to the paypoint so we can complete the final formalities and leave you to enjoy your day.'

Outside in the pedestrianised high street, The Old Writer squinted and peered, reassessed features of the grubby urban world.

The pox of gobbed gum that afflicted the shoddy block paving did not seem to him any sharper.

The vomit-map of Cuba splashed on the steps of the derelict library remained unpleasantly low resolution.

THIRD TOWN CHURCH BLAZES, blared the headline on the paper-seller's hoarding; he deciphered its scrawl from across the street no more easily than before.

So that was four hundred and fifty-five quid well fucking spent.

Helen, bored with his intermittent headaches – or at least with his weeks of complaint and gruff resentment of Cormac, on whose turnip attack he persisted in blaming his discomfort – had despatched him to the optician. A plump child had shared an intimate garlic memory of her evening meal, exhaled as she leant close to study his inner optical workings. Stoically non-committal on the subject of headaches, she had advised that his astigmatism might benefit from a slightly stronger prescription and passed him to Alice for specialist cash-extraction.

The Old Writer reviewed the experience now as he strolled in casual search of his car. He felt mildly violated, as if a naive anxiety had been callously taxed. Ageing baby-boomers were going to fuel a twenty-first century Capitalist bonanza; he should buy shares in parasitic US healthcare corporations.

Sirens howled somewhere beyond the market square, diminished in retreat. Muffled inside his heavy coat, a persistent double-bleep chided his neglect of electronic duty. The Old Writer searched four pockets before he found the phone. Its screen announced a text from Rude Jude. A drip of adrenaline curdled his blood as he keyed the message open with a clumsy finger.

hi - on mway heading sth mite cum and c u l8er

The sub-literate composition stirred irrational annoyance, just as Jude knew it would. Borderline dyslexia was no excuse for wilful language mutilation, or for punching sarcastic teachers, getting expelled, and then running away with a busload of raggle-taggle ravers to test your iron constitution with a five-year Ketamine binge.

Ten years ago The Old Writer and Helen had thought their youngest son lost, waited in dread resignation for the inevitable news of death or incarceration. But Jude, it appeared, was bulletproof. Bored, eventually, by poverty and the travelling life, he had 'come ashore' to set up shop in Hackney, renting sound systems to outlaw party-animals for both fun and considerable profit. An impressive achievement in an uneducated force of nature, The Old Writer grudged, worried Jude's penchant for high-end gangster chic betrayed interests in riskier business.

The Old Writer shivered in the pissy car park stairwell, blinked baffled at the ticket machine. He had used his card at the opticians' not twenty minutes before, so why now was access denied to the slot in his brain where his PIN was habitually stored?

Mental fingers scrabbled for clues. It was the year of Helen's birth with digits reversed? No. His telephone area code minus the zero? No. Someone shuffled impatient behind him; rattled, he stabbed random keys.

The machine extruded his card like an insolent tongue. 'Please select an alternative valid means of payment,' its robot voice insisted. He fed it a note fumbled from his wallet, took his ticket, relieved.

Change clattered in the chute as he stalked to the stair. Embarrassed to turn back, he abandoned it, an offering to the demon Dementia.

A worm of trepidation turned in The Old Writer's belly. Rude bloody Jude and his crazy fucking static; even at long-distance the bastard still had the power to spin his father's fragile mental compass.

The Old Writer parked his stolid old Volvo in the chill shadow of the obsidian starship docked considerately – by Jude, he assumed – a nanometre from the porch. His mouth puckered in envious disgust. The thing was a monster of pure arrogance; just like its fucking driver.

There was barely enough room to open his door. The Old Writer disembarked clumsy, squeezed past the massive vehicle, scraped gleeful zips along its deep-shone flank. Caught in a tinted window close-up, his reflection winked: a malevolent old fuck, crooked mouth cracked with childish spite.

There was something inside on the backseat; something disconcerting.

Curious, The Old Writer leaned close, shaded his eyes to peer dark through the glass. It took him a frowning moment to be sure what he saw, and then fear seized his balls, wriggled its frosty finger in his sphincter.

The body was stretched out stiff, mummy-wrapped tight in a blanket. A naked foot poked from a teasing cleft in the extremity of the winding.

The Old Writer saw chipped green varnish on toenails, a slave bracelet closed with a tiny gold padlock. He felt sick. Flies buzzed dark inside his head. Jude's bass laugh boomed out large to meet him as he opened the front door of the house.

He found them in the kitchen. Helen had made tea. She sipped hers, watched wary over the rim of her mug as her son flirted with her mother.

'I'd love to Nan, honest. Fox like you, who wouldn't?'

Jude slid Obscene Irene from his knee, patted her scrawny rump.

'But I took a stupid vow of abstinence.'

Down the table Cracked Jack snorted mirthful, slapped his bony thigh; his nostrils dribbled tea.

'And Granddad Jack is jealous,' Jude said and stood to greet his father.

'Hey, Jude.'

The Old Writer offered the ritual greeting dry-mouthed.

'Hey, man. How're you doing?'

The boy's open face beamed close; his tattooed arms spread possessive. The Old Writer's ribs creaked as Jude's merciless *abrazo* engulfed him; air wheezed from his lungs. He was teetering on the edge of blackout when the iron grip relaxed. Grateful, he sucked a breath, smelled the animal heat his son exuded, the musk of stale perfume and whisky. He smiled. The boy's raw power enfeebled him but swelled his genetic pride.

'I'm doing okay for an old fuck. But I reckon you're doing better—if that outrageous gangster-truck parked outside is anything to go by.'

'Yeah. Cool huh?'

'Bit of a fucking cop magnet down your ends, I'd have thought.'

Jude smirked non-committal.

'So what's the occasion?' his father probed, timid. 'Doing your bit for global warming at ten bloody miles to the gallon?'

'Been up to Leeds, checkin' a club. Investment opportunity—y'feel me?'

The Old Writer looked for tells, the eyelid twitch or tongue-flick on dry lip that would betray a terrible guilt. Nothing; Jude's brash countenance was unperturbed. Perhaps the backseat mummy was a febrile hallucination. Only a psychopathic monster could sip innocent tea in his parents' kitchen while a corpse cooled in his car. Was that what his wild boy had become?

Helen raised a tentative eyebrow. 'No room for romance between the wheeling and dealing?' she asked. 'What happened to that nice black girl—Denise?'

'Denelle. I couldn't afford her crack habit, Mum. She got superseded by Natalya.'

Cracked Jack sneered.

'She sounds bloody foreign too. 'What's wrong with English totty?'

'Their accents are a turn-off you nasty old bigot.'

Jude chastised the old man without malice.

'Natalya's a lovely name. Is she Russian, Jude?' asked Helen.

'Latvian, Mum.'

Jude frowned.

'Or is it Lithuanian? I can never fucking remember.'

'It's a shame she's not with you. It's always nice to meet your friends.'

'She is.'

Jude sucked his teeth.

'But it might be a problem bringing her in. It was a heavy night up north.'

The Old Writer studied his son, imagined the interior turmoil masked by his poker face. Jude grabbed up his keys, jangled for the door.

'Left the lazy tart dead in the fucking car. Not sure she'll be human yet.'

'Thank you, but not to worry.'

Natalya pouted, brushed a flame of hair from snowy forehead.

'The English winter is not so cold for a girl who grows up in Riga.'

She shifted on her stool, crossed elegant legs, tugged down the hem of her tiny green dress with fingernails painted to match. The Old Writer caught himself observing the modest gesture a little too closely.

Helen caught him, too. 'Nonsense, girl,' she said. 'It gives me goose bumps just to look at you. Put on that jumper. You'll catch your death.'

Natalya frowned.

'Goose bums? What are these please?'

'Great British delicacy, babe,' Jude deadpanned. 'We eat them with piccalilli.'

'Jude's teasing you, Natalya,' said Helen. 'Goose bumps are when your skin looks like you've had all your feathers plucked out.'

'You think I have bad complexion?'

Natalya caressed a cheek alarmed.

Helen flushed.

'No, no. I just meant—'

'Stop digging, Mum,' said Jude. 'And don't fuss so much. Natalya's a lap-dancer. She's used to being stared at.'

'This is not true!'

Natalya slid cool from the stool, reached to take the heavy jumper from Helen's flustered hand.

'I am post-graduate student. I read for doctorate—criminology.'

'That's just what it says on her visa.'

Jude helped his girlfriend hide her assets in shapeless knitwear while Obscene Irene tottered up from her chair, lifted her housecoat above rolled stockings, flashed her varicose thighs.

'Lap-dancing sounds much more exciting,' the old lady said. 'I wouldn't mind learning a couple of moves.'

Helen buried her face in her hands. Her mother ground arthritic hips, thrust her ancient booty at Cracked Jack trapped terrified in his chair.

'Dirty, dirty, dirty,' the old man moaned. 'Sweet Jesus, when will my Doris ever come and take me home?'

Jude beat time on a cupboard. 'Go, Nan!' he encouraged, impervious to pathos.

The Old Writer caught Natalya's eye, grimaced apologetic.

'Please—is not problem.'

She shrugged, graceful in bulky wool.

'My family is crazy, also. But they drink very much wodka.'

'Wodka sounds good,' The Old Writer said a little too loud. He was high on relief. His son was not a sordid killer after all; that warranted celebration. 'We've still got a couple of bottles left over from Christmas. I'll break them out and phone for a curry—if you and Jude are cool to stay?'

'Sounds fuckin' top to me, man.'

Jude punched his father's shoulder with sincere but brutal affection.

'Never pass on a chance to get messy.'

six

'I'd love to help, Dad—really,' Jude lied through his teeth. 'But I've got shit to do today.'

Suspended by hooked fingertips from the lintel of the kitchen door, he lowered his taut bulk with focused strength, upper arms massive as tractors.

'Just got to pick up a box of old vinyl from the barn while Natalya's in the shower. Then we're gonna do one.'

'Okay.'

The Old Writer shrugged.

'We'll manage, I guess. 'Course, humping your sister's chaotic life from truck to fucking house could finish your old dad off—but don't let guilt ruin your day.'

'Old? You're only sixty for fuck's sake. A bit of graft will do you good—get you out of that Tower of fucking Babble.'

Jude crossed to the sink. Water rushed. He gulped, throat an open drain, gasped and wiped his mouth dry with his shovel of a hand.

'What are you working on now anyway? Not still that final fucking Leepus book?'

'Yeah.'

The Old Writer tried not to sound defensive.

'Trying to make it last so I don't have to think up anything new. Pretty sure I'll have it finished before you read the first one though.'

'Ouch—wounded.'

His son feigned affront.

'You know I'm fucking bibblephobic. That's why I was shit at school.'

'Bibliophobic, you hopeless arse.'

The Old Writer's sneer was reflexive.

'It's Greek for intellectually bone-idle.'

'Piss off you elitist fuck. Come the dyslexic revolution you book-writing pricks'll be first to hear the death squad's knock.'

Jude rapped the door, headed outside.

'And at least I suffered through the bullshit TV box-set. So you can't say I didn't make an effort.'

'Yeah, well—those idiots missed the whole point of the thing. Leepus was completely miscast. Two totally different characters sharing a name is the best way to describe that shambles.'

But Jude was gone. The Old Writer abandoned his lame hobbyhorse, stepped out onto the back step, blinked in the pallid sun.

He had enjoyed the evening of alcohol and banter. Jude was the life and soul. The boy's routine of scurrilous jokes had rendered everyone helpless. Later, the prodigal sang Beatles' tunes in raucous duet with Helen at the piano, brought a tipsy tear to his mother's fond eye. The party wound up with a latenight poker game. Natalya skinned them all.

The Old Writer and Helen had retired to bed content. He had a vague recollection of some kind of sex occurring but that could have been a dream.

Jude loped down the path from the barn, record case under his arm. He flicked out a casual hand, decapitated a brussels plant as he passed Helen's raised vegetable-bed.

The Old Writer flashed on a three-year-old's mealtime tantrum: green sprouts splattering against a yellow wall. There was no denying the boy knew how to bear a grudge.

Jude shifted his gait, dragged his foot; clay cloyed on the soles of his Nikes, smeared the frayed cuffs of his jeans. 'Fucking dirty countryside,' he rumbled. 'No wonder they invented towns.'

The Old Writer trailed his son round the house. The four-by-four blipped, flashed a greeting to its owner; its tailgate gaped hydraulic. Jude smirked back over his shoulder. 'Admit it, man. You're fucking well-impressed,' he said.

The vast luggage space was crowded: huge speakers and an amp like a racing engine, all gleaming aluminium. Jude threw the record case in.

'Five-hundred watts of bass evil that bad bastard puts out. Involuntary defecation guaranteed within fifty fucking metres.'

Jude waved the key-fob, a manic conductor; the world throbbed in response. Solid sound kicked The Old Writer in the chest, disrupted his cardiac rhythm. Window-glass rattled. Starlings exploded from the roof of the house, flocked overhead, strafed the gleaming black vehicle with a panic-rain of shit.

Jude scowled, keyed the volume down to five on the Richter scale. 'Fucking filthy vermin,' he snarled. 'The dirty flying bastards should all be burned in their stinking nests.'

The Old Writer fished a crusty tissue from his pocket, used it to check his ears for blood, tossed it to his son.

'I'd wipe that guck off pronto. Bird shit'll strip paint quick as bloody acid.'

Jude frowned distrustful, decided not to take the risk. He was still smearing the last of the white mess clumsy across his paintwork when Helen and Natalya came out of the house.

Cheeks were kissed, shoulders clapped, hands shaken. Dotards waved warm behind windows. In response: Jude's blown kiss for Obscene Irene; for Cracked Jack, his stiff good-natured finger.

And then the young lovers were gone in a hail of wheel-spun gravel.

The Old Writer stood with his wife for a minute of silent recuperation. A mild breeze stirred bare poplar branches, carried the distant shrieks of urchins happy from the schoolyard. Birds resumed tentative song.

'So, we live to fight another day,' said Helen.

'Yeah—as visits from Rude Jude go we got off pretty light.'

He squeezed her shoulder affectionate, watched ASBO Angie's beat-up Transit lurch overloaded through the gate.

An hour later the van was empty and The Old Writer had lost the will to live.

'All right there, chap?'

Angie winked, dead ciggie glommed to her lip.

'Just shout if you need a rest.'

The thin steel case of the washing machine cut his fingers to the bone. He stumbled backwards over the barn's narrow threshold, ground his hand between load and frame. 'Too late for rest,' he croaked. 'How are you at CPR?'

'Hah! I might manage a few token chest compressions, pal—but you can forget about mouth-to-mouth.'

The barn was full, garden tools buried by boxes and bin-bags stacked hasty and haphazard. They manoeuvred painful and laborious, jammed the cumbersome load into the last available space. The Old Writer folded weak-kneed onto a rolled mattress, looked up at Angie silhouetted in the door.

'Guess I'll have to settle for a smoke then.'

The woman fished a crumpled plastic pouch from grimy jeans, reached it down to him with a tattooed arm. He squinted up at a small hard tit flashed through the gape of her singlet, waved a vague hand of surrender.

'Roll it for me, huh? I'm fucked.'

Angie ripped off a Rizla.

'Must be crap to be old.'

'Old is okay. The problem is hauling other people's heavy shit around all day.'

She ignored his bait, pinched out tobacco, pulled loosened strands along thin paper.

'And make it a decent size—none of your fucking anorexic prison ciggies.'

They smoked silent. The Old Writer coughed. Angie spat, picked a wisp of tobacco from her lip, studied it on her finger.

'I don't blame you for being pissed off, mate. I want to do better by Vi and the kids—but shit keeps fuckin' up, you know?'

The Old Writer heard the catch in her voice and looked away.

'Family life must be weird after being at war.'

'Yeah. Fuckin' army. Fuckin' Afghan.'

Angie clenched a fist, rapped her skull.

'Bubbled my fuckin' brain.'

The barn was claustrophobic. The Old Writer hauled up shaky to his feet.

'Well a couple of months in the caravan might give you some space to get sorted. Treat it like a holiday.'

Angie glanced sharp.

'Right—life here's a fucking beach.'

The Old Writer clambered for the light.

'Thanks though,' she said in smoke balloons. 'Appreciate the help.'

He turned in the doorway.

'No choice. Can't see my own bloody daughter chucked out on the street.'

ASBO Angie ground her cigarette into her palm. Her eyes gleamed hard in the jumbled gloom. 'I fuckin' love that woman,' she growled. 'I never want to hurt her, man—believe me.'

It was touch and go. The carnage was horrific. But in the bitter end, superior tactics and sheer force of arms tipped the balance in their favour. Carthage crumbled before the might of Rome. The victors burned the gleaming city to the ground of course, slaughtered its vanquished population.

'Yes—sick!'

Cormac revelled grim in the destruction.

'Now our legions march on Thapsus.'

Flushed with hard-won glory, The Old Writer's reflex was to indulge the boy's ruthless quest for empire; the throbbing pulse behind his eye tempered this martial instinct.

'Yeah—but this general needs rest and recuperation. Thapsus is spared till the weekend.'

'No way!'

Cormac's face darkened.

'We need to strike before they reinforce. *Carpe diem*, dude.'

'Sorry, bud—school tomorrow. Mum said nine at the latest. It's already a quarter-past.'

Cormac scrutinised his grandfather's face, recognised the futility of confrontation, switched on his inner diplomat.

'Please. You're the bollocks when it comes to tactics. It'll only take a couple more turns.'

'Saturday—after football. We'll have all afternoon.'

'Can't.'

Cormac swallowed disappointment.

'I'm not even here this weekend. My dad says I have to go and stay—wanker came out of rehab last week.'

'Well.'

The Old Writer groped for an upside.

'It's good he wants to spend time with you.'

'You wouldn't say that if you had to hang-out with the miserable bloody arsehole.'
'Come on. He's not that bad—just a bit messed up in his head.'
'It's all right. I can deal with Druggie Dave.'
Cormac grimaced wise.
'It's just so boring at his cruddy flat. No TV—and he even sold his Xbox to buy methadone last time his bloody script ran out.'
The Old Writer nudged the glum youth sympathetic.
'Thapsus is ashes on Monday—deffo.'
'Right.'
Cormac's face brightened.
'And then we move south, take down the bastard Egyptians.'
A slow heavy footstep on the tower stair. Not Helen's; she always moved silent as a cat.
The door groaned open.
'Uh oh. I think we're in trouble, boy,' The Old Writer mugged as Vile Viola shouldered in bulky.

Cormac departed without protest to spread the news of triumph to the wider world. The Old Writer creaked up from his chair, joined his daughter at the tower window. Light spilled from the old caravan across the dark paddock below, backlit ASBO Angie hunched on its brick step with cigarette and can.
'So—you fit everyone in okay?'
'Just about.'
Viola turned to him, smiled tight.
'It's bigger than it looks from up here.'
'Most things are. Writers prefer a simplified perspective.'
'Yes. You do.'
Viola sniffed, surveyed the octagonal chamber: three walls of dusty books; a shelf of redundant smoking paraphernalia; the cobwebbed display of grotesque masks; framed Leepus cover art; Cormac's early battle pictures Blu-Tacked to smoke-stained plaster.

'I coveted this room when I was a girl—wanted to be Rapunzle, grow my glorious hair right down to the ground.'

'Yeah.'

The Old Writer remembered stubborn petulance, the dark flash of eyes averted.

'You hated me for months.'

'Months?'

Viola's full lips twisted.

'Oh no—it was way longer than that.'

'Sorry.'

He shrugged.

'I needed a proper space to work in. Spent too many years in that poky flat, hammering away behind a screen of your drying nappies, trying to get Leepus off the ground. Felt like I'd earned my sanctuary, you know?'

'It's okay. I'm over it now.'

She flickered a heavy eyelid.

'Mostly.'

The Old Writer chanced an affectionate arm.

'I know you've had a few tough years. Young kids. No money. But maybe things will be better now—with Angie?'

She stiffened. He withdrew.

'Hard to imagine they could get worse,' she said.

The Old Writer bit his lip. He imagined endless disastrous permutations, averted them, superstitious.

'The kids seem happy. Cormac's much calmer.'

'Yes—thanks for that. He gets more of a kick out of hanging out in ancient Rome with you than mooching about in the real world with the rest of his dull family-members.'

'You're welcome—nothing I like better than corrupting young minds. They'll all be mine in the end.'

Viola sucked in a breath through her teeth.

'Angie tries hard with them too. But she's got her own shit to work out.'

'I noticed.'

'Give her a chance. I know she's hard to take—but you've no clue what she's been through.'

'Actually I quite like the little psycho. Compared to her predecessors she's a breath of fresh air. Just hope she directs all her fire at the enemy—keeps pissing out of the tent.'

Viola looked away, hugged herself defensive.

'Right—thanks for the blessing, father. I'll get back down to my hovel now—make sure the peasants aren't revolting.'

The Old Writer stayed at the window, watched his firstborn lumber tired across the paddock.

Vile Viola: the cruel alliteration infuriated Helen but he could not let it go.

Their daughter had earned her nickname at the tender age of three. Perched astride the horse of her indulgent father's foot – a tiny blonde Godiva clutching outstretched-finger reins – she had beamed angelic up at him, paused for effect and then announced, 'I'm making your slipper all slimy and smelly with my vuh-vuh-vagina, Daddy.'

The harsh appellation's appropriateness had received sporadic reinforcement throughout the intervening thirty years.

At six, Viola's parents were summoned to her school. Embarrassed, the headmistress suggested referral to a child psychologist; there was some 'troubling exhibitionist behaviour' that needed to be addressed. The Old Writer and Helen had assumed inappropriate expression of their daughter's inner diva. The head's description of uninhibited defecation, performed for a privileged audience of infant peers in the shrubbery of the village churchyard, had taken them by surprise.

Viola's periods had started two days after her eleventh birthday. She celebrated this biological landmark with a series of florid flower-illustrations daubed in menstrual blood. Diplomatic appeals for decorum were dismissed with shrill accusations of Philistine oppression. For weeks, a gallery of gaudy art had adorned the hallway of their home for visitors to admire.

Viola blossomed in adolescence. Her flesh swelled flesh on flesh; it smothered the delicate nymph of childhood, consumed the ghost of innocence. But while her body billowed outrageous, Viola's intellect had firmed, honed a wit cruel and razor sharp. Stumbling dazed and defenceless from stoned struggle with the obstinate Word, The Old Writer suffered frequent laceration. He countered with craven good humour and obsequious flattery but his daughter's spite remained uncurbed. He was hurt. His empathy with John and Jude was effortless; Viola was a stranger, mysterious and dark.

Helen brushed off his concern, told him it was a phase that would pass in time. He took her at her word, relieved to be excused.

Life passed. The Old Writer kept his distance. Vile Viola did not object; she had her menagerie of animals on which to lavish gross affection.

For several years the barn had housed a fetid ghetto of stacked cages. Rodents lived, multiplied, teemed and died furtive in the gloom.

The Ugly Rabbits of Terror came next. Heedless of his daughter's liberal outrage, The Old Writer had wrestled reluctant rolls of chicken wire and awkward wood, constructed a domestic Guantánamo to secure fraught Helen's innocent vegetables from lapine depredation.

In the long run the effort had been futile. Razor wire and minefields could not have preserved the garden from the cloven-hoofed devils next chosen to suffer the exquisite torment of Viola's love. The image of his daughter – a flushed gumbooted Gaia stamping triumphant from her makeshift manger, smeared in shit and afterbirth and trailing the acrid scent of goat – still spooked The Old Writer twenty years on.

At sweet sixteen, Viola's need to nurture was reassigned to boys. Her appetite was voracious, or so the bus-stop graffiti The Old Writer once passed a furtive midnight-hour erasing had implied.

Her body depraved by hormones, Vile Viola remained strict mistress of her mind, held steady to her academic course through the furious carnal maelstrom. At eighteen she left for university, graduated three years later with a first-class biology degree under her belt. And a foetal Cormac.

Years of furious motherhood followed. Queen Viola ruled prolific. Hapless drones were exhausted in her service. Thriving infants swarmed her hive.

Callum, Carmen and baby Christy joined Cormac on the roll of souls The Old Writer was required to love. He was proud, delighted by their energetic promise. But they crowded him merciless up life's vertiginous ladder, inspired profound resentment and existential dread.

The Old Writer clung on tight and terrified. The black sky of oblivion gaped inevitable above. Below, relentless regenerations howled, hungry for promotion. If children devour their parents' lives, he thought, grandchildren gnaw their aching bones and suck the marrow dry.

seven

'The chickens don't like me. They want to peck my eyes. Don't send me out to feed them, ma. I promise I'll be good.'

'Okay, Jack—I won't let them get you.'

Helen patted the old man's hand.

'Just as long as you cooperate so I can get you into your shirt.'

The Old Writer watched his wife struggle to bend his father's rigid arm. Her patience was shrivelled as thin as the limb.

'Look! His willy's poking out of his pants,' giggled pretty little Carmen at the bedroom door.

'Cover it up quick,' urged Callum cruel behind her. 'A chicken might think it's a juicy worm.'

'Out demons out!' The Old Writer roared.

The children shrieked in terror, fled gleeful down the hall.

He crouched beside the bed, grabbed a wrinkled hairless leg.

'C'mon, Dad—let's get your bloody trousers on. You're damaging young minds.'

'Get off me you fucking queer bastard!'

Cracked Jack's spastic kick caught his son on the side of the head; horny yellow toenails raked his cheek. The Old Writer sprawled, impacted the bedside cabinet catastrophic. A water jug smashed, inundated clothes and floor. Pillboxes exploded tablet shrapnel. A toppled linctus bottle gulped viscous down the wall.

Cracked Jack cackled.

'Christ!' said Helen close to tears. 'Are you totally fucking incompetent?'

'Sorry—just trying to help.'

The Old Writer scrabbled melting gelcaps from the flood.

'Well you're not.'

'I'll go and find a mop.'

Helen hauled up Jack's trousers, reached for a sodden slipper. 'Don't be a bloody idiot,' she said and sniffed dismissive. 'You wouldn't know where to look.'

Stung, The Old Writer smeared the mess of gelatine from his hands with an inadequate crumple of tissue, considered retaliation.

Helen got in pre-emptive. 'Just piss off and write your stupid book,' she said. 'Or whatever it is you waste your life doing up there in your ivory fucking tower.'

The page was blank. The cursor blinked relentless. Pain throbbed in rhythmic sympathy through the hopeless void of his brain. The Old Writer sparked up his guilty joint, sucked smoke deep and desperate, waited for the fog to clear and reveal Leepus' ultimate story.

He smoked on. His headache diminished. His fingers flirted with the keyboard but the page remained frigid white.

Frustrated, he flicked the exhausted roach; embers exploded pyrotechnic on Leepus' face but the bastard did not flinch.

'Fuck it.'

The Old Writer pushed back his chair.

'We all have to die in the end.'

He stood, stared close at the framed portrait. Leepus smirked back, wry behind cool glass. It was the original unlettered cover art for the first book of the series. He had written it in a rush of stoned creativity twenty-five years before. His agent had persuaded a dubious publisher to take a reluctant punt. The gamble paid off. Pure chance, or instinctive genius, had keyed Leepus into the zeitgeist. A cadre of hip young initiates spread the word. A minor cult developed. Devotees demanded more, and more.

The publication of the first Leepus book had ended a dozen years of hack scribbling and part-time 'proper jobs', banished poverty and brought authorial props. The experience had changed his life, reaffirmed wavering self-belief and confidence in his craft, so it freaked him more than a little now that he could not recall its title.

He frowned. It was on the tip of his tongue. He just needed to relax and it would come. He took a breath, held it. Synapses flickered, scanned the fragmented archive of his brain, reported 'file not found'. Alarmed, he reached for backup. Twelve matched casebound editions were ranked dusty on a shelf; his anxious finger hooked down the first.

"AUTO DA FE", the title blazed in a charred forty-eight point font. Leepus smoked cool beneath it, dropped his match still burning meteoric out of frame.

The Old Writer eased back into his chair. He hefted the book, enjoyed its weight, flipped it in his hands. A portrait of The Young Writer brooded up at him, intense. He winced, scanned the hyperbolic blurb.

A village terrorised by carnivorous cows.

A priest devoured by his congregation.

A young teacher tortured by feral infants.

Something bad and weird is abroad in rural England— something it takes a special kind of mind to understand.

A hip proletarian detective with a penchant for high-stakes poker and mind-expanding drugs, Leepus gets under the skin of the modern world and exposes its carnal secrets with sly insight and savage wit.

Smart, cynical and sexy, this darkly comic debut novel transcends the conventions of crime and horror fiction, forges a mutant new genre for our time.

The occult odyssey starts here. Only a fool would miss their chance to get onboard for the ride.

The provocation had done its job. Judged in the court of popular culture and convicted of commercial appeal, he was condemned to literary servitude, sentenced to life in the Tower of Babble. Year on year and book on book his keyboard rattled easy. A million stoned words spilled profligate as Leepus spewed his stories. The Old Writer assumed eloquence would gush eternal. Twelve books were done and dusted; one more would see the series' end.

But then his spring ran dry.

The Old Writer had a superstitious understanding of his craft. Writing was a magical act. A practitioner mined the ore of story at the extremity of human experience. Imagination strung a subtle bridge between the subliminal and the mundane, a bridge that horror might traverse.

As a novice, The Young Writer had relished the adventure, delved deep and reckless, careless of contamination. Writing was a dangerous sport but its risks were his alone.

Later, made vulnerable by innocent dependents casually acquired, The Old Writer learned to fear the infectious power of The Word. He approached the manipulation of its threat with the perspicacity of the adept. Artful incantations were wrought to confine Bad Evil impotent in fiction. Characters suffered torment in Leepus' world so the loved ones of his creator could live happy, safe and free.

The metaphysical strategy paid off. Readers sucked up vicarious despair; his family thrived contented. All was good until, after a dozen years of deathless prose, The Old Writer's mojo collapsed and expired.

"Book Thirteen" was a decade overdue now. Superstitious fans – offended by rumours of the intended demise of their hero – blogged that Leepus had blocked his creator with a curse. The Old Writer suspected they were right. Silence had coshed him from behind, left him dumbstruck in the wilderness, abandoned by The Treacherous Word, his canon incomplete.

The years ground by. Day after day, alone in his tower, The Old Writer smoked and despaired. Sometimes lost eloquence echoed, inspired him to prod chimpish at random keys; more often he just stared.

He grew to dread his morning plod up the futile spiral stair, but he feared, if he left his watch too long, the chaotic elementals of imagination, no longer constrained by his magic words, would undermine his precarious castle-walls, ravage his vulnerable family and burn his life down to the ground.

The phone rang. He opened his eyes. He picked it up. He held it to his ear. The empty world whirred wordless down the line. It was night outside. The room was dark. The computer was asleep. He tapped a key to wake it up and see what he had written.

The page was blank. The cursor blinked relentless.

The house was dimmed and quiet. The Old Writer crept abandoned rooms, sniffed lonely for signs of life. Sofa cushions, tidy and plumped. TV remote stood-by on coffee table. Crocks on draining board, dry. Kettle, cool. Covered plate by microwave. He read the scribbled Post-it note: *nuke it 3 mins then let it stand.* He was hungry but it seemed like too much trouble. He grabbed a handful of biscuits from the jar, munched, trod crumbled fragments guilty into carpets as he wandered back upstairs.

The bedroom door was ajar; it oozed soft light, a purr of respiration. He peeped in. Helen was propped on pillows: eyes closed, jaw slack, glasses cliffhanging at the end of her nose. He moved to rearrange her with delicate precision: slipped the book from the limp hand on her lap, reached deft to unhook the glasses from her ear, tripped the creaky-floorboard IED.

Helen exploded from sleep, shuddered, flailed, gibbered terrified.

'Wuhwhassamatterhouseonbabyfire?'

'It's alright,' he said soft. 'You dozed off reading again. Give me your specs. I'll put the light off—you go straight back to sleep.'

'What time is it?'

'Late, I think. Sorry I missed dinner.'

'I called you twice—assumed you were making progress and wanted to be left alone.'

'Yeah. Something like that.'

'There's some shepherd's pie under a plate.'

'Right—I saw it. Might heat it up in a while.'

'Sorry I snapped at you earlier. No one else to take it out on.'

'I know.'

'You're really not totally incompetent.'

'Thanks. But you were right. I couldn't find the mop.'

Helen smiled wry.

'It's okay. You wouldn't have known what to do with it if you had.'

'We should think about hiring someone in to help with those crazy ancients,' he said. 'Buy you a bit of time for yourself.'

'Mum's no trouble really—and Jack only kicks off big-time when you get under his skin. God knows what kind of a kid you were to inspire so much latent fury.'

'Even so, a couple of tough Polish girls to give him a bed bath now and then might quieten the old bastard down. Don't want you worn out prematurely. I might have need of that TLC before too bloody long.'

'Right—think I'll take my chances with Jack today and save the Polish girls for your incontinent dotage. I plan to pass my graceful seniority squandering the kids' inheritance on gigolos and world cruises.'

'I suppose I could do worse. Some of those Eastern Europeans are pretty hot.'

'Right.'

Helen narrowed her eyes.

'Natalya got your attention.'

'Natalya's cool. Good for Jude, I think. Funny and smart. Gives as good as she gets.'

'But a *femme fatale* if ever I saw one. Let's hope it doesn't all turn *noir*.'

'Jesus.'

He brushed off the thought.

'Give the boy a break. We've got enough to worry about with Jilted fucking John.'

'And Viola—you saw all those bruises on her arm?'

'No.'

'She said she tripped over some Lego in the caravan.'

'But what?'

Helen chewed her lip.

'ASBO fucking Angie?'

'I hope not,' Helen said and picked a loose thread from the quilt. 'But something's not quite right.'

'Shit.'

The Old Writer moved for the door.

'Don't go.'

Helen turned back the cover.

'I want you here in bed.'

He stooped, kissed her cheek, inhaled a sweet gust of body-heat. 'Okay—just let me have a pee,' he whispered.

He was less than five minutes in the bathroom but Helen was already snoring when, mouth-washed and intimately sluiced, he slipped naked into the bed. He snuggled close and cupped a heavy breast; she murmured and shifted her arse against his groin. He waited for further invitation but the deepening rhythm of her breath made it clear his more energetic attention was no longer required and he subsided into sleep.

eight

The Old Writer had woken early and unusually refreshed.

Spring sun pushed into the kitchen, flared from the hanging copper pans, scattered the walls with light. He set coffee to brew, made tea on a tray and delivered it upstairs.

Cracked Jack sniffed at his mug, cursed a negligent deficiency of sugar.

Obscene Irene blessed his saintliness, winked and invited him to feel under her quilt to locate her misplaced teeth.

Helen blinked confused, accepted the proffered loving cup, grateful but suspicious.

'Thanks. So what's the occasion?'

The Old Writer flung curtains wide, flooded her with light.

'Don't know.'

He flashed a smile.

'Random benign impulse. Make the most of it, darling—it probably won't last.'

He left her to sip and ponder, jogged whistling back downstairs. He whistled on as he trucked outside, bagel toasted to perfection and 'Best Granddad Ever' mug brimmed-dark with aromatic promise. But it was not until he sat, face upturned heliotropic at the rickety patio table, that he identified his refrain. *Daybreak on the land...*

He flashed back: a 'seventies highland road trip; a campfire and shooting stars; a cassette-player warbling a Grateful Dead soundtrack to an acid epiphany that peaked as red dawn light bled through gashed clouds, ignited a mountainside, filled a loch with molten bronze.

The magnificent incandescence had suffused him with crazy joy, moved him to mount an ageless tumulus of boulders and stand, arms spread in delirious embrace of an ineffable Universe of possibility, until a treacherous plane of granite conspired with brutal gravity to bring him down hard and break his arm.

The Old Writer finished his coffee. He was tempted; while Leepus dropped cognition enhancers by the handful it was decades since he had tripped himself. Would a psychedelic renaissance spark his own creative fire, or just choke out its last faint embers in a chill vacuum of doubt?

Sudden ennui threatened his solar mood. He never used to be so timid, so disabled by mortal dread. Somehow the world had grown heavier and time had made him weak. But the freshness of the day infected him with vigour. He stood, inhaled the taint of hopefulness deep and whistled shrill defiance. A virtuoso song thrush took his challenge, trilled back loud and mellifluent from a nearby holly tree. He abandoned the patio stage with grace, ambled easy across the paddock to the gate with a creaky spring in his step.

It was his habit to walk in the forest. He knew the hidden trails where mothers feared to lead their shrieking infants, where filthy dog-cultists had not decorated every other tree with pendulous offerings of bagged canine shit. He knew the secret ponds, where muntjac drank and newts surfaced to breathe from submarine depths uncluttered by crushed cans and drifting confectionary-foil. He knew the blasted oak whose roots had buttressed the badgers' tubercular citadel for a thousand coughing generations, and the hawthorn-hidden stone pits where forgotten peasants toiled and cursed to raise church and manor to rule them.

At large in the wordless wood, he knew the value of silence and answered only to himself.

It was his habit to walk in the forest but his mood was contrary today. He turned for The Village of Idiots instead, moved by an idle impulse to infiltrate the dismal fleshpot on whose periphery he resided but whose dubious community his misanthropic reflex spurned.

Helen was his neighbourhood spy. Her casual network of informants, established in her years as a District Nurse, kept her in touch with the village day-to-day. Her selective reportage filtered the thin gruel of local gossip and distilled the piquant essence of human suffering which, over the years, had spiced his fictional gumbo with verisimilitude.

The Old Writer knew, for example, that the gaunt, streaked-blonde woman towed now by her string of retrievers toward the footpath behind the church had, ten years earlier, been surprised receiving rough-tongued canine pleasure – albeit in the supposed privacy of her high-hedged garden – undone by her neighbour's spontaneous decision to rake out the dead leaves from his gutter. The Old Writer had employed her disgrace in "What the Crows Know" to inspire a sordid blackmail plot and spark a tragic chain-reaction of misery and murder.

"Viking Funeral" co-opted the ex-police inspector who had devoted five years of his retirement to the restoration of an ancient boat stranded in the driveway of his village High Street home. Each day at three-fifteen – like a clockwork meerkat, it was noted – he poked his head from its for'ard hatch to gaze with hungry eyes, all hands busy below deck, at fresh-limbed adolescents straggling uncouth from the school bus in uniformed disarray. It was rumoured that his brothers on the lodge, concerned by a gathering storm, had advised him to relocate his activity to a discrete berth on the local canal.

The Old Writer had ordained a more spectacular fate: the filthy old seadog tempted into deep and troubled waters by vigilante sirens; they chain him aroused to his vessel's mast and, its tiller lashed on a blazing course to Hell, jump ship as it burns to the water.

There were others whose foibles and misfortunes his literary licence had distorted.

Brigitte the Bike: the intellectually challenged lonely young multiple-mother whose door was open to any sly youth with a comforting spliff and a hard-on.

Punch-it Pat: the brain-damaged gypsy ex-bare-knuckle fighter who, in drink, would snort snot-ropes while pounding lamppost, tree or mailbox with bloody shattered fists.

Phone-sex Phyllis: the resourceful young widow driven to self-employment when her Incapacity Benefit was harshly re-assessed.

And Graveyard Gary – named on account of his haphazard dentition – who nurtured a thriving weed farm upstairs in his fortified terraced home in a social housing cul-de-sac at the bitter end of Scum Street.

It was Graveyard Gary who, with four cans of Diamond White and a sliced loaf crooked under his arm, hailed The Old Writer now as he whistled past The Village Stores.

'Yo, man. Jerry rules,' Gary wheezed and flashed a peace sign.

'Hey, Gary,' The Old Writer acknowledged puzzled. 'Who the fuck is Jerry?'

'Garcia, man—who else? You were whistling his tune.'

The Old Writer watched as Gary fumbled to unchain Grizzly – a decrepit old Newfoundland as big as a bear – from the war memorial railing. The obelisk was a ten-foot oak trunk carved in the form of a howitzer shell. Poignantly apt or brutally crass, The Old Writer wondered, not for the first time. The dog cocked a callous leg oblivious of debate, hosed down the bronze plaque that roll-called The Village of Idiots' dozen shattered scattered sons.

'I was there at Wembley in 'seventy-two. Garcia blew me out of my fucking skull,' said Gary, snaggle-toothed. 'Or maybe it was the four microdots—and the half of Red Leb I smoked up. Man was a fucking hero. Hard to believe he's dead.'

'Right,' The Old Writer said. 'Or grateful.'

Grizzly growled and plodded off; unbalanced by the tightened chain, Gary tottered after.

The Old Writer fell into sociable step with huffing man and dog. 'Rats are all jumping the sinking ship,' he said. 'Beefheart and Bill Burroughs—and poor old Hunter Thompson, blown out of his fear and loathing with his own fucking gonzo gun. Be time to join them soon enough.'

'Fuck off, you cheerful bastard. Old Deadheads never die.'

The Old Writer glanced at the groceries dangled from his companion's dead white fingers.

'Carry-out breakfast today then, mate?'

'Yeah—cider for me and a loaf for the dog. Keep it from chewing my fucking leg off till I can get over the fields for a rabbit.'

They paused on the corner of Scum Street. In an oil-slick front yard littered with old tyres, a tattooed fat-man in boxer shorts chased a naked toddler around a car-on-bricks. The dog panted, stared and licked black lips.

'Grab 'er, Terry,' yelled a woman, massive negligéed bosom squeezed out over the sill of an open upstairs-window. 'Silly little tart gets run over there'll be fuckin' hell to pay.'

'Morning, Liza,' called Gary.

'Awright Gaz,' the upstairs woman squawked. 'I'll be down to see you later, mate—when I've cashed me fuckin' Giro.'

The Old Writer took his chance to walk on, waved and muttered, 'Later, bro'.'

Gary frowned vague disappointment.

'Come and have a cup of tea. It's yonks since you've been round.'

'Yeah. Sorry. Trying to avoid temptation. I haven't smoked in months.'

Gary's eyebrow signified his obvious doubt but he did not call the lie.

'Still on the chink electric fags? Good luck to you. Wish the fuckers worked for me. Quack says ten-to-one I don't live to draw me pension.'

It was rubbish collection day. A light breeze plucked pizza boxes from overstuffed wheelie-bins, rattled plastic bottles across the potholed tarmac. Grizzly scented temptation, pulled free from Gary's frail grip, clattered his chain behind him, reared on hind legs to embrace a bin and rummage his massive head inside. The bin toppled; the dog growled eager, seized its chicken-carcass prize and bone-crunched up the street.

'Dirty old fucker.'

Gary sighed. Weary, he righted the bin, stooped to scoop scattered domestic debris single-handed from the verge.

'Still, could be worse. Cunt scoffed some kid's shitty nappy out of one last week. Breath would've killed a fucking horse.'

'Beats me why you keep the brute.'

'Company,'

Gary wiped his hand on his shirt.

'And security. No tow-rag's gonna crack my crib and blag my weed if they know Grizzly's ready and waiting inside to gnaw on their fucking skull.'

Gary led the way through the rusty wrought-iron gate in the unkempt ten-foot privet hedge that screened the house from casual observation. The dog sprawled on an old mattress by the steel-plated front door, watched Gary prod at a keypad. Electric bolts snapped. Gary pulled a keychain from his greasy jeans, worked locks high and low, leaned his shoulder to the heavy door and beckoned his guest inside.

'Jesus.'

The Old writer choked on a thick sweet soup of dope and dog.

'Where do you keep the breathing apparatus?'

'Got forty plants in full bud, man,' said Gary. 'New hybrid called The Church. Be ready to crop in a couple of days, I reckon. Sit yourself down in the front. I'll bring you some tea and a sample.'

The Old Writer eased into the sparse-furnished sitting room. The huge hound snuffled at his heels. A persistent thin-yellow flare of sunlight penetrated the barrier of high hedge and grimed glass and fell – striated by the shadow of iron window-bars – across dog-hair-matted purple carpet and matching split-seamed sofa. Tentative, he sat.

Casting around for distraction he noted the .22 rifle propped in the corner, the enormous wall-mounted TV wired to the open laptop on the coffee table. Its keyboard was half-buried in drifts of ash and flaked tobacco: a tiny Pompeii of dope-debris. The dog loomed over him abrupt, cleared its throat and stared into his nervous face with crusted eyes as big and dark as eight-balls.

'Just keep your fucking distance, mutt,' The Old Writer growled defensive.

The dog sniffed his fear, and then his balls, laid its engine-block head mournful in his lap. Its tail twitched elephantine, thumped the dormant laptop into life.

Fixed rigid by canine weight and terror, The Old Writer spent his next five minutes engrossed in a glistening HD demonstration of virtuoso lesbian sexual technique presented for his widescreen delectation by www.filthygash.com. Fortunately for his self-respect the immediate proximity of Grizzly's septic jaws to his groin forestalled any gross manifestation of arousal.

Gary lurched in sudden, fat spliff drooped from his mouth.

'Fucking twenty-first century is far-out, ain't it man?'

Tea slopped as he set down mugs.

'Time was you could only get this hardcore shit smuggled in on wagons from Holland at ten-quid a fucking tape. Now it's a wank-fest twenty-four/seven—and you don't even have to pay.'

Gary squatted on the sofa, reached out a claw for the laptop.

'Have a squint at this mad shit I watched last night. "Fat Fruit Fucks"—this one black tart does a whole fucking hand of bastard ripe bananas.'

The Old Writer reached to take the spliff.

'I'm not that big on racist grocery-porn, mate. Internet poker is my preferred pointless pastime.'

'Fucking intellectual prick.'

Gary sniffed scornful but, in deference, logged off. He watched his squeamish guest exhale a blue-grey cumulus across the room, waited for a connoisseur's opinion.

Gary knew his craft. The weed smoked smooth and potent; it oozed cool through The Old Writer's blood, tickled a sweet spot deep in his brain, provoked a silky secretion that smothered the grit of the nascent headache, whose niggling inception he only now noticed, with a pearly anaesthetic pleasure.

'Very nice, Gary.'

He grabbed another toke and passed back the spliff.

'I reckon you're getting the hang of this job.'

'Job? It's a sacred fucking vocation, man.'

The Old Writer leaned back, at peace enough with his world to scratch the dog's head in his lap with gentle affectionate fingers. The brute moaned, drooled its slimy gratitude incontinent onto his chinos.

'So, been anywhere good since I last saw you?'

Gary was not the travelling type. In a decade or more, to the best of The Old Writer's knowledge, he had not ventured further from his bunker than the benefit office in the nearby town of Dismal. But, although largely incurious of the world beyond the village stockade, he seemed to get a vicarious buzz from the imagined glamour of the occasional international voyaging of his 'world-famous mate' that it felt churlish not to indulge.

'Not really,' The Old Writer eventually replied. 'Just the Belgrade Book Fair last autumn.'

'Belgrade?'

'In Serbia.'

'Right.'

Gary stubbed the dead roach of the joint and reached to make another.

'Bit fucking chilly, was it?'

'Most people were friendly enough—but it felt kind of weird being interviewed for a culture show across the street from the TV station NATO bombed to rubble.'

Gary sparked the new spliff, studied its tip thoughtful as he held in smoke.

'Wolves.'

'Huh?'

'Saw a documentary about this old Russian guy studying wolf-packs out there in the frozen wastes. They can run down a fucking snowmobile, man.'

Gary sucked sharp.

'Thought you might've seen some.'

The Old Writer took the outstretched spliff, frowned puzzled as he inhaled, finally made the connection.

'No, mate—that's Siberia. You're anagrammatically confused.'

'Go easy. They never had words like that in Janet and fucking John.'

'Anagrams are when you mix up letters into different words.'

Detecting a risk of perceived condescension The Old Writer passed back the joint with an apologetic shrug.

'Serbia's in the Balkans, mate—part of the former Yugoslavia.'

'Me an' Grizzly dig the wildlife channels,' Gary said unfazed. 'Nature looks fucking amazing in HD when you're stoned—almost as good as the porno.'

The conversation had come full circle. The Old Writer fished out his wallet, extracted two-hundred in fresh twenties, tucked them under the sofa cushion, eased the dog-head deadweight from his numbed thighs and dizzy, swayed erect.

'Thanks for the taste, mate. Give us a shout when it's cut and dried and I'll be round to top-up my stash.'

'It's all good, man.'

Gary wafted smoke.

The Old Writer's head was inflated; it wobbled, a balloon tethered in a breeze. He limped to the door, grasped its greasy handle with extenuated fingers.

'Fucking rabies, right?' said Gary from the sofa about a hundred feet below.

Some sort of stoned non sequitur related to the dog, The Old Writer mused dismissive and toddled on outside. He was halfway down the path to the gate before he worked it out.

He looked back over his shoulder. Gary flashed a peace sign from the doorway, cracked his graveyard grin.

'Anagrams—I shit 'em, man. I could've been a writer too, in another fucking life.'

Helen – bent from the waist and balanced taut-limbed on the terraced rockery beside the barn – stabbed the soil aggressive with a hand trowel. The Old Writer considered sneaking past to hole-up safe in the tower, but her firm round arse and the cant of her hips inspired him to reckless affection. He crept close and was still poised, undecided between goose or slap, when she straightened up and turned – face flushed with exertion, shirt clung alluring to soft, perspiring skin – and wrinkled her nose in disgust.

'Nice walk?'

Her enquiry was neutral but her eyebrow arched a warning. Stupid; Helen had the olfactory capability of a drug dog. With the reek of Gary's weed still tainting his clothes he was busted before he got close.

'Yeah—went round the village for a change.'

'See anyone?'

'Bumped into Gary coming out of the shop. He made me go back for a cup of tea.'
'And?'
'We watched girl-on-girl porn and smoked some spliffs.'
'Right.'
Helen peeled off her gardening gloves, looked him up and down.
'That explains the bleeding-stigmata eyes.'
He took a shot at a helpless boyish grin. She stepped up close, as if for a kiss, brushed past and swung off graceful down the path.
'And the damp patch on your trousers.'

They sat at the patio table, sipped silent tea in the sun. Her hair caught fire in the light. It was dyed these days, of course – Florida Honey, according to the bottle in the bathroom cupboard – but it framed her handsome Viking features no less finely than the natural blonde of her youth. He reached out and touched a curl. Her narrowed eyes mooned over a cup-rim horizon, assessed him cool and blue.
'Love you,' he stated, truthful. 'What can I say? I'm weak.'
'Love you too,' she said, and stood. 'But if your filthy cough keeps me awake all damn night I'll put a pillow over your head.'
'Fair enough,' he said to her departing back. 'And it was dog-drool on my trousers, by the way.'
She laughed abrupt. He caught her up, encircled her waist with an arm. She frowned mild curiosity, impatiently detained.
'Do people really watch pornography at ten in the morning— on a perfect day like this?'
'Graveyard Gary does.'
He bent to whisper in her ear.
'But then he hasn't got a gorgeous wife to passionately commune with.'
She twisted in his arms, scowled and pushed herself free.
'No. And neither have you, you bloody old fool.'

'Oh.'

He grimaced rueful.

'No chance of a quick knee-trembler behind the barn, then—before I lose my high?'

'None—I've got gardening to finish before Jack and Mum wake up from their naps and the kids get back from school.'

'Okay. Just a thought.'

He was disappointed, and relieved.

'But, talking of behind the barn—'

Helen eyed him shrewd.

'Was it you who trampled over the rockery and squashed my new bulb shoots flat?'

She gestured with her trowel, indicated the vandal's route up the barn-side of the terrace to the old cherry tree and the derelict beehive beneath it.

'Not guilty,' he said instinctive, touched by a faint shiver of déjà vu. 'It must've been one of the kids.'

'With bloody great size-twelve feet? Anyway, the kids have more respect. Maybe it was a prowler. We should get security lights.'

'Or a guard dog.'

He imagined Grizzly gnawing skulls.

Helen ignored his whimsy. Brisk, she pulled on gloves.

'I'll be working for a while,' he said and ambled down the path.

'Ask me again later if you're still in the mood,' he thought he heard her murmur scarcely audible over the breeze. But when he glanced back she was already down on her knees engrossed with trowel and dirt.

Sequestered in his tower The Old Writer passed the afternoon diverted from the need to write by an online-poker tourney. Three hours of solid grinding, and then he called a final table all-in shove from 'ShipItSean' with pocket kings, found himself facing Big Slick, got taken out in sixth place by a sick ace from space on the river. He was almost relieved; not only was he twelve dollars and twenty-three cents richer but, freed from the devious thrall of the game, he was finally able to deal with the insect whose persistent drone and repeated tiny window-glass head-bumps had bugged him for the last twenty levels.

It was a bee. He forgave its bumbling irritation, ushered it to hesitant liberty with a generous waft of his hand. It zigzagged away down across the roof, erratic on the breeze, perhaps to dance, on the threshold of an industrious hive, an artful interpretation of its baffled redundant hours.

Inspired by the child-developmental potential of organic honey production, Helen had been a casual apiarist a couple of decades back. But, after a brief honeymoon of sweetness and stings, her bees had been fatally infected by a parasitic mite. The exterminated hive – a silent waxy catacomb of delicate shed wings and crumbled brittle cadavers – had been abandoned to decay, forgotten until an entrepreneurial teenaged Jude had spotted its potential as an asset to nefarious business.

The boy had been sixteen: surly, self-absorbed, secretive and stoned to virtual catatonia for most of his waking hours, whether imprisoned in school or haunting village recreation ground, lurking at large and hostile with his dead-eyed zombie tribe.

It felt like a kind of meta-game that they played, a jostling for rank. The Old Writer versus The Usurping Son: who could stay up later and more stoned?

Night after night, long after Helen had departed pragmatic for bed, The Old Writer would wait – sofa-sprawled, chain-smoking junk TV – until Rude Jude lurched in, weed-wrecked but safe, home from the outlaw night.

Usually they would exchange edgy platitudes or snarl a brief routine of tired repartee, and then Jude would yawn, blink bloodshot eyes and stagger off, sometimes pausing to vomit in the bathroom *en route* to his oblivious bed.

Only then, content that his family was locked-down secure behind shot bolts – and that if his son should die in the night of some new-fangled designer overdose, at least it would be curled up quiet in his laundered bed and not face down in a filthy ditch – could The Old Writer suck up a last soporific joint and retire in hollow triumph.

Rude Jude was always shrewd; he had a dominant mercantile gene. Astute – if not blatantly exploitative – trades with less-alert primary-school pals had routinely multiplied his modest parental allowance. Top Trumps cards; Match Attax stickers; scavenged motorway-crash detritus; intricately painted Warhammer figurines: Jude recognised the commercial potential of them all. So it was obvious, and of nagging concern to his father, that he would finance his adolescent peccadilloes by dealing a little dope. An eighth here, a quarter there. Not good, but Jude was sharp. Most likely he would get away with it; there was no need to worry his mother.

The Old Writer had been engrossed in the novelty of Late Night Poker on Channel Four – seeding his own new addiction – when Jude loomed abrupt in the sitting room door.

'Shit, boy—you nearly stopped my bloody heart,' he had blustered. But answer came there none.

Annoyed, he had turned to look up at the ignorant youth. Rude Jude swayed backlit in the doorway, gulped, toppled and fish-flopped on the floor. Mobile phones skittered across the faded Afghan carpet. Three of them; surely excessive for legitimate purpose.

The Old Writer had stared confused, wondered if it would be quicker to grab one of them up than cross the room to summon paramedics on the landline.

But Jude was on his feet again in one embarrassed bound.

'Fuck. Sorry. Bit of a whitey. It's smoky as shit in here,' he said and swooped to gather scattered wits and phones.

Rattled, The Old Writer had spluttered incoherent as Jude pinballed in slo-mo out the door and blundered upstairs to bed, a blizzard of silvery confetti fluttering vague in his turbulent wake.

Confetti?

The Old Writer had frowned, crawled and peered myopic.

No. Wings; twenty of them, maybe more.

He had picked up a tiny veined-transparency, studied it like a jeweller between puzzled finger and thumb. It was from some kind of fly. Or bee. How the fuck could the boy have got bee-wings all over his clothes?

Subtitled sex had long since superseded TV poker when he recalled Helen's abandoned hive.

Cunning little sod, he had thought and ransacked kitchen cupboards for a half-remembered torch.

Balanced atop the rockery in the surreptitious night, he had removed a dilapidated honeycomb from the warped old wooden hive. Shone dim into the depths of the necropolis the torch had revealed, not the anticipated innocent handful of five-quid deals, or modest Ziploc bag of skunk buds, but two nine-bar soaps of commercial Moroccan hash, a smiley-face-stickered Nescafé jar half-filled with tabs of E, and a roll of twenties in an elastic band that he reckoned at about a grand.

Outraged, halfway to the house and primed to confront his son with the enormity of his crime, a sudden spasm of self-preservation had sent him clambering back to the hive, alert to the paranoid possibility of guilt by forensic association.

Fingerprints wiped and stairs quietly climbed, his passion had subsided, somewhat. He had crouched low over the rank snoring youth to prod and whisper urgent but resisted the vindictive temptation to douche him from stubborn sleep with the water glass of hangover prophylactic at hand on the bedside table. More effective perhaps, he had considered, to avoid a spontaneous eruption of nocturnal violence and negotiate the fine points of drug etiquette in the cool clear light of morning.

When finally he slept that night, The Old Writer had dreamed he was incarcerated in a vast Panopticon of waxy cells in which malevolent stoned screws tormented restrained inmates with the stings of giant bees.

He woke late. Jude had already departed for school. By the time the rude boy slouched home a few hours later, telephonic news of his disgraced expulsion from that institution had already disappointed Helen.

The Old Writer had felt it counter-productive to intensify the general angst with supplementary charges. They endured a fraught month of impassioned debate and sullen intoxication until – rational advice shrugged bullish aside – Jude declared unilateral independence. Within hours he was gone, dull domesticity spurned in favour of precarious adventure On the Road.

Shell-shocked in the aftermath of their son's abrupt desertion, The Old Writer had withdrawn to his tower to sulk in a fog of dismal smoke. Left alone to mourn in her garden, Helen nurtured sympathetic plants. Later, dope-fogged conscience pricked by her irritable summons, he had shared the awkward comfort of dinner with his wife, the guilty secret of Jude's criminality subsumed in the global aura of dejection. A couple more days of careless anaesthesia and he had forgotten the hive completely.

It was his logical assumption now, a decade down the rocky road to familial equanimity, that the devious desperado remained carelessly unaware that his security had ever been breached.

It was cloud-blackened midnight. Bulb shoots avoided assiduous, The Old Writer picked a precarious route from stone to rockery stone. The new torch was tiny and solar charged. Its LEDs radiated a subdued lunar light that seemed to flatten perspective. He felt as if he walked on the moon.

Curiosity had nagged him since he had realised the significance of the mud on Rude Jude's trainers, but he hesitated before he lifted the rickety lid of the hive. Snooping on his adult son felt kind of low, and risky; some secrets it was best not to know.

Then again, revenge promised to be sweet. The bastard deserved a good headfuck. Let him sweat for a while when he rocked up to recover his cache and found it blatantly looted. Jude's conflicted fury and relief – when after due interval of anguish his stash was returned with ceremonial mockery – would be marvellous to behold, a phenomenon whose memory might warm The Old Writer's corrupt soul long into bleak senility.

Anyway, he thought as he hooked the lid with anticipatory fingers, Jude knew his dope. At the very least he would carve himself off a smoke or two of something nice as a token of restorative justice.

The package he delved from the shadowed chasm of the hive was not quite what he expected. Vaguely triangular, gaffer-taped tight in thick plastic and dense with a sinister weight, it did not feel like any dope The Old Writer had ever handled. He placed it on the ground and plucked loose the tape, groaned soft as the thick wrapping unfurled, a monochrome alien flower.

Blue-black, heavy and squat in the cool torchlight, the gun oozed a sick radiation, infected The Old Writer with nausea and shivered him with dismay.

Other than that their primary function was the delivery of sudden death, The Old Writer had little knowledge of guns. For a while in early adolescence, he had indulged a primitive urge to slaughter hapless sparrows with a clandestine airgun that he had purchased with funds embezzled from the golf-ball box of saved florins and half-crowns his father hoarded in his wardrobe. In the due course of spiritual evolution, savage bloodlust had matured into a more sophisticated passion for drugs and sex. At fifteen, he had traded the redundant rifle for a sticky ounce of Afghan black.

Later investigations of replica weapons for the purpose of literary research had taught him enough to recognize that the pistol was a semi-automatic, with magazine in place and safety-catch engaged.

Uneasy, The Old Writer craned erect, checked the night for surveillance. The caravan was quiet and dark. Curtained windows in the house glimmered soft and dim. He waited as a suspect car prowled past on the road beyond his gate; its headlights swept the crowding forest trees with sudden vibrant green. He trembled, tensed as the dark closed in again, and then lunged in urgent reflex, snatched up the weapon from the ground, like a heron takes a frog.

The gun had a cold seductive weight. Its lethal potential excited the nerves of his arm. He lifted and aimed it at the shy new moon unveiled by a sudden teasing breeze, denied a savage impulse to bust a cap in its innocent face. He crouched furtive, chilled by a creeping sense of betrayal and disgust, bundled the thing guilty in its wrapper and hurried it back to the house.

nine

'You need to talk to Cormac,' Helen said and passed him toast.
'Yeah?'
The Old Writer sighed.
'What's the devious little sod gone and done this time?'
'I don't know. But something's on his mind.'
He stirred his cup of *maté*, stirred it some more, created a translucent green whirlpool that threatened to suck him down. He endured a dozen dizzy revolutions, forced himself to lift his head, meet her chilly stare.
'What?'
'We're having a conversation. I speak, you're supposed to respond.'
'Right. What about Cormac?'

He bit his toast. It was wholegrain; a crunched seed jangled his sensitive tooth. He frisbeed the slice toward the bin, scowled silent blame at his wife.

'God, you're an arse this morning.'

'Yeah.'

'Why?'

'Don't know. Bad night. Headache. Fucking dismal rain.'

'Your dad shat the bed. Come and help me change his sheets. That'll cheer you up.'

He swallowed a mouthful of lukewarm *maté*, dumped the rest into the sink.

'I need coffee.'

'Help yourself,' said Helen. 'The rest of you is irritable enough. Your bowel might as well be too.'

'At least I don't shit the bed.'

'The first time you do I'm calling a lawyer.'

He compromised, spooned granules of instant into a fresh cup. It was too much trouble anyway to prepare a proper brew.

'Should rub his goddamn nose in it. Teach the dirty old fuck a lesson.'

'Stop it! You're being vile.'

Angry now, she scraped back her chair, gathered noisy plates.

'I know,' he said. 'I'm sorry.'

'He can't help it. He's a sick old man. You should show a bit more compassion.'

'Right.'

He grimaced contrition. Helen ignored him, busy at the sink.

'So, I need to talk to Cormac?'

'Yes. I found him earlier, when I took the rubbish out, crying by the bins.'

'What about?'

'I don't know. He wouldn't say.'

'Shit.'

The Old Writer watched the rain. Fat tears rolled down the window. He thought about children. He thought about guns.

'Okay. I'll catch him later, after school.'
'He's not at school.'
'Why not?'
'Because it's Sunday of course.'
Helen sneered.
'Get a bloody grip!'

Less than three minutes Internet research informed The Old Writer that the pistol was a nine-millimetre Zastava CZ99, manufactured in Serbia sometime after nineteen ninety. Fifteen minutes more and he had absorbed a comprehensive YouTube tutorial on its maintenance and operation presented, in the interest of public safety, by ex-US Marine Corps weapons specialist, Thomas 'Gunny' Graham. The impressive devastation of a pumpkin was a salutary visual bonus.

Competent now as an armourer, he slid back the false-spine facade of a Collected Works of Shakespeare that concealed his safe in the wall behind the bookcase. He keyed the required digits and opened the heavy door. It occurred to him, as he extracted the gun, that its dark presence added considerable hardcore cachet to the friendly collection of life-enhancing drugs responsibly preserved there out of curious juvenile reach.

Not to mention a potential extra five fucking years in jail.

He unfolded the wrapper on his desk and lifted the cold squat weight, fumbled with nervous fingers to extract the weapon's magazine. It was loaded, charged sinister with dull copper seeds of murderous violence and mayhem.

Surprised that he felt no need to refresh Gunny's video advice, he worked the slide to clear the breach, checked both visual and manual, deconstructed the death-machine, easy, like a pro.

It was only then that he noticed the USB memory-stick taped inside the crumpled wrapper.

The Old Writer touched tongue-tip to lip. For a moment he was Leepus, hot for the thrill of revelation. He slipped the stick into a vacant CPU slot and clicked the requisite icons. The fucking thing was encrypted of course, locked behind a password.

Frustrated, he typed manifold permutations around the theme of Jude's chaotic life: birth date, anagrams of 'Natalya', even old movies he had loved as a kid; but he failed to find the magic word before, panicked by a sly creak of stair, he was forced to abandon the game.

'Hey, mate!' he called as he stowed the stripped-down weapon safe back behind classic camouflage. 'You going to skulk out there like an assassin for hours or come in and say hello?'

The Old Writer walked with his grandson. Around them the sodden forest dripped rank with a tropical musk. Glimpsed ragged through the treetop canopy, grey sky became vague blue. Beneath their feet, the path steamed as the re-emergent sun recycled puddled rain.

'How far do we have to go, then?'

Cormac scowled.

'My trainers are already soaked.'

'Stop moaning,' said The Old Writer. 'Wet feet aren't going to kill you.'

'Yeah, but Mum probably will. If I go home with them ruined the blame's on you, okay?'

'Okay.'

He ushered the boy from the wide track. They sprang a briar-tangled muddy ditch, pushed through a curtain of wet hazel, stepped into a dark sepulchre of beech that ringed a despondent pool.

Cormac stared hard into the black water.

'It looks deep.'

'It is.'

'How deep?'

'No one knows.'

'If you fell in, would you drown?'

'Depends.'

'Depends on what?'

'On whether Old Razor Mouth grabbed your skinny leg before you could drag yourself out.'

Cormac eyed him, dubious.

'What's Old Razor Mouth?'

'Can't say. Never seen him. Just know he's been lurking there to ambush the unwary for at least a hundred years.'

'Yeah—right.'

Cormac quick-stepped back from the perilous edge.

'Believe it or not,' The Old Writer said, and then led off on a slotted deer trail between lichen-mottled trunks.

They walked on silent for a while, cleared the beech to tread a soft needle-floor beneath colonnaded larch. A tinnitus of long-tailed tits kite-tailed bright through the shadows.

Cormac stepped heavy, snapped a dry twig, froze rigid as a raucous jay shrieked unseen alarm. 'What the hell was that?' he murmured pale.

'Evil-spirit of the woods,' his grandfather reassured. 'Hang onto your mortal soul, lad. Those buggers can be sly.'

'Have you ever got lost in here?' said Cormac in the gloom.

'No. Not for more than a day or two. It's not as big as it used to be when outlaws hunted here.'

'Outlaws are like robbers, right? Robin Hood an' that?'

'Sometimes, yeah. And sometimes they're just people who don't fit in and want to live by different rules.'

'Mum had some friends in Bristol. We went to see them once. They lived in this big manky old house—kept the windows all boarded up so the cops couldn't throw them out. Said they were antichrists, or something.'

'Anarchists.'

The Old Writer's pedantry was instinctive.

'But yeah, I reckon you could call them modern outlaws, right enough.'

'If you ran off to be one, would you hide in the forest or a town?'

'The forest, I think.'

'But what would you eat?'

'I'd hunt deer with a bow and arrow, trap rabbits and pheasants—and there'd be nuts and berries too.'

They jumped the stream and scrambled the slope up to the nettled clearing. The fat old oak straggled haggard at its centre, twisted arms fisted with hands of sprouting green. Cormac sagged, sat down on a lightning-scorched fallen branch that reared from the scrub like a dragon.

'That's far enough now, Granddad,' said the boy. 'I'm knackered and bloody hank.'

'Hank?'

'Hank Marvin. Starvin'. What've you got to eat?'

Helen had thrust a couple of Fruit'n'Grain bars into his hand as they had left the house an hour before; he tossed one to the grateful boy. They munched. Cormac studied the oak.

'Looks like one of those mad tree-giant things out of Lord of the bloody Rings.'

He shook the last crumbs into his mouth and handed his grandfather the wrapper.

'How old do you think it is?'

'Probably five-hundred years or more. It's called The Sanctuary Tree.'

'Why?'

'Because it's hollow inside. They say people used to hide there.'

'Outlaws?'

'I wouldn't be surprised.'

'Cool.'

Re-energised, Cormac slid from the log. The Old Writer followed him to the ancient tree. The boy slapped its twisted trunk, heard the dull resonance of the void beneath the creviced bark. 'Give us a bunk-up,' he commanded. 'I want to see inside.'

The Old Writer cupped compliant hands. A cold muddy trainer smeared his face as the boy kicked up into the crook.

'Wow,' Cormac said as he peered down inside. 'It's as big as a bloody room.'

'Any outlaw skeletons?'

'Dunno. The floor's all covered in leaves and twigs. I'd have to get in to see.'

'Give it a go if you want,' said The Old Writer. 'You probably won't get stuck.'

'Uh—maybe we could come back another time.'

Cormac wavered on the brink.

'Bring a torch and some rope.'

'Good plan.'

His grandfather sidestepped as the boy star-jumped reckless from his perch, commando-rolled into nettles. 'Ouch!' he said and grinned sympathetic. 'Bet that bloody stings.'

'Not as bad as falling backwards onto gravel off a bike,' Cormac muttered stoic.

'Look before you leap.'

The Old Writer crouched to squeeze dock juice onto thin rash-encrusted arms.

'You think those old know-alls made up their sage sayings just to be bloody annoying?'

Cormac peered at the sky. 'Maybe we should head home now,' he murmured. 'It's getting sort of dark.'

'Yeah—could be another shower before morning.'

The Old Writer squinted up, flinched as a lightning razor-slash disembowelled the bloated sky.

They ran down the slope, dived into a dense hawthorn-bunker and hunkered down, thunder-shocked but dry, as stormtroopers machine-gunned helpless foliage with a fusillade of hail.

'Now what?'

Cormac tensed for the next detonation. The Old Writer peered out at the solid roar of rain.

'We'll be okay here till the worst passes over.'

'But a big tree might get struck and fall on us. What would we do then?'

'Curse the gods that mock us and die squashed to jam, like bugs.'

Cormac huddled chilly, watched him gather leaves and splinter twigs to spark a friendly fire. They fed the flames and wafted smoke, silent for a while.

The Old Writer studied the tired anxious boy, judged him conditioned for interrogation. 'So,' he opened, casual. 'How's life in the old caravan?'

'Okay.'

Cormac poked the tiny inferno with a thoughtful stick.

'Bit crowded. Mum gets the chin if we don't keep everything neat and tidied away.'

'It won't be forever. And summer's coming—you've got plenty of space outside.'

'Yeah. I want to practice with the trebuchet. But Mum says I'm banned for busting your head with that bloody frozen turnip.'

'Okay. I'll have a word.'

'I'd really like to build a ballista. That would be totally wicked.'

Reluctant to disappoint, The Old Writer pantomimed due consideration, lined up boring excuses before he spoke.

'Sorry, mate. Not possible. We're technically incompetent to tackle a job like that. Ballistas are complicated bits of kit—not to mention bloody lethal.'

Cormac waited, watched a flame lick up his stick almost to his hand, and pounced. 'How about a longbow then? I could practice cool outlaw skills.'

'Hmmm.'

'I'd only use it in the paddock. We could set up a bunch of targets and stuff.'

'Well, you do have a birthday coming up but—'

'Yeah. Thanks, Granddad.'

'Slow down. We'll have to see what your mum says first—and Angie.'

'Mum'll need some persuading.'

Cormac considered tactics.

'But Angie's cool—she'll help me wear her down.'

'So you like having Angie around?'

'Yeah. She's kind of nuts—but way more fun than all our other boring dads.'

The boy paused, lifted his head; distant thunder circled. 'Though you can't really call a woman 'dad', can you?' he qualified.

'Strictly speaking, I suppose not,' The Old Writer agreed. 'But the title's not important as long as she does the job.'

'She has bad dreams. About the war, I think.'

'Yeah?'

'They make her moody. Then Mum gets cross and picks on her for drinking. And Angie gets upset.'

'Do they fight?'

'Yeah—sometimes. Kind of.'

'Does that bother you?'

'Of course it does. I don't want Angie to leave.'

'Do you think your mum does?'

'I don't know. She's made it happen before.'

'Did they fight this morning? Is that what made you cry?'

Cormac stood up sudden, kicked at the dying embers of their fire and sniffed.

'That's enough questions. I don't want to talk about it now.'

The sudden resistance wrong-footed The Old Writer.

'Why not?'

'Because it's peoples' private business, Granddad. And I'm not a bloody snitch.'

Cormac clawed out of their bunker; thorns grabbed at his thin clothes. His grandfather sighed and followed the evasive boy out into the drizzling dusk.

They negotiated the dark wet woods in single file without the distraction of conversation. Still mute, they emerged from the tree line. Ahead, the motorway hissed and slithered urgent. Stitched with red and white light-chains, curtains of road-spray veiled the bridge. They trudged across it sodden, side by tongue-tied side. It was not until they were back at the house – shivering guilty and drowned-rat-like to kick off filthy shoes in the porch – that Cormac squinted up shy and let him off the hook.

'Thanks for showing me your outlaw tree. It was ace. And the storm was bloody dread.'

'Hey. Thanks for being with me. I'd have been scared shitless dodging all that crazy lightning out there on my own.

The boy appreciated the mild scatology with a snigger. The Old Writer steered him through the door, firm hand on bony damp shoulder.

'Upstairs and have a hot shower now,' he nudged. 'I'll see what your grandma's saved for our tea.'

'Right,' called Cormac from halfway up the stair. 'Then we can look on eBay—choose what kind of mad longbow I'm going to get.'

ten

'Do you think I brought enough?'

Helen watched him drag the first hay-bale from the trailer onto the paddock grass.

'I could always go back for more.'

'No need.'

The Old Writer panted it into position.

'We're only building a backstop, not Hadrian's bloody wall.'

'Okay.'

She was still dubious.

'I'll leave you to get on with it and go and defrost the meat.'

'Fine.'

He eyed the stacked trailer.

'Don't strain yourself watching the microwave.'

He yanked hard at the second bale, cursed the thin twine that cheese-wired his hand.

'Just remember the bloody trebuchet,' she called in supercilious retreat. 'Better safe than looking stupid with an arrow through your eye.'

By the time the trailer was half-empty The Old Writer hated straw. His temple throbbed and his shoulder ached. His forearms, crosshatched raw by brittle stalks, stung like bloody bastards. He took a breath, assessed the progress of his construction. Two courses were bonded haphazard, only four fucking more to go.

Subject to intensive lobbying, Helen and Viola had performed a rigorous risk assessment on the proposed archery butts. Full compliance with their specification was mandatory before Cormac could be licensed to string his bow.

The Old Writer recalled his own brief ballistic craze. The attitude to Health and Safety had been more libertarian back then. Proper bows beyond their financial reach, his small band of pre-teen outlaw renegades had pillaged canes from the allotments and bent them to their crude purpose with hanks of garden string. Arrows were cut from economic dowels, fletched dextrous with pigeon feathers and tipped with heads filed from solid brass in the metalwork shop at school.

Denied long-range shooting opportunity in the tame wilderness of suburbia, they annexed the small lawn of the local Parish Hall to launch their handcrafted projectiles on a risky vertical plane. It was imperative not to lose track of an arrow as it plummeted to sprout erect from the turf, though it added a certain eye-scrunching thrill of expectation if you did.

One breathless summer afternoon, as aerobatic swallow squadrons wing-flicked slick through insect-clouded air above imagined Agincourt, he had full-bent his heroic bow and loosed its deadly shaft. Rapt, he had watched it soar, slow and hang, plotted its trajectory of descent to inevitable impact point.

There was a wide verge of grass between the hall's enclosing fence and the road; a footpath cut through it to the kerb of a pedestrian crossing. On this, oblivious in fond maternity, a young woman in a floral dress strolled her baby in its pram. He had stared, iced in terror, as his deviant arrow fell.

Panicked recalculation offered no desperate hope of error. Honed to lethal perfection, the heavy arrowhead would penetrate the pram canopy unerring. The infant was doomed to die impaled in sudden silence; its mother, her agony eternal, would scream, and scream, and scream.

Something curled up and died inside him there in the fleet second between life and death: a naive innocence of consequence that could never be recovered. He closed his eyes and waited for the terrible noise to start.

But some compassionate god of reckless youth had stooped to intervene, averted his future Hell of guilt and jail with a miraculous breath of mercy. When he had opened his eyes and looked again the woman still stepped lively, pushed her baby future-ward, ignorant of hazard. A heartbeat behind her, flowered with feathers, the arrow stalked stiff from the verge. He had recovered it with a quivering hand and slunk home to choke down a penitent tea of bilious beans-on-toast.

'Alright there?' a voice asked sudden from somewhere off in space.

'Huh?'

The Old Writer squinted up from his bale, blinked ASBO Angie into focus.

'You look a bit fuckin' pale, mate.'

'I'm fine. Just summoning a last burst of energy to finish my house of straw.'

He stood. Too quick. Pain's arrow pierced his brain. He winced and sat back down.

'Here.'

Angie tossed him her makings.

'Roll yourself a ciggie and catch your breath. Used to help out on the family farm back in the day. I'm an old hand at tossing bales.'

'Farm?'

He tongued the narrow glue-strip automatic – for at least the hundred-millionth lifetime count – and smoothed the sheath of thin paper tight over plump tobacco. Angie jerk-lifted the heavy block of straw above her head, tossed it into position, energetically efficient.

'Yeah. My brother Frank took it on when the old man went walkabout.'

She grunted another bale aloft.

'Pigs. He keeps about a thousand Tamworths—over Sleaford way.'

'You weren't cut out for kicking shit?'

The Old Writer returned her tobacco.

'No,' she said and squatted next to him. 'I thought it'd be more fun kicking arse. So I fucked off and joined the army.'

'And was it?'

'What?'

She idled with her half-formed cigarette.

'The action. All that licensed violence. Did it get you off?'

'Why would you care what gets me off?'

'Sick curiosity. Indulge me.'

'Yeah—sometimes it did.'

She hawked and spat.

'Others, I puked my fuckin' ring.'

'And now?'

Angie cut her head up at him, searched his face with her eyes.

'Now is another fuckin' country, man. I'm still finding my way around.'

'But old instincts die hard?'

The woman stood. Her fist balled, flexed nails into her palm. He was chucking rocks in a minefield; he waited for the bang.

'And your point is fuckin' what?' ASBO Angie said and stared down hard.

He reached out the lighter clutched damp in his fist and flicked a trembling flame. She bent her head towards it, ciggie lip-clamped tight.

'I don't know,' he said. 'Just that sometimes overwhelming force might not be the best first response to provocation?'

Angie sucked fire; it flared in her eye. 'Okay,' she said, 'I get it now,' and took the lighter from his hand.

'Good.'

The Old Writer smiled, relieved by her reaction.

'Because there's some shit it's tough to ignore, and I don't want to have—'

'Hey! Shut the fuck up now.'

'But—'

'You're a nice old twat and you mean well—but whatever it is you think you know you don't have a fuckin' clue.'

She hauled and heaved the last half-dozen bales in a fury of exertion. The Old Writer watched and smoked. Tobacco tar condensed bitter in his throat and trickled sick to his stomach. He choked and coughed, and coughed again. Each violent bronchial spasm hacked a chunk from his frontal lobe. Eventually he calmed his troubled breast, flicked the dead cigarette from self-disgusted fingers, lifted his battered head. ASBO Angie loomed over him, sweating and impassive.

'Well?'

'Not really,' he said. 'But I'll live a couple more hours.'

'You gonna shift your scrawny arse off that last fuckin' bale?'

She grimaced and cracked her knuckles.

'Or do I stick you up there with it, like a fuckin' nasty old gargoyle?'

He moved. She lofted the bale and dusted her hands. Together they carried the archery target from the car and set it in its place.

'Right,' she said. 'I'll go and sort the barbecue out. Birthday boy'll be coming off the bus from school in half-a-bleedin'-hour.'

'Thanks, Angie. I'd have been struggling with that till dark.'

'It's all good, man.'

She dead-armed him with a jab.

'But next time skip the counselling, huh? Or I'll have to start calling you 'padre'.'

They turned towards the house.

'Sorry,' he said. 'Didn't mean to preach. But feel free to find me anytime you need a cat to kick.'

Angie sniffed, caught her breath on the edge of speech, cast a narrow eye around in search of a change of topic.

'Talking of preaching, I see a bunch of Jesus junkies have set up camp in town.'

'What?'

'Yeah—fuckin' god-botherer tent-show on the footie pitches. Saw it when I went up the shop this morning for me snout. 'Army of Light', or some such shit, the fuckin' banner says.'

A distant bell of memory chimed deep in his aching head, echoed unanswered into silence. 'Not thinking of enlisting, mate?' he asked as she veered towards the barn.

'Not fuckin' likely.'

Angie marched on.

'Soldiering's for cunts.'

'Shit! It slipped off the bloody string again.'

Cormac ground his teeth as yet another arrow wobbled down the range, planed high above the target, slapped the hay-wall broadside and fell feeble to the grass.

'This bow is fucking crap.'

'Relax, mate.'

The Old Writer dribbled oil on troubled waters.

'Focus more and curse less. You'll get your eye in soon enough.'

A skein of smoke drifted thin across the range, greased his nasal membrane with the taint of cremated flesh.

'Why don't we give it a rest for now and get the celebrations started. That delicate aroma of incinerated cow is starting to make my mouth water.'

'Yeah. Your mouth, my bloody eyes.'

Cormac glared frustration.

'How am I supposed to hit a target when I can't bloody see it for smoke?'

They unstrung the bow, gathered scattered arrows. The family was assembled fireside by the barn. Cormac squinted at them shrewd through the hanging haze.

'I wonder what Uncle John's brought me. Something weird and dead, I bet.'

'Uncle John?'

The Old Writer caught a whiff of barbecued cat.

'I'm not sure he's coming, mate.'

Cormac frowned.

'Well his van was parked over by the rec when I got off the bus.'

'You sure it was his?'

'Yeah. Unless there's another mad weirdo driving around with a stuffed crow stuck on his dashboard.'

'I texted them both,' said Helen in the kitchen.

The Old Writer watched her adjust the candles on a *testudo* of Roman legionaries wrought artful from iced cake.

'Jude sent fifty-quid in an inappropriate card, but I haven't heard from John.'

'Inappropriate?'

'Lad's mag picture of some pouting sex-mutant babe. She opened her shirt to show her huge tits when you turned it in the light.'

'Hah. Clever. Should enhance the boy's cred at school.'

'I don't think so. Viola put it through the shredder and gave him ten minutes on the proper respect of women.'

'Right.'

The Old Writer fumbled for his lighter, adjusted his position.

'Good for her. When you're talking potential role models Jude doesn't make the cut.'

Candles flickered waxy above raised shields as the *testudo* slow-marched ceremonial up the garden path to the barn. Cormac stared, caught awkward between childish delight and insouciant adolescence.

'Thanks, Nan,' he breathed, and stooped to study intricate candlelit detail. 'Tesco cakes are getting better.'

Maternal, Viola cuffed him.

'Don't be so rude. It took your grandma a whole day just to ice the eagles on those shields.'

'All right.'

Cormac shrugged her off.

'Nan knows I'm only winding her up. Her cake's the bloody bomb.'

'Language,' cautioned Helen, pleased. 'Now let's all sing Happy Birthday and you can blow your candles out.'

The sugar shields of the *testudo* were inadequate defence against the keen assault of Sheffield steel and grasp of hungry hands. The cake was demolished in short order, hapless legionaries mutilated and devoured in barbarous celebration. Enthroned chiefly on his garden recliner with the land's best wine in hand, The Old Writer indulged the loud revelry of his tribe, distant but benign.

The music – conjured mysterious via Angie's iPhone wired devious to a cunning amp and boomed-large through tiny speakers – was alien but familiar. The Old Writer caught echoes of diverse tunes from decades passed buried deep in cacophonous confusion. He drummed spasmodic fingers on his thigh but the new rhythms were elusive. Around him, excited children chased and danced to the turbulent beat, innocent pleasure uninhibited by shades of future doubt.

It was not only the children who danced, he noticed. Obscene Irene had hauled Cracked Jack to his feet and now held his hands and swung his arms as she jigged and jived to the music. The old man leered and twitched in jovial response, intoxicated by the heavy throb of bass and a bottle of strong cider.

'Looks like your mum finally tweaked the old bastard's romantic nerve,' The Old Writer muttered to Helen and, surprised by a sickly whiff of skunk on the air, turned to find it was Jilted John whom he had sensed moving to stand beside him.

'Hey, boy! Good to see you,' The Old Writer greeted his son, outstretched a supplicant hand. 'Got a toke there for your old mooch of a dad?'

John passed him a soggy roach.

'Sorry I'm late. Got halfway here before I realised I'd forgotten Cormac's present. Didn't think it would go down too well if I turned up empty-handed.'

The Old Writer read the shift of his son's eye that betrayed his lie but let it pass unchallenged. The boy was still fragile. He had probably lurked for hours round the corner in his van, smoking up enough skunk courage to broach the family circle.

'Well, you're here now. Have you seen your mum?'

'Yeah—I just got ambushed in the kitchen and maternally scrutinised.'

'She'll be pleased you made the effort.'

'She nagged me for being thin.'

'Right.'

The Old Writer nodded toward the smouldering barbecue.

'You grab a nourishing hunk of fatted-calf. I'll go and fetch you a beer.'

Helen was busy at the kitchen sink, plunged elbow-deep in the comfort of suds. The Old Writer plucked a towel from the rail and reached a warm plate from the drainer.

'What's wrong?'

'Nothing,' she replied with a sniff.

'It's good John came.'

'Yes.'

'He seems okay.'

'Really?'

She clattered a handful of cutlery onto stainless steel, wiped a tickle of hair from her forehead with the back of a soapy hand.

'It's hard to tell. He could barely look at me.'

'He was never the most demonstrative.'

'He's just so pale and tense.'

The Old Writer stacked dried crocks conscientious in the cupboard. Helen wiped the surfaces down, frowned, relocated the plates to a more appropriate shelf.

'C'mon now, love.'

He steered her gently, hand on hip.

'Let's go and join the party before it ends in tears.'

'Look what Uncle John got me, Granddad.'

Cormac treasured a small dense object on a reverent clammy palm.

'It's real Roman. From about two-hundred years BC.'

'Cool.'

The Old Writer peered, genuinely impressed, at the wedge of verdigrised bronze.

'It's an arrowhead from Carthage,' Cormac enthused. 'It might have been used at the battle of Zama, when Scipio Africanus beat Hannibal, you know?'

'Well that's according to the description on eBay.'

John smiled shy.

'We've no way of knowing for sure.'

'Looks genuine to me,' The Old Writer judged. 'You can even see where one of the barbs is bent—as if it was fired and hit something hard.'

'Yeah. Probably a Roman skull.'

Cormac mimed an arrow's flight; it impacted between his eyes.

'Pretty bloody unlucky, huh—if that was the last thing you ever saw, coming down straight at you out of a scorching desert sky?'

'I hope you thanked your uncle for buying you such a special present,' Viola said and drained her wine. 'Just make sure you keep it safe in its box. It's for looking at, not shooting.'
'What happened to the music?'
Irene tottered from the shadows.
'The party's hardly started and Jack's still hot to trot.'
'The little ones have gone to bed, Mum,' said Helen. 'Maybe you should too.'
'Not without Jack.'
Irene smirked sly.
'I'll see if the old chap's ready.'
'You too, birthday boy,' Viola marshalled Cormac. 'Time's arrow is pointing to sleep.'
'God, Mum,' the boy said sullen. 'It's only bloody eleven o'clock. Why are you so boring?'
'Because that's the curse of mothers, brat.'
Viola rolled her eyes.
'Now move—or you'll be bored for a week while you're grounded for disrespect.'
'I'd go now,' said The Old Writer. 'Before Irene comes back for her birthday kiss.'
'Good plan.'
Cormac stifled a yawn and slouched off to the caravan, Viola close behind. Muted conflict grumbled momentary inside, coerced his reappearance.
'Thanks for the wicked presents everyone.'
The boy called his reluctant encore from the step.
'And the sick bloody party, too.'

eleven

The Old Writer had made it to about three a.m. before the steady attrition of wine and skunk finally collapsed his composure.

There had been an hour of stoned shit talked with John as the barbecue embers dimmed and died and the rest of the household slept. Back inside at the kitchen table, he had blathered on, all reference to cats evaded. John humoured him with an occasional gnomic response, engrossed in his meticulous rendering of the panoramic Battle of Zama sketch that Cormac's pleading flattery had earlier extorted.

A diligent but incompetent host, The Old Writer had burned toast and boiled the kettle dry, soldiered on to the dregs of a last, superfluous, bottle of wine. But compliance with John's unreasonable demand for a Sharpie – required to ink the blacks of his epic work – had proved a hospitable bridge too far.

The Old Writer recalled his legless collapse down the kitchen wall: a tray dragged clumsy from Helen's kids' art-supply cupboard, an avalanche of coloured pens clattering down around him onto the cold stone floor.

John had hauled him to his tangled feet, prodded him up the funny stairs, left him to crawl, sick and stupid, along the landing to bed.

The Old Writer looked at the bedside clock; it was ten thirty-two. He thought about getting up but the oppressive deadweight of the duvet pinned him uncomfortably inert.

He had dreamed the house had been raided: a panic of sirens, blue light strobing, shouted orders and pounded doors, cops with smirks and handcuffs dangled.

He thought about John and his crucified cats. He thought about Angie burning cars, about Jude's fucking gun in his safe. He felt the need to vomit; he just could not be arsed to move.

It was ten thirty-four. He buried his face in the pillow, listened to his heart beat sluggish blood through the veins of his aching head.

'Half-past bloody one in the afternoon and it's still not shaved and dressed,' snarled Cracked Jack, his whereabouts uncertain. 'Where's your damn self-respect, you idle little shit?'

'Hangover, Dad.'

The Old Writer reached for the kettle.

'We had a family party last night. Did it slip your simple mind?'

'You should take a bit more water with it, boy, if you can't hold your bastard drink.'

The Old Writer took his time. He checked the filled kettle was plugged in, switched it on, and then turned to face his father's shrivelled scorn. It took him a bemused moment to locate the old man. He was folded awkward on the floor in a chilly pool of fridge-light.

The Old Writer blinked incomprehension. Limp ham-slices were plastered to floor-tiles in an ochre smear of mustard; a brace of cold-grinning mackerel swam through a lurid reef of shattered eggs. Cracked Jack glared up defiant, waved a stainless-steel carving knife smeared with buttery blood.

'Shit, Dad.'

The Old Writer stared.

'What the hell are you doing down there?'

'Making a ham sarnie for my lunch. What does it bloody-well look like?'

'A plate might've been a good idea. And some bread to put the meat in?'

He disarmed his father, clattered the knife onto the drainer, seized the old man under his arms, hauled him to his feet.

'Now stick your hand under the tap while I find a plaster for that cut.'

Cracked Jack waved him away, frowned at the bead of dark slow blood that oozed from his hand and shuffled to the sink.

'And mind you don't step on that bloody fish,' The Old Writer said too late.

His father frowned at him, mournful.

'If you'd been here to help me like your missus said you would I wouldn't have got into a mess.'

'Right.'

The Old Writer plucked the backing from a plaster selected from the first-aid box he had located in a cupboard with gratifying ease.

'It had to be my fault.'

Impatient, he turned on the tap, thrust Jack's hand into the torrent; sprayed water soaked them both. The tea towel looked less than sterile but there was nothing else to hand. He dabbed the wound, pressed the dressing into place on slack and mottled skin. His father's hand was damp and cold; it squatted in his like a toad. The Old Writer shuddered, let it drop.

'Where is Helen anyway?'

He bundled ruined food from floor to fridge, clunked shut the heavy door.

'Shopping. With Doris.'

Jack curled his lip, pointed a hooked finger.

'Can't you bloody read?'

The Post-it note was concise. *Taken Irene for a doctors' appointment. Jack will want his lunch at about 12:30. Get the washing in if it rains.*

The Old Writer uncovered a pre-prepared plate of crustless sandwiches, carried it to the table, pulled out a chair and gestured Jack to sit.

'Irene,' he said, deadpan.

'What about her?'

'Helen went out with her today—not Doris.'

A flutter of panic crossed his father's face.

'Doris was your wife, Dad. She's been passed away five years.'

'Liar.'

Jack's clenched fist thumped the table, caught the rim of his sandwich plate and flipped it.

'Do you think I'm fucking stupid?'

'No—just nasty old and demented.'

The Old Writer reassembled sandwiches.

'Now shut up and eat your goddamn lunch. I can't be arsed with your spiteful shit today.'

He re-boiled the kettle and brewed *maté*, washed down Paracetamol. Behind him, Cracked Jack stared at the wall and chewed his silent cud. Rain squalled sudden against the window. The Old Writer cursed and shouldered out the door.

'Are you sure?'

'About what?'

The Old Writer spat out a mouthful of pegs, dumped the armful of retrieved underwear and socks jumbled onto a chair.

'About Doris going and changing her name. You'd think she'd have bloody told me.'

'Wipe your mouth, Dad,' The Old Writer said. 'You've got ham fat on your chin.'

Jack's lips writhed spittle-flecked. Fear flitted his red-rimmed eyes.

'Being old is shit, boy. It makes you all bitter and twisted.'

'Yeah—well you were never Mr. Happy, were you?'

He reached out a fist. Jack flinched. He smudged the detritus from his father's face with a bent protruded knuckle.

'I did what I was supposed to.'

Jack jutted his jaw, defiant.

'I went to work and paid my way. Gave up my dreams for my children.'

'Did you? Really?'

'Yes. I wanted to go to Australia and work on a ranch, live free in the great outdoors—somewhere that wasn't so bloody crowded dull and cold. I had all the money saved.'

'What stopped you?'

'Doris wouldn't have liked it. She wanted babies, and a house.'

'You loved her though.'

'Couldn't help myself, could I? The woman was too bloody nice.'

Jack sucked a shuddering breath.

'I was fond of her damn children too—whatever they were called. But they still went and used up my one and only sodding life.'

'I'm sorry, Dad.'

He laid his hand on his father's nape, felt vertebrae knotted beneath dry-tissue skin.

'Don't pity me, you smug lump of shit.'

Jack flexed him off.

'One day it'll be you knocking at Death's door all disappointed and alone. Then you'll damn-well be sorry.'

'Right. Thanks for that encouraging word.'

'Don't tell me you don't feel it too, Mister Clever-Dick-Rich-Writer. You act like the wise old king-of-the-castle with your happy tribe around your feet. But I've seen that trapped look in your eyes, smelled the fear that rots your guts.'

'Everyone has their off days.'

The Old Writer mustered a grin of resolve.

'But it's families that make us human, isn't it? They're the reason that we care?'

Cracked Jack laughed his teeth out. 'You saying you don't hate yours then?' he sneered, dentures cupped in hand.

'What? Don't be daft.'

The Old Writer swallowed.

'Of course I fucking don't.'

Cracked Jack thumbed his plate back into gummy position, raised up hunched on shaky legs, glared down vulturine. His breath was a gust from an opened tomb; his son inhaled his doom.

'You will, boy. Believe me,' the old man rasped. 'It's only a matter of time.'

twelve

'You're sure it was Shy fucking Skye?'

'Yes—the police car pulled out of the rec car park as I was driving past with Mum. She was in the back with some weird rock-star Rasputin-type—all mirror shades and mad Christian bling. She stared me right in the face.'

'Did she acknowledge you?'

'No. She looked utterly terrified. And her eyes were red-raw from crying.'

'Shocked, I guess,' The Old Writer said. 'They could've got torched with the tent.'

'Yes. I suppose they were bloody lucky.'

Helen grimaced, finished re-upping her mother's medicine dispenser with tablets decanted from a fresh prescription pack before she spoke again.

'Their Army of Light camper-van was on the back of a low-loader. The paint was all scorched and blistered down one side—and it had cat-paw shapes daubed all over it, like a weird graffiti rash.'

The Old Writer took stock through the kitchen window: young Cormac practising diligent at the archery butts in the paddock; Callum and Carmen, happy in the sandpit by the caravan fighting with plastic spades; Baby Christy watching delighted from his pram as – lofted skyward on the old garden-swing by the effort of Cracked Jack – Obscene Irene kicks her legs and giggles girlish.

'How do you know it was arson?'

'Michaela-in-the-chemist's said. Her son's a fireman. Apparently the signs are obvious if you know what you're looking for.'

'Any suspects?'

'Fingers have been pointed at young Paul Brady—that Goth boy who got caught spray-painting mystic sigils on gravestones last Halloween. But his mum says he's been ill in bed with a stomach bug all week.'

'And what time did it happen?'

'The sirens woke me about half-past four. I tried to rouse you from your drunken stupor—but you just mumbled some shit about victimless crime, farted and turned over.'

'Right.'

The Old Writer studied his wife, assessed the level of her suspicion. She frowned and met his eye, rose to stow surplus medication safe on the high 'pharmacy shelf'.

'So what time did John leave?'

'I don't know.'

Helen dumped packaging in the bin.

'He was gone when I got up at seven. Left a note on the table with Cormac's picture, saying thanks and he'd call us soon. Why?'

'Just wondered.'

'Strange that Skye was so close by. Good job he didn't know, I suppose. It might have spoiled the party.'

'Yeah.'

The Old Writer stepped close and embraced her. She was warm against his chill.

'Be best if we keep his visit quiet, if anyone comes asking questions.'

Helen bit her lip and turned from his arms. They stood together, momentarily silent, looked out into the paddock. Obscene Irene, dismounted from the swing now, tiptoed to fix a yellow rosebud in Cracked Jack's buttonhole.

'I found one of Mum's slippers under your dad's bed this morning,' said Helen shifting ground.

'He thinks she's Doris.'

'Okay.'

Helen rolled her weary eyes.

'I wonder if she knows.'

The sensation was weird, a cross between pain and emotion. It turned like a worm in The Old Writer's brain, undermined a minor foundation.

He winced; she saw.

'What's wrong?'

'I don't know. I'm just feeling a little bit fragile.'

'What can I do?'

She touched his hand; her compassion moistened his eyes.

'Take me to bed and shut the world out,' he said, trembling and feeble. 'Hold me close in the lonely dark and make love to me like you used to.'

The Old Writer drifted, suffused with primal bliss. Confusion resolved and contradictions reconciled, he was calm, fulfilled, complete. The struggle was over, the long-awaited climax triumphantly achieved. The unruly world was ordered; everything made sense. There was nothing left to do now but rest comfortable, in peace.

If only he could stay submerged, asleep in the opiate deep.

But sharks of adrenaline cruised his hypnagogic ocean. They drove him to the surface and tore his dream to shreds, stranded him, drowned and disappointed, on the deserted shore of the bed.

'Fuck,' he croaked as he opened his eyes to the half-light of the room. 'Fuck. Fuck. Fuck.'

He remembered the warmth of Helen's hand as she led him upstairs to bed. He remembered how she undressed him and held him huddled cold in her arms. He remembered the weird black void in his brain that had gaped and sucked him down. But he had no recollection of her leaving, or of how long he had slept alone. Light fingered past the curtains, infiltrated gloom. But the world turned relentless day on day. He could have slept the clock round for all he fucking knew.

The Old Writer sat up, swung leaden legs from the bed, swallowed a brief nausea and invoked the will to stand. The limbs were pale and scrawny. A vein pulsed blue on a thigh. He shivered, reached for trousers and covered his alien flesh.

Cormac was in the kitchen mooching biscuits from his nan.
'About time.'
He turned to The Old Writer with a mercenary eye.
'I've been waiting since I got in from school.'
'Sorry. Getting too old for late-night parties, boy. Had to grab a nap.'
'Three-and-a-half hours in the afternoon?—that's more like a bloody coma.'
'Language.'
Helen cuffed the youth as she caught his grandfather's eye.
'Coffee's on.'

'Thanks.'

The Old Writer raised an eyebrow.

'That's an unexpected treat.'

'Heard you blundering about in the bathroom. Thought you might need a wake-up shot.'

'Right.'

He yawned.

'Got an amphetamine kicker, too?'

'Amphetamine is like speed, right?' said Cormac brushing crumbs.

'Yeah. Though I'm not sure you should know that.'

'It's like a really strong energy drink. Makes you a superhero for a while, but it stresses your heart big-time and messes up your brain.'

'Okay. I'll settle for coffee on its own.'

He took the cup from Helen, nurtured its warmth in both hands to cover up his tremor. Cormac eyed him narrow.

'Have you ever taken speed, Granddad?'

'Do you think I'd tell you if I had?' The Old Writer parried clumsy.

'So that's a 'yes'.'

He swallowed coffee, invoked respectful silence with an over-the-cup-rim glare.

'What about crack? Or charlie? Did you ever do base, or Es?'

The coffee was good. He swallowed another bitter mouthful.

'Smack then? Or weed? You must've smoked a ton of weed.'

'Enough with the dope talk,' he said impatient. 'You're spending too much time with your dad.'

'Wrong.'

The boy tightened his lip, jutted his jaw.

'We had a Drug Awareness talk at school the other day. Dave never goes on about that stuff. But sometimes you look all weird and skanky, just like him—and I worry 'cause you're getting old.'

The Old Writer clasped the skinny youth's shoulder.

'Well, I appreciate the concern, boy—but really, I'm doing fine.'

Cormac squinted up, doubtful.

'Promise?'

'Cross my heart and hope to—'

'No! That's not funny.'

The intensity of the boy's sudden embrace surprised him. He slopped coffee onto the tousled head thrust hard against his chest. Cormac clung on tight and turned his face up fierce.

'I don't want you to die, Granddad. I love you. I want you to be here forever.'

'Well, I love you too, boy. Immortality might be a bit of stretch—but I plan on seeing a few more winters.

'Cormac?'

Helen intervened adroit.

'Help me get this lid off, there's a love. My wrists aren't strong enough.'

Cormac clenched his teeth and twisted, handed the open jar back to his nan with a grin of self-satisfaction.

'Blimey.'

The Old Writer took her lead.

'Perhaps you'll make an archer yet.'

'Hope so.'

Cormac flexed a scrawny arm.

'I've been practising for hours.'

'Managed to hit the target yet?'

'Yeah—and I've had at least three bull's.'

The flicker of calculation was back in his eye.

'The string makes my wrist and fingers bloody sore though. I really need finger-tabs and an armguard. Can you get me them from eBay?'

'More expense?'

'But I need them. They don't cost much. And it's not as if you're poor.'

'Clear off now and leave me in peace, you gold digging little bugger. If I can stay alive until after my tea I might try and have a look.'

'Thanks, Granddad. Make sure they're good ones,' Cormac called, already out the door.

The Old Writer subsided to a kitchen chair, watched Helen spread a slab of pastry thick with crimson jam. 'Fuck,' he said and sighed. 'That kid is good.'

'He knows a pushover when he sees one.'

'What? All that vulnerable neediness is just an act to set me up?'

'No.'

Helen dusted flour from her hands.

'I think it's real enough. But he's not too proud to exploit it for economic gain.'

The Old Writer craned, caught his reflection in the mirror.

'Do I really look weird and skanky—three steps from my fucking grave?'

'More like you've just crawled out of it after being dead for a couple of years.'

'Thanks.'

'A shave and a shower might help. You've got time before we eat.'

The Old Writer supposed he should make the effort. He stood, drifted door-ward, hung back on the threshold. 'Sorry for being a useless arse,' he said. 'Earlier, you know?'

'That's okay, I'm used to it. As long as you've perked up now.'

Her smile was warm but her eyes appraised him cool.

'It's just sometimes I get scared I might've lost the fucking plot,' he croaked and zombie-shuffled off.

'I really thought I'd finally done it—found that elusive clear spot.'

She wriggled, impatient, held back from the edge of sleep.

'And then I woke up.'

'As you do.'

'Yeah, but normally it's the restless dreams that fuck me up. Consciousness calms the crazy shit down. The disappointment was profound.'

Helen rolled, released his numb hand from the hot clamp of her thighs, raised up bleary on an elbow and blinked down.

'Perhaps I'm tired, but you're not really making sense.'

'No. I know. Nothing does anymore. That's the goddamn problem. But in my dream it did. The bastard book was finally finished. Everything was under control.'

'Everything?'

'Yeah. You know. Jack and Irene. Us. The kids. Their bloody kids. The whole fucking troublesome human chain-reaction commonly described as Life.'

'Control?'

'All the characters true to themselves, playing their part in the drama—the story running smooth.'

'Conforming to your preconceptions—saying what you want to hear? Making you feel good?'

'Yes. No. Sort of. Jesus, Helen—don't you understand? If "Book Thirteen" doesn't get written soon, everything could just spin apart.'

'Hush,' she said. 'Listen'.

'What?'

He strained his ear but all was quiet.

'Thought I heard Yeatsian Rough Beasts slouching up the drive. Probably just a fox though, scavenging the bins.'

She exhaled – part sigh, part laugh – slumped back to her pillow soft and tired.

'Laugh all you want. But it feels like some fucked-up twisted story's taking shape—and I'm not writing it.'

'Idiot. How could you? Your family aren't characters in some stupid book you're writing. You're just a simple hack, man—not God's guiding bloody hand.'

He looked up. A crack-river snaked the ceiling plaster to a shadowed-corner delta. His eye swam upstream, explored the crazed confusion of jagged tributaries. It seemed like half a lifetime before he discovered the lost source, veiled by slovenly cobwebs that trailed from the flex of the light.

'Hack is a bit harsh.'

'Okay. I take that back. But the rest is dead to rights.'

His cock was in her hand then, her breast against his face.

'Now get a grip and fuck me if you can,' she growled. 'Or shut up and let me sleep.'

thirteen

He had enjoyed the drive, at least.

Motorways relaxed him; guided by autonomic reflex The Old Writer became thoughtless, at one with time and distance, his spatial awareness focused in the evolving moment of the road. The sat-nav's blunt announcement of imminent arrival – whether on right or left – was always anticlimactic.

Conveniently located on a decayed commercial reef submerged an hour-deep inside the chaos of a vast drowned conurbation, the 'exciting new leisure hotel' was modelled from snot-green plastic and glass, and staffed by humourless clones. Suave in sympathetic corporate livery, a fish-skinned trainee-manager officiated the brusque ritual of check-in deaf to repartee. The Old

Writer noted a discreet scar at the youth's temple that suggested his capacity for ad lib had been surgically removed.

The Old Writer's room was an injection-moulded egg of soothing aquamarine, highlighted by sparse soft furnishings in radioactive lime. It had a distinct hygienic air. He imagined robot maids routinely expunged the organic trace of departed inmates with jets of cleansing steam.

The room's window was a 'porthole'. The murky view it offered – of some shadowed interior space traversed by a sculptural tangle of functional tubular steel – implied that his ship was sunk.

Perched prominent on the sterile bedside shelf, a triangular 'Strictly No Smoking' sign triggered Pavlovian rebellion. The Old Writer rolled himself a neat spliff of Gary's weed, appreciated only post-ignition that respect for his personal comfort and security demanded the porthole be hermetically sealed.

He took his smoky pleasure in the bathroom balanced on a stool, exhausted guilty fumes purse-lipped into a ceiling extractor-vent. Stoned, he withdrew to the polyester sanctuary of the bed with TV remote clutched clammy. He recycled the eclectic menu of digitised distractions for twenty compulsive minutes but found nothing he preferred to sleep.

The room-phone roused him, chilly and confused. It was seven o'clock, already. Downstairs in the lobby, his hosts waited to take him to dinner.

Tony was a thin neo-beatnik boy, friendly enough but nervous. His girlfriend, Shula, was perfumed with mild hostility and outweighed him three-to-one. Exchanging a cool handshake with the black-draped girl, The Old Writer thought of rubber.

'Really glad you could make it,' Tony said and blinked his glasses up his nose. 'Shula and me are both massive fans.'

Shula's sniff was almost imperceptible.

'We thought Indian, if that's okay with you? Our budget is really quite modest.'

'Well, I usually insist on three Michelin stars, and at least a couple of hookers and a gram of good cocaine.'

Tony smiled unsure. Shula whirled her knitted shawl around her shoulders, led out into the gathering gloom as the lobby doors swished wide.

'But hey.'

The Old Writer shrugged resignation.

'The new era of austerity demands humility of us all.'

The restaurant was hot and loud with vaguely northern accents. The combination of jalfrezi and Kingfisher beer made him both weary and dyspeptic. They sat by a window rattled by rain, The Old Writer distracted from their stilted conversation by ribald posses of raucous girls who – tottering high-heeled and wind-lashed, barely clothed – trolled the greasy Friday-night street on the hunt for testosterone.

'So,' Tony solicited mild, while his partner scrutinised, then queried, the bill presented by the waiter. 'We've scheduled your interview for three p.m. tomorrow, onstage in the lecture hall— to be followed by a signing session where you can meet and chat with fans. Is that okay with you?'

'Cool. Is that before or after Neil Barker?'

'Ah, Neil cancelled, I'm afraid. Something about a pressing deadline.'

'Oh. Shame.'

'Yes, a lot of people will be disappointed,' said Shula, counting change. 'Though, if he hadn't, we wouldn't have been able to accommodate your late acceptance of our invitation. Our budget is—'

'Modest?'

The Old Writer raised an eyebrow.

'We got small grants from the council and the student entertainment fund, but advance ticket-sales have been kind of limited.'

Tony grimaced apologetic.

'But we did get your name added to the website last week, so we're hoping plenty of Leepus fans will turn up on the day.'

'Right—good of you to fit me in. Sorry to leave you so long in suspense. Pre-occupied with pressing domesticity, you know?'

'I'm looking forward to your interview,' said Tony, pushing on. 'Shula's been rereading your stuff all week to come up with interesting questions.'

'I'm flattered.'

Shula ignored his winning smile.

'I should really have been working on my thesis, but Tony's a hopeless fanboy. His objectivity couldn't be trusted.'

Tony covered his embarrassment, stared out, retaliatory, at raw weather-beaten girls.

'What's your thesis on?' The Old Writer asked.

Shula pushed back her chair and stood, loomed silent large and dark.

'The working title is "Dead Blondes: the perennial role of woman as victim in mystery fiction, from the nineteenth century to the present day",' said Tony, somewhat glum. 'It's very comprehensive and insightful.'

'Snappy.'

The Old Writer winked wry.

'Appreciate the heads-up. I'll be alert for ambush.'

Resisting his hosts' diffident invitation to seek 'somewhere safe' for a nightcap, The Old Writer excused them to run for their last bus, strolled off melancholic in search of his plastic bed.

It was midnight in the city and the nocturnal economy boomed. The street was a recreational warzone. There was vomit; there was blood; there was broken glass. Youths bellowed and tore their hair in rage, punched faces and stamped on heads. Girl's goaded, screeched and scratched at eyes, squatted and pissed in gutters. Bouncers marshalled unruly queues and muttered into headsets. Hi-vis steroid-inflated cops sprayed CS gas and hurled berserkers into vans, while paramedics swarmed after them to sweep up the dead and wounded.

Against the odds and grateful for his luck, The Old Writer made it back to his hotel bunker, shaken, shocked and a little awed, but physically uninjured. To his room for a civilised, soothing bathroom spliff, or two, he thought, and then to sleep, in pointless preparation for the tedium of tomorrow.

Bloody Helen. He should never have let her talk him into it. A Celebration of Mystery Writing at The University of the Midlands was always going to be dire.

No more, he had promised himself after that last dismal signing at the bookshop in fucking corpse-cold Inverness. No more personal appearances at low-rent gatherings of genre afficionados, organised by 'nice people' for the benefit of their friends. No more vague guilt for inadequate public performance, where audiences shuffled out in silence, nebulous expectations of literary wit-and-wisdom painfully unfulfilled.

The Old Writer had once enjoyed the mild masochism of occasional expenses-paid trips to Festivals of Literature in exotic foreign cities. He took pleasure in alien cultures glimpsed, in convivial intoxication with hosts and other scribblers on leave from their solitary confinement, in the warming reassurance of polite admiration bestowed by grateful readers.

But the novelty of travel paled with familiarity and age. The Old Writer had tired of sweating through airports, anxious that molecular traces of forgotten contraband might adhere to his clothing or luggage, set the tails of drug dogs wagging, get his arsehole probed. He resented the need to X-ray his shoes and confiscate his lighter, to have his ID mechanically scrutinised, his biology scanned, his destinations and purpose interrogated by a succession of supercilious security staff.

Bloody Helen. Okay, so maybe he had got a bit stir-crazy, let the old Black Dog worry at his equilibrium, chew his interior world ragged. Perhaps it was true that he 'needed to get out more', 'refresh his perspective', 'get his creative libido energised by some admiring young literary tart' – he assumed the suggestion was figurative, but you never knew with Helen – but it was already dismally obvious that this trip stood slim chance of accomplishing that.

Bloody Helen. Even a holiday would be better. Fuck, yes. Why not? He would sort it out when he got home from this horrible debacle. Peru, perhaps; she had always wanted to see bloody Machu Picchu. Getting there would be a massive mission but the benefit would outweigh the cost. They could get respite care for the aged impediments-to-recreation, let the kids worry about their own chaotic lives for a change. Viola's brood would survive a while unguided by grandparental wisdom. "Book Thirteen" would fester on in his subconscious. Tanned and relaxed, he would come back to his Tower of Babble inspired, intellectually energised and productive.

Bloody Helen. He loved her. He should crawl down out of his own fucking arsehole and spend time making her happy.

The Old Writer was waiting for the lift; the lift appeared detained. The lobby floor was a dizzy green swirl of seaweed washed by tide. He felt a little sick, jabbed at the button with his thumb, and jabbed at it again. But no motor whirred encouragement; the doors did not glide wide.

'Fuck this shit,' he muttered and looked around for stairs.

'You need to put your room card in,' a girl said meek from behind.

'In where?'

He frowned impatience, disconcerted by an embarrassing 'seventies-flashback evoked by a whiff of patchouli.

A pale hand poked from a ragged Afghan cuff. A chewed black-painted fingernail pointed to a slot.

'There. It's a security thing, innit? To keep the robbing scumbags from getting to the rooms.'

She was short, somewhere between sixteen and twenty-one. Her eyes were dark; their lashes, crusted with mascara, fluttered like startled bird-wings in the magenta foliage of her fringe. Her body – sheathed in a knitted purple dress beneath unbuttoned sheepskin – was a couple of years shy of tubby. Twin blisters of pallid thigh-skin mooned through holes in tight black leggings. She looked up at him expectant, flickered a wet pink tongue-tip along the dark plum of her lip.

'Hi,' she said coy and looked back down, toed the floor with a boot skinned from the leg of a juvenile yeti.

'Hello.'

'Don't recognise me, do you?'

'You do look slightly familiar—but sorry, no, I don't.'

'I changed my look.'

She fingered fluorescent hair.

'Do you like it this new colour? I nearly went for blonde.'

'It's fine.'

He sensed she wanted more.

'You'd be hard to lose in a crowd.'

'Good. I wanted to get it right for you.'

'For me?'

'It cost a whole week's JSA. Glad it wasn't wasted.'

'What? Fuck. I mean, are you sure I'm who you think I am?'

'Yeah—absolutely. Know you anywhere. You think I'd come on to just any leery old fucker?'

The girl smiled, tiptoed up to kiss his cheek and whisper, 'I'm Crystal, your ever-lovin' soul-mate, man. Shall we have a drink in the bar first—or go straight up to your room?'

The Old Writer elected option one.

A tired middle-aged woman in a lime-green waistcoat tended the desolate hotel bar. He ordered a gin and tonic. Crystal called for vodka and Red Bull, 'Because I didn't have time for tea.' The woman served them without comment, followed their retreat to a shadowed booth, eyes hooded with disdain. He slid onto the cold plastic bench, waited for her to grab the phone, summon Child Protection.

'Didn't expect to see me here, I bet?'

Crystal clashed her glass with his.

'It's been a while since I heard from you, yeah. So it is kind of a surprise.'

'A nice one though?'

Her mouth was a bruise. Purple lipstick flecked her teeth.

'I thought about you loads, love—but I didn't have my Internet, stuck in the bastard hostel.'

'Hostel?'

'Yeah. It was going okay 'til LeRoy got himself lifted jacking some old tart's Audi.'

'LeRoy? The Temazepam guy?'

'Right. Did I tell you about him? History now. He got banged up for five. I got done for the pills in our flat, and bailed to the fucking hostel.'

'What happened?'

He didn't really want to know. But then again, he did.

'Probation. Drug-treatment program. My dad came through—told the court I could stay with him.'

'Lucky for you.'

'Not really. He lives on a farm in Wales with his mad Wiccan old lady. They used to have a cool converted barn but the roof came off in a gale. So they moved into some skanky old yurts they put up in the yard. Rats came in when it got cold. I stuck it a week, then did one.'

'Where did you go?'

Crystal winked.

'The situation was well bollocksed up, so I had to get a bit snide. Hitched to my big sister's place in Bourton-on-the-Water. She's married to this posh banker prick. Told them I'd cook and do childcare for room and board—and he bunged me two grand to fuck off.'

Crystal waved her empty glass. The barmaid shuffled over.

'Result, huh? Paid the deposit on my new bedsit and kept me in Lamberts and beans-on-toast until I got my benny sorted.'

The Old Writer signed for the drinks. Crystal's glass was empty again before the woman was back at the bar. He studied the girl. She studied him back with eyes that glittered manic.

'So, life's better now?' he ventured.

'It could be.'

She bit the dark fruit of her lip.

'If I wasn't always so fucking lonely and hung-up on killing myself.'

The Old Writer took a breath and held it, considered his response. He tried for concerned but non-committal.

'That doesn't sound so good. I think you should get some help.'

'Why do you think I'm here, luv?'

Her hand was a black-toed spider; it squatted over his.

'Because—'

He wanted to laugh but it was not funny. He wanted to run, but the sick voyeur inside him insisted that he stay.

'I don't know why, Crystal—and I don't think you do, either.'

'It's Fate, stupid.'

She scathed him with wide eyes.

'Our destinies are interwoven for all eternity across the astral plane.'

'Whoa.'

He gulped.

'Slow down. You're getting things out of propor—'

'No! It's true! Don't say it's not! I knew it the first time I ever read a Leepus book. He's so deep, and dark, and sexy. He can strip off your skin with his razor-eyes, reach all the way right up inside you and touch your secret heart.'

'Crystal. Hey. Leepus is just a smart-mouthed character I wrote. Don't mix him up with the sad old reality of me.'

She scowled, squeezed her glass. He waited for it to shatter.

'But it was you who answered my emails and understood my pain. And Leepus must be a part of you, otherwise you could never have made him so totally fucking cool.'

'But—'

'Anyway, you saved my miserable life, man. So now I'm yours forever.'

'What?'

Inside his head: a heartbeat, alien and cold.

'I was looking at suicide sites on the web—trying to figure the best way to do it. Suddenly your name was in my head, so I typed it into Google.'

'Right.'

He winced. The heartbeat was a fingertip now, picking a cerebral scab.

'Must have been a web angel looking out for me,' Crystal continued, breathless. 'The link said you were on at this uni gig a couple of bus-rides down the road. I just knew I'd find you here waiting for me and my dreams would all come true.'

'Crystal. Hey.'

He looked for a convenient exit.

'Maybe we should talk this through later. I've got a filthy headache coming on and I'm feeling kind of shit.'

'Poor babe.'

She frowned concern, seized his hand and stood.

'So let's go up to your room now and I'll love you 'til you're better.'

The Old Writer stood with her, retrieved his hand, met her eye and shook his head.

'Sorry, Crystal. That's not going to happen.'

'What do you mean? Why not?'

'Because it would just be bloody wrong. I've got a family, and stuff.'

'Love's never wrong.'

'Love? Christ, girl—I'm too old for that. Look at the damn decrepit state of me. I could be your fucking granddad.'

'So what if you're old? It's not like it's illegal. You think I'm some sweet little virgin who doesn't know the score? My body's younger than yours, okay, but I've got an ancient soul.'

'Look.'

Her desperation scared him. He steered her towards the door.

'I'm tired—you're drunk and a bit mixed up. You need to get yourself home now.'

'No. Please. I don't want it to be all messed up again—like it will be if you send me away.'

'Write to me in a couple of days and we'll talk this through more calmly.'

He offered a friendly wink.

'But no more naked pictures, huh? My feeble old heart won't take the shock.'

'You don't want me.'

Tears softened her mascara.

'You think I'm a cheap little slag.'

'That's not true.'

His arm was around her shoulder now. He moved her into the lobby.

'You don't even have to fuck me, if I don't turn you on.'

The desk clerk smirked and raised a fishy eyebrow. The Old Writer flipped him a finger behind his back. Crystal twisted in his arms, nuzzled meek against his chest.

'Just let me stay one night with you. I'll curl up on the bed like a puppy, cosy and quiet while you sleep. I just can't stand to go home alone.'

'I'm sorry.'

The Old Writer pried her trembling arms from his ribcage.

'The answer is still 'no'.'

The lobby doors swished open automatic. Outside, the night yawned wet.

'Please.'

She huddled childish.

'It's too late to get the bus now, and I'm scared to walk on my own.'

'Here.'

The Old Writer riffled notes from his wallet.

'I'll get the desk guy to call you a cab.'

He felt like a callous bastard, but if fifty quid would buy her off it was cheap at the fucking price.

She looked at him as if he had spat in her eye, clenched the notes rolled tight in her palm.

'Don't bother,' she said and turned out the door. 'I'll flag one down on the street.'

'I'm sorry, Crystal,' he said, sincere. 'It's not that I want to hurt you.'

'No. But you still cut my bleeding heart out—you dirty-fucking-shit-let-down.'

She scuffed sullen across the threshold; the doors slid shut on her heels.

'Good luck,' he murmured under his breath as she faded into the disappointed night, dissolved by acid rain.

He had handled it as well as could be expected, The Old Writer considered, smug. Crystal was lucky she had picked him as the bizarre focus of her infatuation. There were plenty of sleazy old moral bankrupts in the world who would have grasped the sweet promise of that juicy young flesh in both eager horny hands. He had not even considered it. Not for more than a nanosecond.

He supposed in a way he should be flattered that his dark creation had the power to evoke such passion, even in a child as obviously lost and deranged as Crystal. But power demands responsibility; the opportunity of advantage must be tempered by mature restraint.

The Old Writer curled up warm in his sanctimonious bed, tried to ignore the provocative finger palpating the sore lobe of his brain. He was balanced on the crumbled edge of sleep when Leepus nudged him sly, dared him to risk louche adventure in an alternate reality.

Younger, more vigorous and drunk, it was conceivable an unguarded man might be aroused by such vulnerable temptation, take a willing young girl to his bed to exploit her promise of versatile vigour.

Later – sweaty in the aftermath of reckless lust, exhausted by the vacuum of her need – he would let sleep drag him from her clinging arms, glad to evade the tedium of awkward pillow talk.

He would wake alone in pre-dawn monochrome, snared in guilty sheets, assume she had slipped from the bed, dressed silent, considerate of his rest and, grateful for her brief moment of generous love, crept off to call a cab. Relieved of his duty of care he would ease cool from the bed to gain similar relief for his bladder. That comfort achieved, doubtless he would return to sleep-sound for several more dreamless hours.

The Old Writer would have been content to abandon his tasteless delusion there. But that was not the way things happened, not in the dark parallel world of fucking Leepus.

His avatar grinned harsh, seized control of the prurient script and deleted its last anodyne sentence.

Stepping from bed to bathroom – the rewrite picked up – a troubled man might wonder why, if the object of his predatory passion had departed discrete into the night, the rank sheet strewn twisted on the floor was tangled with frail feminine garments.

Disconcerted, he might hesitate a moment outside the open-mouthed bathroom. Perhaps the girl was in there taking a pee of her own; why then did she not answer his nervous croak of enquiry? Was she hiding? Had she slipped and fallen, passed out drunk, or worse?

A man might feel a tug of cold anxiety then. He would pause naked and dread-bound at the door, lunge, snap-on the light and stumble into stark-tiled vacancy.

Strangely, the inevitable denouement would be postponed while he took time-out to stand and piss alone in chill mirrored anticlimax.

And then he would understand.

The shower was where the horrific revelation lurked, of course, behind its green-curtained proscenium.

Sphincter tight and scrotum shrivelled, he would pad the clammy floor, extend his reluctant finger and tease-open the plastic shroud. He would peep down then as she gazed back, vague in her weightless world: a wide-eyed nude Ophelia drowned in a stone-cold bath. The plunged syringe would sway erect, still tethered to her vein: a poignant, translucent marker buoy tagging the wreck of her sunk life.

There would be police of course, interrogation and arrest. Later, the dead girl would leave by the service-lift, discrete in a body bag. But her abuser would check out in handcuffs, despised by cold-staring staff.

The Old Writer spent a Kafkaesque lifetime in jail, remanded to await inevitable conviction for crimes of literary dereliction.

Amused by his predicament, Leepus visited now and then, to listen supercilious as The Accused rehearsed yet one more stammered revision of his plea of mitigation. Invariably the bastard shrugged dismissive, tossed his condemned creator a new dense tome and left in a clang of iron.

Abandoned, the prisoner would retreat again to his comfortless bunk and scour the latest cryptic title, desperate to discover clues to improbable new lines of defence. But however hard he pored impenetrable texts in the half-light, the words always blurred and danced. Sense shifted as sentences morphed anarchic, provoked his head to throb, beat him down defeated into tortured restless sleep.

The Old Writer woke cold-sweated and dry-mouthed, sprawled in wan porthole light. It took him five blinking minutes to banish the torrid confusion of the night.

'Thank fuck,' he breathed and rolled free from the bed's guilty grip, grateful his self-righteous squeamishness had at least ensured that poor fucked-up Crystal's potential O.D. would occur in some other sick bastard's bath.

But he still sniffed the air for the taint of patchouli, paused wary at the bathroom threshold before he eased open the door.

fourteen

Showered, shaved and late-breakfasted, The Old Writer tipped his friendly freckled waitress and sauntered off to find the venue.

Outside, the flood had subsided, the drowned oppression of the urban night replaced by the optimistic clarity of delicate early autumn sun. Peaceful in calm pursuit of commerce or recreation, civilised humans now navigated the airy streets that had channelled primitive bloodlust.

The Old Writer checked his watch. He had a couple of hours to kill before he was due onstage, time to relax and prepare himself for the ordeal of interrogation.

A mediaeval church – glimpsed serendipitous down the throat of a crooked passage – offered an opportunity for secluded contemplation. The Old Writer nosed into its graveyard and was only mildly disappointed to discover it already harboured refugees. A straggle of flushed dipsomaniacs reclined against a wall, eked comfort from a bagged bottle in the quiet company of the dead. He greeted them as he passed them by to sit on a sunlit bench. Polite, they hawked and nodded back.

The Old Writer enjoyed the warmth on his skin as he smoked a small pre-rolled joint. Pigeons purred and clapped spasmodic, hidden in the ancient yew clumped cool and green in the corner. He studied the tree; its trunk writhed in subtle torment against the crumbled stone of a wall, reached past huddled redbrick to finger ceramic blue. He imagined it mirrored subterranean, roots sucking slow nutrition from the mouldered husks of buried lives.

The Old Writer sat a while in thoughtless meditation. Suddenly sentimental, he fished out his phone, flicked away his burned-out roach and texted *I love you* to Helen.

The churchyard was a pleasant place, he thought as he rose and ambled off. He might almost be content to pass eternity there if not for the tedious presence of God.

The interview – conducted in a tired university auditorium degraded by the pursuit of knowledge – was not quite the embarrassment he had dreaded.

Trepidatious in the wings as Shula introduced him, The Old Writer had scanned the tiered ranks of assembled heads for a magenta flash of warning and, no immediate threat apparent, found himself encouraged onstage by a ripple of warm applause.

Further relaxed and flattered by Shula's perceptive introductory review of his body of work, The Old Writer was moved to reward a receptive audience with subtle and expansive insight of his craft. His loquacity surprised him. Even the rehearsal of his pet theory – pirated from Bill Burroughs – that writers were the helpless hosts of vile disease, chronically infected by the insidious Word, for once seemed to make an artful sense.

Well-judged self-deprecating humour and the occasional sly dig at brother and sister genre rivals subverted the potential for pomposity and kept the gathering on his side. Even the inevitable sting in Shula's inquisitorial tail failed to unsettle his equilibrium. The Old Writer met her anticipated challenge on the supposed 'stereotypical portrayal of female characters in the Leepus books' with a plausible, if extemporised, rebuttal. His occasional provocative characterisations were justified, when not ironically post-modern, he argued, by direct personal experience and sympathetic observation of vulnerability victimised by corrupt societal expectation.

The moderator sniffed. Her eyebrow spiked in a brief impulse to contradict but, disarmed by his insouciance, she declined to call his bluff.

Her prepared topics addressed and scheduled-time filled, Shula gathered the reins of the proceedings, invited closing questions from the floor.

The Old Writer deployed his standard facetious response to the inevitable routine enquiry after the origin of his inspiration. He was non-committal on the subject of his personal belief in the 'existence of supernatural forces', and content to concur with an offered opinion that the TV adaptation of his work was a 'sick travesty' of the original.

Then, just as it appeared that the curiosity of the audience was sated, a gaunt forty-something with an academic haircut wafted a theatrical hand, expressed tight-lipped exasperation with the glacial progress towards completion of the thirteenth Leepus volume. Emboldened, the wit's lover – a corpulent sly-bespectacled Buddha in a rainbow knitwear jacket – hypothesised, to audience sniggers, the longevity of the author might prove insufficient to encompass the work.

Off-guard, his weak spot probed, The Old Writer responded reflexive, claimed that the ultimate Leepus book was finally all but written. His instinct was to cover the lie with justified retaliation. With effort, he refrained, choked back the harsh observation that the insolent fat fuck's future reading pleasure would doubtless soon be diminished by the self-inflicted early-onset of diabetic retinopathy.

Proud of his professional restraint, The Old Writer sat back, waited for Shula – who glanced at her watch – to thank the audience for their kind attention and invite their final applause.

'Perhaps.' She smiled sweet. 'As we've got a few minutes to spare, you'd give us a hint of the plot?'

Trapped, The Old Writer cleared his throat to stammer some bullshit evasion, found himself listening, fascinated and appalled, as his arsey unconscious hijacked the mic and delivered a reckless ad lib.

'Leepus feels jaded. His instincts are dulled by age. He's spent a lifetime navigating the precarious no-man's land between the ethereal and the mundane but he's starting to lose his balance. He retreats from the supernatural fray for a while, hides away playing online poker, invariably running bad.'

Too close to home, The Old Writer thought. He should put a stop to this shit. But curiosity and a vague weird hope stifled his timid objection.

'An opponent who calls herself PokerTart haunts him from table to table. Eventually, intrigued by her cryptic chat and the bold cut and thrust of her game, Leepus is seduced into playing her heads-up. Their trysts become nightly. Leepus is soon obsessed—he gets off gambling one-on-one with her in a kind of combative surrogate sex.'

The Old Writer checked the audience. They looked happy to hear more. Shula watched him, curious. He pictured her playing cards.

'One night, as a passionate battle nears its climax, PokerTart drops offline. Leepus waits impatient but his antagonist doesn't return. Frustrated by successive unrequited nights, Leepus blurs the line—calls in a debt from an adept phisherman to hack her account and track her down.'

Enough. The Old Writer was getting sucked in too deep. If he did not silence this craziness soon he would be committed to writing it.

'In real life, PokerTart is a sick woman in a world of trouble. Leepus weighs the odds on extracting her life intact, decides the risk is too great to justify a bet and coldly folds his hand. Harshly abandoned, poor PokerTart suffers a fate inevitably tragic and disconcerting.'

The Old Writer groaned internal. Was he insane? This stuff was all unedited, too raw for public release. And it seemed that, this time, the anarchic inner-voice took note as – suddenly self-conscious – the creative download stuttered.

'So, well, Leepus is, uh, left tortured by his guilty failure to intervene. He needs to make amends, sort of restore the, uh, messed up balance of his karma. So he takes up his altruistic psychic sword again to vanquish the demonic influence in a couple of innocent lives—but, uh, that doesn't stop fucked-up PokerTart stalking him vindictive from beyond her restless grave.'

'And, well, that's all she wrote—so far,' The Old Writer wrapped up, breathless but back in control. 'If you want to know how the shit gets worked out you'll have to buy the damn book, or steal it.'

'Well.'

Shula eyed him askance.

'Thank you for the privilege of that fascinating insight. I know I'll certainly be stealing my boyfriend's copy of "Book Thirteen" as soon as he's ripped it from The Pirate Bay.'

The audience chuckled and applauded. Relieved, The Old Writer stood a little shaky and shuffled from the stage.

The Old Writer spent the next hour signing multiple dog-eared copies of his ancient works for disparate loyal Leepus fans and autistic autograph-speculators.

He smiled and exchanged pleasantries, shook proffered hands, accepted both compliment and occasional gauche rudeness with routine impenetrable charm.

He offered sincere but worthless authorial advice to hopeful novice novelists, declined – apologetic but resolute – their earnest invitations to critique treasured manuscripts, all the while distracted by an old familiar excitement that quickened his slow blood.

Leepus stalked by a demented dead girl? Leepus stalking her back? Lost souls gambling in Limbo? Sleazy supernatural sex? Was there a ghost of a chance he could weave a slick story from those tenuous inspirational threads, a shroud fit to wrap his intransigent avatar for his deserved eternal rest?

Why not? He had worked with worse in the past, imagined many less-promising cultures into shocking virulence. Perhaps the damned dumb dam had finally cracked; and now the murmurous creative trickle would surge again full-throated into flood.

The Old Writer's optimism was tentative but persistent as – final flyleaf scrawled on and ink of goodwill spent – he relished the large gin and tonics with which beatnik Tony rewarded him in the scruffy students' union bar.

'We're really pleased with the way it's gone,' the goateed impresario schmoozed. 'You really boosted our take on the door. There's a chance we'll be able to make it an annual event now—get even bigger names next year.'

'Great. Perhaps Neil will be able to make it.'

The Old Writer tipped a wink to the boy's *faux pas*.

'I'll put in a word if you like.'

'I really enjoyed your interview—and from the way you described it the new book will fucking rock.'

'Thanks. Worth waiting for, you think?'

'Absolutely. All those starved Leepus fans are going to be really psyched.'

'Talking of the interview.'

The Old Writer was magnanimous in drink.

'I wanted to thank your girlfriend for the smooth job she did. Only I missed her in the aftermath and I haven't seen her since.'

'Shula's a workaholic.'

Tony grimaced and adjusted his specs.

'She's gone home to transcribe the interview recording so we can get it straight up online.'

'Online?'

'Yeah. We publish a little cult webzine called "Gut Wrench". I don't suppose you've come across it?'

'Sorry. I should probably pay more attention.'

'It's got a pretty good following among horror and mystery freaks—we cover movies, comics and games as well as genre books. The info on the new Leepus story is a massive scoop for us.'

Tony paused as The Old Writer frowned.

'You don't mind having it on the record?'

The Old Writer thought for a moment. A provincial audience of less than a hundred was harmless enough to ignore, but the worldwide fucking web was a totally different order of magnitude.

Oh well, he surrendered inward. Fuck it. If he didn't subconsciously want to be held to his word he wouldn't have blurted his thoughts uncensored.

'Not at all.'

He gestured expansive.

'Publish and be damned, man. I'm flattered you think it's of interest.'

'Great. Thanks.'

Tony was on his feet.

'Sorry but I'll have to dash now. I'm due onstage in a couple of minutes to host Vera Violenz. She's doing a PowerPoint on her latest Hell Whores graphic novel. You're familiar with her stuff?'

The Old Writer drained his drink. His ignorance was plain.

'You should really check her out, man. She's sharp and well-fucking dark. This new one's called "Hell Whores versus The Taliban"—some kind of twisted satire on global culture-war, I think.'

'Perhaps I'll call by and eavesdrop,' The Old Writer offered, distracted, for no apparent reason, by a figure hunched alone in a corner sipping Red Bull in a hoodie.

'Cool.'

Tony waved and turned away.

'You can pick up a signed copy of her book, and then we'll meet Shula and the other guests for pizza and shots to wrap things up.'

The Old Writer watched the skinny hipster slouch away, contemplated another gin but decided a nap would be more beneficial. He had drunk enough alcohol already to inhibit the possibility of legal vehicular escape from the threat of celebratory fast food and crude liquor.

He stood, jarred the table with his thigh. An un-drained tonic-bottle toppled, spurted feeble effervescence. The liquid wriggled across greasy Formica, dribbled, precipitous, to spatter down on his shoes.

The Old Writer needed to piss. He blinked blurred eyes into long-range focus, located the required iconography above a door across the room, limped towards it awkward. He was drunk and a little unsteady. His hip hurt from sitting too long cross-legged, and although his head was not quite aching yet there was a presentiment of pain.

But so the fuck what, The Old writer thought as he pushed through the door and descended a fetid stairwell. He might be a little frayed around the edges but the hit of creative excitement that now buzzed his veins was a tonic for tired blood, a long-missed vital antidote to sclerotic obsolescence. He had a viable story at last. He just needed to get home to his tower now and write the bastard down.

Machu Picchu would have to wait. It had been there for millennia; it would last another six months. He might even take genuine pleasure from the trip if it marked his triumphant retirement from the war of fucking words.

A short, doglegged tiled tunnel channelled The Old Writer into the unoccupied subterranean toilet. The air was hot and thick. A ventilator wheezed emphysemic, unequal to the fug. He tasted disinfectant and stale piss enhanced by subtle hints of vomit. The row of stainless-steel urinals that lined the far wall shifted in the stuttered light of an exhausted fluorescent tube. He reached automatic for his zipper, moved towards them crab-like, forced to circle an unhealthy pool that – lapped by a pale tongue of unravelled bog-roll – leaked from a shit-smeared stall.

The Old Writer sighed as his bladder drained. His face – carved harsh by flickered light in the smeared mirror above the urinal – was not a pretty sight. He closed his heavy-lidded eyes and swayed, focused on the minute shift of his balance caused by liquid evacuation. His flow was steady and strong. He might be superficially eroded, he reassured himself, but at least his fucking prostate was holding up, so far.

The Old Writer shook, retracted and re-zipped. The ceiling tube pinged and flickered dark. He winced as a sympathetic shadow pulsed across his brain.

Something was wrong.

He squeezed shut his eyes.

Lysergic Paisley pyrotechnics fluoresced his ocular orbit.

He stepped back.

Jarred from the urinal step.

Stared wide, blind, lost in absolute black.

The ceiling tube pinged.

Light snapshot a squat figure: hooded, small-handed, black-nailed; Chef's knife gripped tight-fisted.

Oh fuck.

Oh fuck.

Oh.

Fuck.

Fear-frozen, mired for sightless millennia in pitch.

And then the ceiling tube defibrillated; cold neon hollowed the dank mausoleum.

'No,' The Old Writer blurted hopeful.

'Yes,' she said, stripped hood from magenta head. 'Got you again, didn't I? You limp-dick phony fuck.'

Her pupils were black puncture wounds; they oozed pink into yellowed sclera. Her mouth was a purple sphincter. It puckered bitter in her freeze-dried face as she lifted the steel shard and kissed it.

'Fuck's sake, Crystal.'

His voice caricatured dismay.

'What the actual sweet fucking Christ in Hell are you going to do with that goddamn knife?'

'Stab you the fuck up, dude.'

She jutted the blade towards him.

'Cut your cunt heart like you cut mine. Then I'm necking the rest of my bastard pills and going to sleep forever.'

'Fuck,' he said. 'Please don't.'

But Crystal was past hearing.

Instinctive, The Old Writer turned and crouched, clasped his nape terrified-ape-like. Snake-crazy, the poison-girl hissed and struck, plunged a savage blaze of venom hilt-deep in the cheek of his arse.

The Old Writer bellowed. Electrified tendons tautened, drove his skull against the wall. Stained glass exploded kaleidoscopic in his head. Blood-blind, he flailed air, buckled and collapsed face down in the pissy flood.

Thank fuck, he thought as the rank waters closed over his head. He would be drowned in deep dark oblivion before the mad bitch could stab him again.

fifteen

Too much information in too short a space of time. Data was compressed, scattered clusters corrupted, irretrievably lost.

Propped semi-reclined on an examination-room treatment couch – stripped of soiled clothing and chilly in hospital shift – The Old Writer strove to comprehend the shock twist with which Fate had subverted his life.

Pumped full of opiate mercy, he was pain-free at the moment; it was not always so.

He remembered an agonised consciousness regained reluctant as irrepressible life force buoyed him from the dark panic-room where he had taken desperate refuge.

Rebirth was traumatic; he had squirmed like a harpooned seal, floundered in filthy bloodied water transfixed through the arse by fire. But the pain that dominated his perception had blazed deep inside his skull; a fury of cold-burning phosphorous, it crackled inextinguishable, drilled a shaft of terror down to the sacred core of his brain.

Elsewhere in the Emergency Admissions Unit another hapless casualty gave voice to their distress. The Old Writer shivered, recalled his own arias of agony re-echoing shrill in the claustrophobic reverb-chamber of that miserable lonely toilet.

His one-man Pandemonium had first summoned upstairs-drinkers down to peer timid and ineffectual.

A whimpered lifetime later and a cursing campus-security guy is tugging him from the flood; he props him in a corner, apologises and retreats aboveground in pursuit of a radio signal. The Old Writer drifts in and out of horror for another day or two. Eventually, two burly lesbian paramedics rock up reassuring. One probes his wounds with rubber fingers, the other his lucidity with an incomprehensible string of questions. Competent and cheery, they scoop him onto a stretcher and haul him deft from the pit. He flashes on a gaggle of gawkers grabbing shots with phones; and then he is strapped in the ambulance, lured to sleep by sirens.

Now The Old Writer remembered flickering awake in a dazzle of white light, the focus of attention for a blue-gowned brisk efficiency of medics.

He remembered a stern Chinese doctor who leaned close and examined his eye. It appeared she had forgotten what year it was; strangely, so had he. Eager to please he improvised glib, informed her that they were cursed to live in the Year of the Vicious Snake.

He had wept as they cut off his clothes and revealed his pale age-slack body. It looked so vulnerable lying down there exposed on the blood-smeared gurney. It had been a helpless baby once, full of hope and promise. Now it was just as helpless again but with the promise all exhausted.

He had felt anaesthesia circling as they rolled him on his side, sick as a cold tool was roughly deployed to plumb his buttock wound. But the last image he recorded as his world dissolved to nauseous black, was the face of the Chinese doctor, who – palpating the raw lump on his head – said in a quiet curious voice, 'This might be a cause for concern.'

Alone in the examination room, The Old Writer shifted tentative, parted the provocative split of his gown and flashed a thigh, scrawny but attractively bronzed by copious iodine spray-tan. The small neat dressing taped to his arse-cheek was a bit of an anticlimax. He felt a little cheated; surely the heroic endurance of such a violent ordeal deserved the recognition of an honour significantly more dramatic.

The Old Writer was thirsty. He craned to look for water. The movement turned a millwheel in his head; it did not hurt exactly, but he could tell that there was damage. He lifted an exploratory hand, snagged the IV drip-line plugged into the cannula taped to his wrist, lifted the other instead. No doubt his perception was distorted by sensitivity of touch and swathe of bandage, but the mental reflection he perceived was of a lopsided fucking Mekon.

Cool, he thought. At least that will distract attention from the ignominy of an arse-wound.

The Old writer closed his eyes for a moment. And then a neat bright nurse was beside him, busy taking his pulse.

'Just need to do your obs,' she said, pen to clipboard chart. 'Then we'll find you a bed on the assessment ward and get you settled in.'

'Ward? Is that really necessary?' he tried to say. But his tongue would not cooperate; words slimed thick from his mouth, like drool, puddled incoherent.

'Don't try and talk if it's too difficult.'

The nurse smiled with practised compassion, wrapped his hand around her fingers.

'Just squeeze once for 'yes' and twice for 'no' and we'll get along just fine. Okay?'

He twitched.

'Good. So do you know where you are and why you're here?'

He twitched again. All conversation should be so easy.

'And the details in the ICE file on your phone are up to date as far as you know?'

The fucking what file? The Old Writer frowned, flashed on a memory of Helen in the kitchen fiddling with his phone. She was fresh back from the bloody speed awareness course she had opted to do when stealth-cops in a camera van tagged her not paying attention as she nipped past the village school.

She had muttered that one thing they'd told her seemed like a good idea. They should all have next-of-kin and medical histories in their phones to enhance their chance of survival and ease busy first-responder workloads 'In Case of Emergency'.

Belated, The Old Writer signalled affirmation.

'Okay. The police recovered that information. I'll ask them to inform your wife. A couple of them have been waiting to ask you a few questions about the assault but I think it's too soon for that.'

The Old Writer agreed. He needed some time to consider his options. If they had not already captured Crazy Crystal – supposing she had even survived her pill-provoked passion for self-obliteration – was it cool to unleash the dogs of law, get her committed to some harsh institution to be predated by dead-eyed psychotics?

His interior fundamentalist snarled that justice must be served. They should whip her naked through the streets and raise her severed head on a fucking pole.

But the bloodless liberal inside him cringed from such brutal commitment. Perhaps it would be more noble and magnanimous – not to mention far less hassle – just to shrug self-righteous and whimper, 'I forgive you, child'.

'Right then.'

The nurse slipped her hand from his.

'That's everything we need for now. I'll be back when we've sorted your transfer up to the ward. A doctor will talk to you in due course and go over the results of your scan.'

Scan? The Old Writer searched, found no relevant memory-file so slithered back to sleep, there to wander naked and confused, lost in a weird swamp-city of brute sub-humans whose language he could not speak.

The Old Writer woke in a crepuscular fug of antiseptic-masked disease, in a bed he did not recognise, with pale curtains drawn around. He lay still for a stifled moment, assessed his new situation. His nostrils flared in quest of air, caught a faint but familiar scent that evoked a longing for lost comfort.

'Helen?' he heard his voice croak, still clumsy and distorted but at least intelligible, he thought.

Cheered by a grunted response, The Old Writer smiled as, vague in his periphery, his wife stirred awake on a chair.

They embraced in a long mutuality of need, lost in a wordless communion of grateful love. Reassured by the delicate weight of her hand lingered on his chest, he closed his eyes for a moment then, and sneaked off for another nap.

The Old Writer surfaced to a loud day-lit irritation of busy care delivery and malodorous demand. His curtains were drawn back. The bedside chair was empty, Helen nowhere to be seen.

There was cereal sodden in a bowl and a plastic cup of evil tea awaiting delectation on his table. He choked the dismal repast down as an antidote to boredom.

'Hello.'

A massive black nurse hip-rolled up. 'Any pain for you this morning, darlin'?' she offered with a smile.

The Old Writer weighed his need.

'No thanks.'

He tried to wink.

'The headache and the fire in my arse will be sufficient for now, I think.'

'You want some medication?'

'A shot of morphine and a ciggie would be nice.'

'Only Paracetamol.'

'Okay,' he said. 'But you're no bloody fun.'

'Bedpan?'

It sounded like an insult; he bit back a childish impulse to respond with 'enema bag'.

'You want to open your bowels?'

She rolled her tired eyes.

The Old Writer felt contrition. The nurse spent her life mopping up the shit and blood of decrepit fucks for a few quid to feed her kids. She did not need her day complicated by a tedious old prick who thought he was bloody funny.

'No. Thanks.'

He smiled cooperative.

'I could do with a quick pee though, if you could point me to the khazi.'

'Urine bottle.'

She nodded to a compressed grey-paper receptacle stranded like a miniature whale in the surf of sheets at the foot of his bed.

'Strictly bed-rest only 'til the doctor says you're fit to stand.'

'Okay—that'll do, I guess.'

'Something else you need? Pillow? Blanket? Personal entertainment-console vouchers—six-pound each or buy-five-get-one-free?'

'I wouldn't mind a word with my wife if she's anywhere around. I'm pretty sure she was here last night. But it might've been a dream.'

The nurse detached a clipboard from the bed frame, frowned at it arm's-length.

'Name Helen?'

'That's the girl.'

'Letter here.'

She passed him a Post-it note, his wife's preferred means of communication. *Gone back to your hotel for a shower and change of clothes*, he read, comforted by her familiar neat script. *Don't give those nice nurses any shit and I'll be back in a couple of hours.*

The Old Writer was still busy under the sheet, fumbling his shrivelled cock into the dry mouth of the bottle, when a slim Asian girl in a crisp white coat forestalled his expected relief. She reviewed his chart in silence, inspected the dressing on his head and shone a penlight into his eyes, and then interrogated him, rapid-fire, in a clipped 'voice of authority'.

The Old Writer answered without resistance. He was distracted by the Burnt Umber depth of her eyes, incredulous that a child of no more than fifteen could be a qualified registrar.

'Very very lucky,' she was saying when he started to pay attention. 'All the signs suggest that the bleed was only quite minor.'

'Right,' he muttered. 'Not too many major arteries in your backside, I suppose.'

'Backside?'

She frowned impatient.

'I'm not concerned with your backside you foolish man. I'm talking about your brain.'

'Brain?'

'Of course.'

She flipped a page on his chart, her nail a surgical blade.

'Symptoms such as those presented are indicative of potential haemorrhagic stroke.'

'Stroke?'

'CT scan confirms the presence of blood in the cerebellum.'

'My cerebellum?'

'Indeed.'

Her thin lips stretched, revealed delicate incisors.

'Such contusion might result from simple extra-cranial trauma, but more likely from a pre-existing condition exacerbated by the shock of a blow.'

'Such as?'

'Cerebral aneurysm is most probable—blood pressure forces a weakened artery to bulge, become vulnerable to spontaneous rupture.'

She studied him, pen poised.

'Recent history of headaches?'

'Yeah. I put them down to stress.'

'Previous cranial injury?'

The Old Writer thought. An innocent frozen turnip soared parabolic through his mind. 'Nothing significant,' he said.

'Very good.'

The doctor stood, breast-pocketed her pen.

'Anything else you need to know?'

'What happens next?'

'The standard protocol requires close observation of the patient for a minimum ninety-six hours to ensure recovery is persistent. Hopefully discharge from the care of this facility will follow in due course.'

'That's it? I had a bloody stroke and got away with it?'

'In the short-term, apparently so.'

She showed her teeth again.

'But referral to a consultant of neurology is routine in circumstances such as this. Ongoing monitoring is strongly recommended in order to anticipate any recurrence of the condition.'

'You're saying it could swell up and pop again?'

'The possibility certainly exists—but it is beyond the scope of my expertise to suggest range of probability.'

The Old Writer stared at his feet. Tendon-knotted, rope-veined and amber-nailed, they reared tombstone-erect and bloodless beyond his inadequate sheet. He flashed on one huge crooked big toe flagged with a future mortuary-tag.

'Well, thanks for injecting some dramatic tension into an otherwise mundane life,' he mustered gruff.

When he looked up, the doctor had moved on. The Old Writer watched her as she scrutinised the ochre luminescence of a bloated catheter-bag held up to window sunlight. He remembered the cardboard bottle still nestled at his crotch, closed his eyes and tried not to strain his brain as he pissed himself to sleep.

The Old Writer stressed the positive when he reported his news to Helen. She studied him, inscrutable in silent bedside thought.

'Could be a lot bloody worse, eh love?' he prompted. 'Any thoughts you'd like to share?'

'Oh, I was just wondering about insurance,' she deadpanned. 'Whether we kept your old life-policy running.'

The Old Writer guessed she was telling the truth, his love undiminished by the thought.

'Sorry for scaring you, sweetheart.'

He reached to squeeze her hand.

'So you bloody well should be.'

Helen shook her head.

'How the fuck did you manage to get yourself stabbed in your stupid arse?'

'Dunno. Just lucky I guess. It could've been through the heart.'

'And you haven't got a clue who did it—or even an idea why?'

'It's all a bit fucking hazy.'

'I talked to a boy called Tony. He said the police have been taking statements, but with no CCTV or witnesses coming forward their best guess is random nut.'

'Right—trust me to be the victim of crime in the only place in the country not under twenty-four/seven surveillance.'

He glimpsed a shadow flit her face: a thought denied expression.

'What?'

'Nothing.'

'Everything all right at home?'

She sighed. 'Do you want the bad news first, or the worst?'

'Break me in gently—unless it's one of the kids.'

'No. They're all alive and kicking, I think.'

'So?'

'Graveyard Gary's dead.'

'What the fuck?'

'They busted him the day you left to come up here. Took twenty of them half-an-hour just to get past his steel door—and Grizzly.'

'And what? Don't tell me he fell down the stairs resisting fucking arrest.'

'No—they took him in and charged him for his plants. He was bailed in less than twelve hours. That's what Liza his neighbour said anyway, if she's a reliable witness.'

'She's not. But never mind. What did for bloody Gary?'

'Apparently, when he got home his power was off—and there was a notice on his metre to say his service had been suspended due to 'unauthorised modifications by unqualified personnel'.'

'Figures—his grow-room was wired like electric spaghetti.'

The Old Writer signalled her to continue, eager for the sorry end.

'It was about ten at night when the house went up. The whole village heard the bang. He'd bodged a gas ring to a cylinder of propane and tried to boil some spuds. Something must have leaked—according to Michaela's fireman son.'

'Jesus. What a fucking idiot,' The Old Writer muttered sympathetic. 'What about the bloody dog?'

Helen shuddered.

'It came out of the house like a meteorite, old Barry Douglas said. Headed for the forest in a howling ball of fire—came to grief on the motorway, squashed flat by a Tesco truck.'

'Shit.'

The Old Writer mourned his pal if not his dog.

'I'm sorry.'

Helen squeezed his hand.

'He was the only person in the village you ever volunteered a word to, so I know you're going to miss him.'

'Yeah.'

He squeezed back and winked.

'Good job I thought to top up my stash when I bumped into the old fuck last month.'

Helen looked off distant across the ward, at an awkwardness of relatives who hovered – caught between impatience and concern – around the bed of a slack-jawed ancient.

'So,' he invited, reluctant. 'If that's the lesser of your evils I don't want to guess at the fucking rest.'

'Your dad passed away the same night as Gary.'

'Ah. Poor old Cracked Jack. No cops involved, I hope?'

The Old Writer felt a twist of self-pity.

'Another rung up the rickety ladder of life. I'm not far from the bloody top now.'

'That's not all.'

Helen chewed her lip.

'Irene took it really hard. She's shut herself up in her darkened room—refuses to eat or say a word.'

'Too close to home I guess. The old girl probably feels Grim Death snapping at her own less-than-agile heels.'

'Maybe.'

Helen did not seem convinced.

'And now Cormac's acting up as well.'

'Go on. The suspense is fucking killing.'

'Viola says he had one of his 'episodes' this morning—ended up punching her in the face, and ran off and hasn't come back.'

'Great.'

The Old Writer swallowed queasy. Was it possible he had looked away for just too long, and now the neglected world of imagination had seeped back to infect his life?

'I grab five minutes to survive a life-threatening trauma and everything fucking kicks off.'

'I don't think it was planned.'

She sounded calm but Helen could be deceptive.

'Sorry,' he said. 'That probably sounded selfish.'

'I feel I should stay here with you but they need me back at home.'

Helen's eyes fluttered over her phone screen.

'It took three hours to get here on the damn train. What the fuck am I going to do?'

The Old Writer surveyed the sick misery around him. Ninety-six hours was four fucking days. To be confined on a claustrophobic hospital ward that long was beyond the limit of sane endurance. Besides, only a spineless arse would leave his wife to struggle with such a shit-storm alone, not to mention fail to exploit a perfect opportunity for escape.

'Okay.'

He mustered calm authority.

'Check out of the hotel and pick up the car. Bring some clothes back here to me and I'll sort out getting discharged.'

'That's stupid. You're sick, man. What if you have another stroke?'

'I won't. The doctor said my recovery was phenomenal.'

'You told me she said your artery could blow again anytime, and the risk couldn't be assessed in the short term. Are you sure you're not in denial?'

'I was exaggerating for dramatic effect.'

'Liar.'

'Trust me. Honest, I'm fine.'

She wanted to believe him.

'And anyway, I can't lie here in bed on my arse for days when you need me at home with you.'

Helen looked around the ward in search of a second opinion; The Old Writer maintained momentum.

'Hurry up and get moving now, and we can be back before it's dark.'

'I don't know.'

She bit a hesitant lip.

'I'm not convinced you're fit to travel.'

'Two hours sitting down? I think I can cope with that.'

He winked an afterthought.

'I'll even let you drive, love—if you're confident handling that old beast of a car on a busy motorway.'

sixteen

'I can't believe they'd just let you out.'
Vile Viola glared suspicious.
'Are you sure you had a stroke?'
'Early release on grounds of compassion.'
The Old Writer leaned against the kitchen wall, desperate to dampen the fire that raged between hip and ankle.
'Now tell me what's happened with Cormac.'
Viola's full lips wobbled. She blinked a blackened eye.
'We've searched the house, been all over the village and phoned all his friends from school. Angie's driving round one last time before we call the police.'
'Any clues why he took off?'
'Who cares about his damn motivation?'

Viola swept back a blind, peered into the obdurate night.

'He's been lost for bloody hours now and I just need to get him back.'

'Come and rest on the sofa,' said Helen and tugged his arm. 'You look a bit washed out. Don't you think so, Viola?'

'I don't know. A bit, I suppose. I just don't know what he's doing here. Like we haven't got enough to worry about already?'

'Your father just wants to help. Now put the kettle on for some tea.'

'A fucking drama junkie is what he is,' he thought he heard her mutter under her breath as he limped off in pained retreat.

Left alone in the sitting room, The Old Writer took a sentimental moment to relish his survival. His head was bruised and confused. His buttock throbbed in repeated remembrance of cold-steel penetration. But he was alive and he was home again, freed from helpless hospital dread and safe on familiar sofa.

Emotion dampened his eyes as the kettle rumbled in the kitchen, muffled murmurous wife and daughter. He had time to get a grip, he hoped, before they reappeared with tea.

The caring authority of the NHS had not been simply undermined. His delusional demand for liberty confronted by stiff staff resistance, The Old Writer had been forced to abandon reasonable persuasion in favour of bloody-minded bluster.

The staff nurse had heaved her outraged bosom and muttered dark prognostications, looked on sullen as – obstinate and unaided by hovering Helen – he demonstrated his vitality by struggling into his clothes. Eventually girded sartorial, he had smirked and lurched for the door, only to find his proud egress impeded by a stern phalanx of reinforcements.

Impatient doctors rationalised.

Worried nurses implored his trust, appealed to wavering Helen.

Ruffled bureaucrats procrastinated, whispered and shuffled dense pages of protocol in support of their outrageous claim that arcane legislation granted them the prerogative, in the face of abusive rejection, to summon crude security staff to enforce their duty of care.

Frustrated, The Old Writer deployed his weapon of last resort, bludgeoned the opposition into sulky submission with a bombastic invocation of the Charter of Human Rights.

Another fifteen wrangled minutes and – institutional liability waived with shaky signatures applied to tersely presented forms – The Old Writer was declared officially free to fuck off and die elsewhere.

Energised by victory, he had hobbled fluorescent corridors in hot pursuit of exit signs. Helen held on to him tight, still rubescent with embarrassment but stout in loyal support.

Outside in the ochre-lit car park night, The Old Writer relished a dank lungful of urban air as his wife fumbled to unlock the Volvo. She had fired the engine as he slid in beside her and slammed the door, giggled as he rewarded her with a celebratory kiss delivered proud to her dry lips. Excited, sucked into his juvenile game, she had quick-checked the mirror professional, popped the clutch and tire-squealed off, a natural-born getaway driver.

'I've used half a tank of diesel crawling around for hours, checked each and every bastard road a thousand fuckin' times.'

ASBO Angie bent to suck up tea.

'I even had a quick squint up a couple of forest paths—but it's dark as a black cat's arsehole out in those bleedin' horrible woods. Wherever the little prick's bunkered up he's not planning on getting found.'

'But we can't just leave him out there on his own.'

Viola paced the room.

'Anything could have happened. What if someone's got him?'

'C'mon now, babe.'

Angie felt her lover's pain.

'There's no point doing your head in imagining the worst.'

'How the fuck do I stop myself? I'm his mother you silly bitch.'
'Viola! Please.'
Helen's glance was sharp.
'You've got every right to be scared and upset, but not to abuse Angela when she's doing her best to help.'
'It's okay.'
Angie took Viola by the hand.
'Give me a minute to finish me brew and I'll get back out on the hunt.'
'What's the point?'
Viola pulled away.
'We need the police and a helicopter—with one of those thermal imaging things.'
'Seems a bit extreme don't you think?' said The Old Writer, soft. 'Might be a bit traumatic to get flushed out by airborne cops and dog teams if the poor lad's just laying low to work out a domestic grudge?'
'Easy to say when he's not your son,' flashed Viola, vindictive.
Angie eyed him narrow.
'Any idea where the kid might piss off to if he wanted time alone?'
'I might have.'
The Old Writer summoned his inner outlaw.
'Okay, here's the deal. Go and see if his bow and arrows are wherever he usually keeps them. If they are, fair enough—go ahead and call the cops. But if Cormac's taken them with him I'm pretty sure he's safe. Everyone should just go to bed and I'll fetch him back in the morning.'
'Makes sense.'
Angie drained her cup and stood.
'Sit tight and I'll have a shufti.'
Helen watched him curious; Viola, with wary scorn and a scintilla of desperate hope. The Old Writer closed his eyes, waited for Angie to come back from the caravan and validate his hunch.

'Yep. You called it,' Angie said several taut minutes later, gusting back on a chill draft perfumed with the refreshing reek of tobacco. 'The bow's not on its hook—and there's a sleeping bag and a gas-lighter that seem to be AWOL too.'

'Okay,' The Old Writer said. 'Let's turn the tension down a notch. A night out alone in the forest won't kill the boy. He'll find a good place to shelter.'

'Well, you're the irresponsible arse who thinks it's clever to fill an impressionable young boy's head with stupid 'wisdom of the woods'.'

Viola sniffed resentful, bundled for the door.

'So it's on your bloody conscience if my son comes to any harm.'

'He won't,' The Old Writer assured his now absent daughter, too tired to entertain the possibility of doubt.

'Come on.'

Helen tugged him to his feet.

'Well done for calming things down but it's time you got to bed.'

'Yeah. Nice one—for an addled old sod with concussion.'

Angie winked sly and punched his arm.

'Heard some fucker cut you a new arsehole too. Must've been a hell of a party. Glad you got yourself out alive.'

'Make sure I'm awake before it gets light.'

The Old Writer settled his throbbing hip in the bed, adjusted his dressed head on the pillow.

'You're sure you know where to find him?'

Helen's hand fluttered between quilt and mattress in uncertain search of his. He trapped it with bony fingers, massaged her palm with his thumb.

'Fucking hope so,' he said and held on as she rolled to kill the light. 'Or I'll have to hide out forever, won't I? Banished beyond the pale of tedious human angst to the peace of the outlaw wildwood—there to abide, guilty and alone, but safe from Vile Viola's righteous fury.'

'You should be so lucky.'

He drifted for a while, matched the pulse of his inflamed leg-nerve to the soft rhythm of her breath.

'I don't mean it when I call her 'Vile',' he whispered in the dark. 'It just hurts that I can never seem to reach her. Feels like there's something always between us—something too big to see clearly.'

The Old Writer waited for wifely wisdom. Helen offered only snores. He fled into troubled somnolence, pursued through groves of blasted trees by the shade of his dead dad.

seventeen

Six-thirty, an opaque autumn morning, the forest hunched dark around them, smothered by a sodden gloom thick enough to drown in.

The Old Writer gestured silent, extorted a half-smoked roll-up from his driver, sucked nicotine fortification.

'You sure you're fit for this mission?'

ASBO Angie smeared window-fog with cuff-gripped sweatshirt sleeve.

'You look fuckin' well fucked-up, man.'

The Old Writer coughed damp smoke.

'It's only half-a-mile. If I can find it in this shit.'

'Want me to come?'

'No need.'

'Don't want to share the honour, huh?'

'Or the blame,' he countered. 'Best if I talk to him alone.'

"Kay.'

She pulled tobacco from her pouch.

The Old Writer grabbed the walking stick bequeathed him by Cracked Jack, creaked open the door of the old Transit, slid stiff to sopping grass. He limped round the concrete anti-traveller berm that had halted the van's off-road progress and pushed into the muffled murk.

Dense sentinels of conifer flanked the muddy bridleway but The Old Writer could not see them. Behind him, radio pundits argued faint in the van. One claimed the nation was sullied by complicity in rendition, the other that harsh expediency had saved it. He hobbled another twenty tortured paces. The futile debate dissolved unresolved, fog-faded into silence.

The damp-cobwebbed algae-slick four-by-four post was adorned with an asterisk icon; arcane to the casual walker, to The Old Writer it marked a waypoint crucial to his progress. A drenched dog rose sagged across his path. He parted dew-jewelled grass fronds with a swing of his dead dad's stick, ducked and followed through, circumnavigated the scrub-camouflaged perimeter of an eroded Iron Age ring ditch.

He anticipated Cormac's interest in this historic echo to be engaged on their return, and then shrugged off the hopeful notion, superstitious of premature chickens.

The Old Writer winced with each buttock-flexing stride. He imagined the wet lips of his stab-wound gurning sympathetic, blood bubbling slimy to saturate his dressing and dribble cold down his thigh. His skull felt raw and tender as stoic he marched on, cerebral contusion disregarded, potential for spontaneous arterial eruption necessarily ignored.

'Fuck.'

The Old Writer floundered calf-deep into a slew of evil black slime masked by a litter of bright fallen chestnut-leaves.

'Fawk,' mimicked a sardonic crow from its eerie fog-bound perch. 'Fawk. Fawk. Fawk.'

The monochrome miasma thickened as he tracked the muddy streambed through the hawthorned gully to the foot of a wet briar-snarled incline. The Old Writer paused, deep-breathed saturated air, attempted oxygenation of his tired blood sufficient to fuel ascent to the Sanctuary Tree. Gills might be more beneficial, he thought, clinging pale to his ice-pick walking stick less than halfway up. Or a fucking aqualung.

The haggard oak spread its delta of branches black against the grey; like an X-rayed tarred lung, he mused a little dizzy.

The Old Writer ducked past the head of the fallen-branch dragon, stepped up to the scabrous trunk of the tree in a fugue of expectation. He sniffed; was that a faint lingering of woodsmoke, the damp ash of last night's fire?

'Come out you ungrateful insurgent whelp.'

The Old Writer exhausted tension in a billow of cloudy breath.

'Come out and submit to justice.'

No rustle in hollow interior. No scrabble of bony hands. No pale tight face poked out to peer down shy from the crook.

'Come out! Come out!'

His frantic stick thrashed unresponsive bark; The Old Writer gulped cold disappointment. It was not supposed to turn out this way. He had plotted a happy ending.

'Come on—come on out now.'

He extended a supplicant palm, touched wood, bent his head close to the silent tree as dread crystallised his marrow.

'Please. I know you're in there boy. Where else could you fucking be?'

'Half a bow-shot behind you, sucker. Ready to nail you with my deadly arrow.'

The Old Writer spun, buckled as his hip spasmed with hot pain, crumpled to his knees.

'No need to grovel.'

Cormac rose vague from the fogged cover of a grass-clump, relaxed his poised bow, lowered its nocked shaft.

'I only kill corrupt sheriff's men, not honest old dudes like you.'

'Christ. That's a relief.'

The Old Writer was sincere.

'Now get over here you sly little bastard and get me back on my feet.'

They sat together on the dragon log. Cormac choked down an emergency chocolate bar, quick as a starved dog, while another hungry hound of pain gnawed on his grandfather's leg-bone.

'Nice ambush.'

'Heard you coming a mile away.'

The boy disparaged him with a smirk.

'Thought you were some kind of animal—maybe a mad wild boar.'

'You weren't worried it was your mum? I'd be a lot more scared of her.'

'Who said I was bloody scared?' said Cormac, white-faced and chocolate-lipped. 'Anyway, how would she find me? No one knows this place—'cept you. And you're meant to be mashed up in hospital. What are you doing here?'

The Old Writer winked.

'Hospitals are for wusses, boy. I decided to get better.'

'Don't look better.'

Cormac scrutinised his grandfather's bandaged head.

'What's a stroke?'

'Who said anything about strokes?'

'Mum. She said Nan told her you'd had one when she phoned. Said you probably wouldn't be able to walk, or maybe even talk.'

'She told you that?'

'She was arguing with Angie. I was just hanging around.'

'Your mother's too pessimistic. I can walk and talk just fine.'

'Yeah?'

Cormac was unconvinced.

'So what's with the bonkers walking stick—and all that mad bloody limping?'

'Well, I got a bad cut on my butt-cheek if you must know. It's inflamed the nerves of my leg is all—nothing to do with strokes.'

'Cut how?'

'Knife.'

Cormac stared, processed information, understood and widened eyes.

'Someone stabbed you? In the arse?'

'Yes.'

'Wow. Dread.'

Cormac was impressed.

'Strayed into some bad postcode, did you? Got cut for disrespect?'

'Something like that.'

The Old Writer refocused on his mission, groped pockets for his phone.

'But, talking of respect, it's not cool to punch your mother.'

'I know that.'

Cormac slid from the log and stood back-turned and shoulder-hunched.

'But pissing someone off so bad they lose it's not that cool either, is it?'

Got him, The Old Writer keyed. *Give us 20 minutes.*

'You blacked her eye. What pissed you off so seriously you'd do a thing like that?'

'Everything.'

Cormac scuffed the ground.

'Great-granddad Jack with his face covered up getting carried out on a stretcher. Nan all upset but trying to be brave 'cause you were sick in the hospital and she was worried it was bad. Mum having a bloody epi at me for not feeling like doing my homework—then starting into Angie again for saying she should lighten up.'

'I can see you were under pressure, mate. But thumping her and legging it is still a pretty extreme reaction.'

'But she always has to fucking go and do it.'

The boy spun on the edge of tears.

'She just keeps on pushing and pushing and making it worse. The more people try to calm her down, the more she has to fight.'

'People?'

'Boyfriends, girlfriends—anyone who wants to be our dad. Like, Angie doesn't mean to swear and shout but Mum just drives her crazy.'

Cormac blinked exasperation.

'Why does she always have to mess things up? Why can't she just chill and be happy for once? What makes her so mad she wants to hurt anyone who tries to like her—scare them and make them so angry they have to run away?'

The Old Writer stretched out his hand. Cormac accepted its scant comfort.

'I'm sorry lad, I can't answer that. Perhaps it's some kind of test.'

A sudden vibration in his palm; a message from ASBO Angie.

Any fear of a sitRep? I'm frzng my fkn tits off.

He had forgotten to hit 'send'. Thumb-jabbed, the phone beeped acknowledgment of his delayed despatch. Cormac turned suspicious.

'Who are you texting?'

'Angie. She's waiting in the van. I told her we won't be long. Unless you're set on spending another night alone out here?'

'Nah.'

Cormac screwed up his face.

'My sleeping bag got soaked. And there's nothing to bloody eat. I thought I could shoot a deer like you said but I never even saw one. And it might be fucked-up and weird at home sometimes— but at least there's no giant silent white ghost-birds flapping around all bloody night.'

'Thank god for that.'

The Old Writer winced to his feet, leaned against his grandson.

'I don't think I've got enough zip left to make it back on my own.'

Enfeebled by exhaustion, pain-hobbled between sturdy youth and old man's stick, The Old Writer crab-walked happy down the hill.

'It's going to feel weird seeing my mum,' Cormac worried aloud. 'I know she's going to be well pissed-off, but I'm not taking any shit.'

A faint high disc of brightness spun, shimmed shades of grey from the fog. They staggered another few steps.

'I suppose I ought to say sorry—for scaring her, you know?'

'Whatever you think is right, boy. She'll be happy to see you whatever.'

'At least Angie will be there.'

'Yeah.'

He squeezed his grandson's nape with an affectionate bony talon.

'Angie doesn't scare easy.'

'Sometimes things work out good, don't they Granddad? It's not always as bad as it seems when you're all on your own in the dark?'

'No, not always.'

The Old Writer felt the pulse in his head, heard a buzzard cry thin in the distance.

'But it's only natural to worry.'

'Right.'

They bridged the stream together. Below, a swamped white feather circled helpless in an eddy.

'By the way.'

The Old Writer smiled wise.

'It was probably an old barn owl that spooked you in the night. They can hear a mouse fart from fifty feet—drop on it without a sound.'

'Barn owls are cool.'

'Yeah.'

They lurched on through resolving trees.

'Sudden silent death from above. I can think of worse ways to check out.'

eighteen

The Old Writer slept the clock around. He woke clear-headed: no snared-birds of dream semaphored fragmented dispatches from his subconscious, fluttering dark and distracting in the periphery of his day; no persistent maggot of discomfort grubbed between brain and skull. A finger slid beneath dressing found his stab-wound tender but scabbed dry. When he stood, poised in search of balance beside the bed, the twinges that flickered down his thigh were more invigorating than corrosive.

Buoyant, he showered and shaved, flattered by a bloom of sunlight flared through etched window-glass. He even stooped, considerate, to scoop soggy bloodstained dressings from the shower drain before ambling naked from the bathroom in careless search of clothes.

'God,' said Viola, nose wrinkled in disgust, stout ascent halted a few steps shy of the landing by pendulous paternal genitalia.

'Sorry. Took me by surprise.'

The Old Writer crouched to take the lunch tray from extended forklift arms.

'I wasn't expecting breakfast in bed.'

'Just as well.'

His daughter averted her gaze, heaved up and shouldered past.

'Because this is for Grandma Irene.'

'Right.'

He followed her down the bedroom corridor.

'The old girl must be feeling a bit better if she's got her appetite back.'

'She hasn't.'

Viola lumbered on.

'We just bring up her meals in case.'

'Oh.'

The Old Writer paused to grab Helen's bathrobe from the back of their bedroom door, sashayed after Viola wrapped swish in skimpy silk.

'All quiet on the home front now?' he asked as he caught her eye in the mirror on the wall just before she turned the corner that led down to Irene's flat. He thought he saw the ghost of a smile but it was gone when she turned round.

'That's supposed to be better? Do you know how ludicrous you look? It barely covers your arse.'

'I asked about Cormac. Did you manage to make peace?'

'More like a grudging detente.'

'Did he tell you he was sorry for thumping you? Because I'm pretty sure he was.'

'I think you should go and get dressed now.'

Viola sniffed dismissive.

'It's like being stalked by a comedy porno-Roman and I'm getting a little bit spooked.'

'Okay.'

The Old Writer would have to be content with her short shrift.

'I'll go and scare your mother.'

'That would be marginally more appropriate,' she muttered dry as he turned away. 'But still a fundamentally disturbing image.'

A rustle inside and a draft from the ajar door bristled The Old Writer's sparse leg-hair as he padded past Cracked Jack's room.

Helen, perched on the edge of the dead man's stripped mattress, looked up as he poked his head in. 'Hello. Welcome back to the land of the living,' she said without irony.

'Thanks,' he said and stepped in. 'A good nap was all I needed. Woke up a whole new man.'

'So I see.'

'Don't—I've already been reviled by Viola. Additional scorn is redundant.'

'Come here.'

'Why?'

'I want to see your arse.'

'What do you think?'

He craned to look down as she lifted his hem and peered silent.

'Feels like it's healing okay.'

She prodded gentle with a finger, gasped disgust and recoiled.

'What?'

Her reaction was perturbing.

'Jesus,' she muttered, hand to queasy mouth. 'I think it might have got infected. There are things wriggling under your skin.'

'Wriggling?'

He groped and twisted, neck cricked in pursuit of perspective.

'What the fuck do you mean?'

Anxious, he pawed at his wound. Helen collapsed horizontal to the mattress, undermined by mirth; five seconds of mock-revulsion was as much as she could manage.

'Gotcha!' she snorted helpless. 'Hook, line and bloody sinker.'

'Nice.'

The Old Writer was relieved if mildly nettled. The wind-up was an art form usually eschewed by Helen. She was behaving out of character; perhaps showing signs of strain? He sat down on the mattress, inventoried the room abandoned by his father while his wife stifled her hysteria.

Scant trace remained of the old man's eighty-five years. A stack of musty clothes neatly folded on the chest of drawers, destined for delivery to a local charity shop; likewise, a crumpled paper sack of dead man's tired shoes. Filed in a battered shoebox, faded and dog-eared documents awaited assessment of sentimental or pecuniary worth. A supermarket 'bag for life' wilted on the floor, half-filled with redundant pharmaceutical supplies cleared from the bedside cabinet. On this, a wedding photo framed behind cracked glass: Brylcreamed Jack and toothy white-veiled Doris ducking awkward and confetti-flecked beneath a church-door arch. Above the bed, a badly painted highland landscape hung crooked. It had been purchased – The Old Writer recalled, engulfed in a sudden dank midge-swarmed musk of peat – on a 'sixties family holiday, from a gift-shop near Glencoe.

And, bed-shadowed on the faded rag-rug at his feet, a book.

The Old Writer frowned. Cracked Jack was not renowned for his literary appreciation. Curious, he bent and retrieved – anonymous *sans* dust jacket – the abandoned casebound volume. He flipped to the title page, stared down surprised at his name.

Fuck, he thought. In all the years he had spent manipulating words for love and money his father had never hinted he had read even a cover blurb, let alone offered an opinion on the merit of a published work. Now here he was reading "Leepus: Badger Boys" in bed. Evidence of secret admiration, or undercover scorn? The Old Writer would never know now; but it was some kind of recognition.

'What's that?' said Helen nosing round his shoulder.

'Just some smut the old fuck was reading.'

'You're crying.'

He blinked and riffled pages. The book opened at page forty-five, place-marked by an old facedown photograph. Jack had not managed to get far into the story, then; perhaps he had finished others.

The Old Writer flipped the photo, time-travelled straight to suburbia in nineteen fifty-nine.

It was hot in the panel-fenced garden at the back of the pebble-dashed semi; bees droned Harry Belafonte songs between hollyhock and nasturtium, and a ghost of pipe-smoke haunted torpid air as, out-of-frame next door, old Arnold Crowley striped his lawn with a rattling push-mower.

Doris – bob-haired, trim in gingham and strap-sandals, knitting in her lap – looked up shy from her deckchair in the shade of pampas grass. At her feet, two boys. One, three years old and golden, beamed beatific camera-ward and played a toy piano; the other – five years older and darker, trapped restless in stultified youth – was the juvenile Old Writer.

A gust of stale resentment percolated the room.

'I suppose someone had better tell Ollie-the-evil-Organist, The Old Writer said, lip curled instinctive.'

'Stop it.'

Helen stiffened.

'We're not going there again.'

'No. Okay.'

'Anyway, I emailed him already.'

'Very prompt.'

'Jack was his dad too.'

'What did he say?'

'Said to let him know the funeral date and he'd sort out getting over.'

'Right. Suppose we'll have to stump up the prick's fucking airfare—like we did when we lost Doris.'

'I think he's doing better now, since he got the Director of Music job at that cathedral.'

'You're up to date.'

'It was in his Christmas card last year.'
'I must have forgotten to read it.'
'Talking of the funeral—'
'To switch to a lighter topic.'
'I found a RestWell pre-payment plan tucked down the back of your dad's sock drawer.'
'Right.'
The Old Writer smiled weak at his wife.
'Sorry for getting arsey—again.'
'It was over thirty-five years ago and you still feel insecure?'
'Music always touched a spot in you that words could never reach.'
'Absinthe and spontaneity were influential too.'
'Yeah. Just wish you'd had a gorgeous spontaneous drunk little sister to offer an opportunity for balance.'
'Piss off.'
Helen laughed aloud.
'You could barely manage me.'
The Old Writer thought about managing her there and then. Helen saw it in his eye and thought about it too. But the ghost of Cracked Jack played gooseberry and the thought remained unrequited.
'So, I suppose we have to pick up the Death Certificate and tell the undertakers to break him out of the morgue?'
'I fetched it this morning while you were still in bed.'
'Oh. Good. Does it say what finished the old sod off?'
'Yes. Your father had a stroke too—the poor old man.'
'Spooky.'
The Old Writer felt his skin creep under chilly silk.
'Like some kind of sick genetic empathy was trying to take me with him.'
'Don't be melodramatic. It was just a weird coincidence. Jack's stroke was ischemic, yours was haemorrhagic.'
The Old Writer stared blank.

Helen stood and said, 'He had a blockage in an artery that starved his brain of blood and killed it. You just had a minor bleed.'

'On top of getting stabbed.'

'It's not a competition.'

Helen turned toward the door.

'Now put some sensible clothes on. I'm not turning up at the funeral parlour with you dressed like a raddled old tranny.'

The decor was themed in lavender, at least three too many shades. The director, Beth, was a wan lank-haired girl; she was dressed in a sombre double-breasted suit she had inherited from her granddad. Her fingernails – ragged on a pale hand slipped limp from an over-long frayed sleeve – were suggestive of premature burial.

They filled out Beth's forms and scanned her brochures, stifled in a twilit cubicle reminiscent of a tomb.

Yes, 'Dad' was to be cremated.

No, additional mortuary treatments would not be required to preserve Dad's demeanour for viewing. The 'basic' coffin prescribed by Dad's plan would be fine unenhanced by decorative brass handles.

Yes, Dad's remains should be recovered and maintained for later collection. No, they would not, at additional cost, like his ashes vitrified and formed into a ring for Mum to remember Dad by forever, because Mum was gone before.

Yes, of course they forgave Beth. Yes, they appreciated her sincere regret for any upsetting indiscretion. No, it really was not a problem.

And no, Dad was not religious. The ceremony would be secular; a hired padre need not attend.

The Old Writer's phone interrupted their selection of a suitable *pro forma* Order of Service. He left the vital decision to Helen while he read the message from Rude Jude.

stbbd up the ars? well fkn hrdcor im fkn prowd of u man – srry abt jack – send funrl dat so me n natalya cn sort out swngng by – J

Hardcore. He smiled, pleased by the accolade bestowed by his gangsta son. And then he remembered the gun. The gun was still a problem. It could not be ignored. But they would get Cracked Jack safely incinerated first, and then tackle the fucking firearm.

The Old Writer signed a cheque for some unspecified additional charges and, soothed by Beth's repeated exhortation that they should, 'Take care now,' they hurried out of the lavender limbo, reprieved to the world of the living.

'Who was your text from?' asked Helen, muscling the Volvo out into the snarl of evening traffic.

'Jude.'

The Old Writer pedalled imaginary clutch and brake.

'He says getting stabbed is hardcore.'

'Oh.'

Helen frowned into the rear-view mirror, distracted by the need to change lanes before the lights.

'Isn't that the psychotic music he was into when he was ten?'

'Yeah.'

The Old Writer smiled, nostalgic.

'The sort that brought his bloody ceiling down after he conned you into buying him a sub-woofer for Christmas by telling you it was a synth.'

'I thought I was encouraging him to find his muse.'

She swung, gunned into a gap, braked hard.

'Had delusions of him in the *avant garde* of electronic composition.'

'Talking of sons and their absent muses,' The Old Writer said. 'Any word from Jilted John?'

'I rang him and his phone was off, so I emailed but he hasn't replied.'

'He's probably just locked in his studio incarnating some new dark artistic vision.'

'Yes.'

She anticipated the light, raced a white van to the roundabout, hauled the big car onto the Forest Parkway slip road. They covered two dark vehicle-choked miles in silence and at speed.

'That's what I'm afraid of,' she finally said, as the car lurched up the exit-ramp signed for The Village of Idiots.

nineteen

Quiet in his Tower of Babble, The Old Writer was absorbed in scientific evaluation of the efficacy of the new absinthe-flavour mega-strength nicotine liquid with which he had just charged his electronic ciggie. More subtle than incandescent tobacco, it delivered the active ingredient just as efficiently, with minimal bronchial agitation. Perhaps it would suffice to fuel the healthy impending construction of "Leepus—Bk13".

The ancient empty file was open on his screen. He rehearsed the PokerTart/supernatural-stalker storyline in his head; in retrospect it was still viable, even eager to be told. But perhaps he should let it simmer subconscious for another week or two, come to it post-funeral when, domestic uproar diminished, he would be free to inhabit The Zone.

The Old Writer inhaled oily vapour, gained nicotine reassurance. Sure, his family saga was still ragged with dangling plot threads but – with a little authorial craft and imaginative manipulation – he could soon get it back under control.

He had already steered the heroic narrator intact through a pivotal twist of peril, expectations of tragedy subverted by the sacrifice of a minor character and the recovery of runaway Cormac. Continuity was being maintained despite the diversion of Cracked Jack's demise. Surely it was not beyond his capability to deflect the potential violence that lurked in ASBO Angie's savage breast, decommission Rude Jude's life-threatening fucking armoury, and guide Jilted John through his dark night of the soul to enjoy a kinder sunrise.

There was still Obscene Irene of course, sequestered in her gloom. It did not look that good for her; they should have asked RestWell for a frequent-shopper discount.

The Old Writer closed the Leepus file, clicked to view his emails. His inbox was a Pythonesque menu. He deleted his way through the tedious scroll of spam, paused at a message from Beatnik Tony.

Hi, hope you're getting better. Me and Shula are gutted you got hurt at our gig. Shula checked with our insurers (just in case we could get you some compo to make it up to you) but unfortunately they say we're not liable for injuries resulting from criminal acts. Also, it might sound cheeky, but someone suggested your take on the whole 'adventure' might make a great piece for Gut Wrench. *We've got space available in our next issue (deadline 25th of this month). We'd be really psyched to have you. Let us know if you're up for it—Tony.*

The Old Writer replied that he would be happy to contribute a couple of dozen paragraphs at a 'mate's rate' of fifty-pence per word (if that didn't sound too cheeky), and would drag himself from sickbed to keyboard just as soon as he received a contract.

Spam, spam, spam, spam, spam; or was it?

PLEASE *PLEASE* READ was the subject line of the message from *ihatemyshitself@freemail.com*. An invitation to indulge in some variety of sick humiliation porn, The Old Writer had first assumed. Maybe it was the redundant repetition in its capitalised entreaty that intrigued his curiosity and made him recover it from the trash. Or maybe his subconscious was just too weak and prurient to ignore the promise of an entertaining new instalment from the sick life of Crazy Crystal the fucking psychotic arse-slasher. He double-clicked the message open.

i bet im the last person you want to hear from – most likely you wish id killed myself with pills like i said i would – well i tried but they didnt do it - i feel like shit for stabbing you – believe me im sorry sorry sorry – i was all messed up and hurting – thats not an excuse – ill never forgive myself for doing it but perhaps you can forgive me one day (i kind of think you might coz you never dobbed me to the cops – thankyou thankyou thankyou – or if you did they didn't find me yet☺) – anyway im feeling more calmer since i started praying regular with morgan (hes my army of light mentor – really wise and well fit too ☺) – and i get it now how evil spirits can lead me to do stuff i shouldnt – like believing in magic and reading bad books that make me confused – not saying you did leepus to lead me away from jesus on purpose – just im weak and easy to fool morgan says – so anyway sorry again for stabbing you up and all that talking dirty (blush) – ive got a bright new future now as a blessed daughter of christ in god's (praise him) eternal shining kingdom so everythings going to be cool – i hope – love you with all my heart forever (but not in THAT way) – sister virginia (formerly known as crystal)

'Fuck.'

The Old Writer sucked hard on his electronic ciggie. Another delusional casualty of emotional confusion recruited by the Army of Light. First Shy Skye and now Crazy Crystal beguiled and enthralled, handmaids for predatory preachers. Coincidence or conspiracy? Perhaps he should not have been so adamant in his refusal of D. C. Mike Jagger-of-Task-Force-Knife-Crime's telephonic request for a victim statement yesterday. Mercy, it seemed, was a double-edged sword; exercised in good faith, it had condemned the hapless child to God's abusive House of Correction.

Spam. Spam offered riches from Nigeria, medication from Mexico, love from a sultry Muscovite, and a penis enlarged to enjoy it. Spam, spam, spam; and one from John, perhaps summoned by the hint of Shy Skye?

Dad: Hi. Sorry to hear from mum about Jack—and your catalogue of physical suffering. Hope you're seeing the funny side by now. Wish I could say I was too—but I'm still on a bit of a weird one, stuck on this fucked-up theme-park ride. I'll be there for the funeral, whatever. Meantime, get well, and don't worry. I'll work through this shit in time.

Love to mum and the others—John.

Don't worry? Shit, The Old Writer thought. Easy to fucking say, boy. If you don't want to be a cause for concern, don't send melancholic emails with disturbing cryptic subtexts.

He turned back to the screen but his search for elucidation was pre-empted by Helen's staircase-muffled voice shrilled with an edge of alarm.

'Mum. Mum, are you okay?'

A fist rapped urgent on distant wood, rattled door in frame.

'Mum, answer me. Let me in, I'm worried.'

The Old Writer pushed back his chair, grabbed a lungful of absinthe vapour and – slowly descending the tower stair – composed a few erudite lines appropriate for the comforting of recently bereft spouses.

'She hasn't eaten or said a word for days. And now she's locked herself in as well,' said Helen as he joined her at the door of the granny flat.

'Let me try.'

He worked the handle. Helen watched, impatient.

'She's locked it. I told you.'

'Come on Irene. Open up. We need to know you're alright.'

The Old Writer knocked authoritative, but with no more effect than his wife.

'You'll have to break it down,' said Helen. 'What if she's had a fall and—'

'Hold on.'

The Old Writer signalled for patience.

'There's a spare key in your bedside drawer, remember? Just let me go and get it.'

The logistics of the hypothetical trip to Machu Picchu seemed simpler by the day, The Old Writer thought as he rummaged for the key. Helen would enjoy it all the more without Irene left behind at home to trouble her filial conscience. Cold-hearted? No, he justified, merely accepting the inevitable and looking for long-term upsides.

Self-satisfied but duly solemn he returned to Helen with his prize.

'Hurry up,' she said.

He worked the key in the lock. Inside, its dislodged twin jangled to the floor. He turned the handle and eased open the door.

'You look,' Helen answered his silent enquiry. 'I found poor old Jack.'

The small sitting room was chilly. Closed curtains filtered daylight, inhibited clarity. Was that Obscene Irene under those spread sheets of newsprint, folded slight and inconsequential in her lonely wingback chair? Squeamish, he pincered a redtop masthead. Smug in loathsome full-page close-up, The Prime Minister smirked as The Old Writer slid paper from dead face and peered. Irene's head was crumpled, lopsided, melted featureless. Christ, how long had she been dead?

He took a breath and peered again. Now it was just a squashed cushion wedged on top of another: the compressed memory of an osteoporotic spine moulded in the corner of the chair back.

'Irene?'

He yanked curtains wide and turned towards her bedroom.

The Old Writer nudged-open the door. The atmosphere inside was sweet and sour. He guessed at alcohol and trace urine. The room was lit by a bedside lamp. He stepped in. Irene whimpered, flapped eerie on the bed: a cartoon apparition, head covered by candlewick bedspread.

'Go away.'

Her voice was tremulous.

'I don't want anyone to see me.'

'Come on. What's the matter old girl?'

He stepped closer, reached a hand to her draped shoulder.

'Aren't you feeling well?'

She flinched from his touch, flung herself flat and, shrouded tight and bony in the cover, burrowed her head into mounded pillows. The movement dislodged a bottle; it slithered from the mattress, clashed harsh with others on the floor. The Old Writer stooped and picked one up, carried it out to Helen.

'Your work I think.'

'What?'

She stared baffled.

'Sloe gin,' he said. 'One of several empty bottles.'

Helen read the label.

'Three years old. They were surplus Christmas presents. I assumed it was Jude who'd looted them from the larder.'

'Not this time.'

'So, what? You found her. Is she—?'

'No.'

He shook his head.

'Dead drunk perhaps but breathing.'

'Oh, Mum.'

Helen sighed disappointment.

'It's been getting on for ten years now. I thought her drinking days were over.'

'She's hiding under the covers. You'd better have a word.'

'I don't know. She's foul when she's on a bender.'

'She's not exactly saintly when she's sober.'

'There's funny obscene and vicious obscene. I took more than enough of her nasty shit growing up. I'm not ready to do it again.'

'Okay.'

The Old Writer smiled at his wife.

'I'll take the bullet for you. Come back with tea in half-an-hour.'

'Thanks, love. Sorry.'

The Old Writer watched Helen plod off around the corridor corner. He had never known her to duck a dirty job; it was not in her nature. So, if she said she couldn't cope, she really couldn't, and the only honourable thing to do was take the weight, for once.

Sweet-talk was cheap enough, The Old Writer thought as he stepped back into the flat. If tender reassurance and gentle persuasion could charm Irene from her bed of misery with dignity restored he was happy to roll his emotional sleeves up and get stuck into the job. But hands-on care was a whole different skill-set. He drew the line at intimate personal hygiene duties. He was not that fucking noble.

'Talk to me, Irene. What's this all about?'

'None of your business. Piss off and let me die.'

'It is my business. The whole family's worried about you. Come out from under that cover now and let's have a look at you.'

'I can't. I'm too ashamed. It's terrible what I did.'

'You're embarrassed you fell off the wagon and let yourself down. But it's not a hanging offence.'

'It used to be—when punishment fitted crime.'
'Getting smashed on homemade sloe gin?'
'No. Don't be so damn stupid, boy. What I did before.'
'You're going to have to tell me, Irene. I'm too bloody dense to guess.'
'Where's Helen? Earwigging at the door?'
'No. We're on our own.'
'She'd always get that disgusted look in her eye—put me to bed like she was cleaning up shit. It made me want to slap her.'
'You're her mum, Irene. She loves you. You think she doesn't care?'
'I don't deserve to be bloody cared about. I don't feel like anyone's mum. I never did. I was always a cheap dirty slapper.'
'That's a bit harsh.'
'You named me Obscene Irene.'
'Only as a term of endearment—because you sometimes get a bit frisky. You shouldn't be offended. I give everyone daft names.'
'You had me bang to rights.'
'No. It was a cheap shot and I'm sorry.'
'You wouldn't say that if you knew.'
'Knew what for god's sake? We're going round in bloody circles.'
'You'll hate me if you know.'
'No I won't.'
The Old Writer sensed the time was right to take the old girl in hand. He sat her upright against the pillows, unveiled her flinching face, finger-combed sparse hair gentle from her clammy troubled brow.
'Hate's an energetic sport. And I'm a lazy sod.'
Irene sobbed. Her shoulders shook. Tears oozed from reddened eyes. The Old Writer let suspense build for a couple of silent minutes.
'It's time to give it up now, Irene. However bad you think it is it's better out than in.'

'Promise you'll never tell Helen. Or throw me out of the house.'
'Cross my heart.'
He pantomimed genuflection, unctuous as any sly priest eager for sinful confession.
'And whatever your guilty secret, it's not my place to judge.'
Irene shuddered a breath.
'I only wanted some company, and perhaps a bit of love. I know old ladies are supposed to be past all that malarkey, but I was never very ladylike—too much of a randy tart with a yen for gin and cock.'
She paused to gauge reaction.
'Sorry if you're shocked, dear. I'm just trying to be honest.'
'Nothing to be sorry about.'
The Old Writer waved absolution.
'We all have our peccadilloes.'
'Very understanding. But then I'm not your wife. If Helen had been her mother's daughter and put the horns on your soft head, you'd probably have buggered off tout suite too—just like her poor old dad did when he caught me in the backseat of Terry Bishop's Rover with my knickers off again.'
The Old Writer flashed on Helen splayed on the keyboard of Ollie's Hammond organ, his brother pounding power chords relentless between her legs. His impulse had been to kill them both. It was lucky he had been so stoned and full of Christmas cheer.
'Enough with the nostalgic reminiscence now.'
He prompted her with a knee-pat.
'You were talking about being lonely.'
'I know he always got nasty when I teased him by being flirty. But I knew that just like me, inside he needed comfort. It was bad to take advantage of him being a little bit barmy—but I really never meant to hurt the poor old man.'
'We're talking about Cracked Jack?'
Irene nodded, eyes downcast.
'He really missed her, didn't he—your mum?'

'I guess he must've loved her in his own mysterious way.'
'It was wicked what I did—tricking him like that.'
'Like what, Irene?'
'I—I told him I could be Doris, if that would make him happy. I shouldn't have. I know that. I just wanted to be close.'
'Close.'
'Yes. Someone breathing beside you in the dark. Someone to reach out and touch when you're old and scared of dying. He was glad to have me with him too. I know he was. It wasn't just wishful thinking—was it?'

The Old Writer had no answer.

'It was lovely for a while.'

Irene wrapped her arms across her chest, hugged herself and rocked.

'But then I went and spoiled it all again by being greedy.'
'Greedy?'
'I only fancied a little cuddle. He seemed to like it—held me tight, made me feel all warm and nice. I got a bit carried away. Thought I'd give the old chap a treat.'
'Treat?'
'Yes. You know.'

Irene flexed her lips.

'Most men seem to like it.'

The Old writer contemplated geriatric porn and quickly wished he had not.

'I was only being nice. I didn't mean to make him angry. He pulled my hair and shouted I couldn't really be his Doris if I'd do a filthy thing like that. I was scared. I said I was sorry. He threw me out of his bed. I put the light on to find my slippers. His face was all screwed up and purple. He held onto his head. His hands were like claws. He stared at me. I felt like dirt. He moaned, and then... and then... and then...'

'And then he died.'

'I felt so bad. How could I ever face you all? I just wanted to crawl away and die as well. I'm sorry, boy. I'm so terribly sorry. I'm sorry I was ever born. I'm sorry I killed your dad.'

She clung to him frail, a malnourished child, as she sobbed against his chest. He patted her back, ineffectual, tried to summon appropriate words while suppressing a fit of the giggles.

Poor old Cracked Jack; the one-and-only blowjob of his life and it blew his fucking mind.

'All right, Irene,' he spluttered. 'Don't cry now. You shouldn't have messed with the old man's head—but it wasn't you who killed him. He had a bloody stroke.'

He held her a while longer. Her sobbing subsided; she drew back and studied his face. He held his breath, chest heaving, stifled a new wave of cruel mirth.

'You forgive me?' she said. 'Truly? You don't think I'm a disgusting old slut?'

'Well, I wouldn't go quite that far.'

The Old Writer laughed aloud.

'But you have to see the funny side, Irene—or else what's the point of living?'

'She wants poached egg-on-toast and a cup of tea when she's finished in the bath.'

'And?'

Helen waited.

'She didn't ask for anything else.'

'Come on. Don't piss around. What sent her back to the bottle?'

'Sorry.'

The Old Writer sidled close to sooth her with a squeeze.

'I'm not at liberty to disclose that. It's privileged information.'

'Bullshit.'

She hunched him off.

'You know I need to know.'

The Old Writer filled the kettle at the sink.

'I think you already do.'

'Your dad?'

He shrugged.

Helen opened the fridge and reached for an egg. 'The sly old cow was with him, wasn't she?' she said and slammed the heavy door. 'With him the night that he died?'

'I promised not to tell.'

'Jesus, she's incorrigible.'

'I wouldn't argue with that.'

'So what exactly happened? It must have been a horrible shock.'

'It was. For both of them.'

The Old Writer choked a disrespectful sob, turned away to cuff-wipe a tear of adolescent glee.

'But maybe we should skip the 'exactly' just for now, huh? There are images of her mother no daughter should have in her head.'

'Right.'

Helen's mouth wrinkled distaste.

'If it makes a sick bastard like you giggle like a smutty kid it has to be bloody appalling.'

The Old Writer watched the kettle boil, tried not to snigger, failed and then failed again. Tight-lipped, Helen loaded the toaster. She cracked the egg into a pan on the stove and stared at frothing albumen, picturing – her husband intuited from her expression – a panoply of grotesque scenarios all starring Obscene Irene.

'I hope to Christ,' she muttered, gelatinous egg poised on slotted spoon. 'That when I'm a demented old bat plaguing my children's lives I maintain a modicum of maternal decorum.'

The Old Writer stepped close as she slopped the egg abrupt onto waiting toast, slid an arm around her waist and nuzzled over her shoulder. 'To be frank and nakedly selfish,' he whispered in her ear. 'If I'm still sleeping with you then I kind of hope you don't.'

'You won't be,' Helen said with certainty, swatted him hard with the spoon.

Long after she had loaded the tray and whisked off to deliver it to her mother, The Old Writer sat alone at the kitchen table and studied, with mortal consternation, the memory-skin back of his old writer's hand still impressed with the livid pattern of hot slotted stainless-steel.

twenty

It was not the sparkling first chapter of the new Leepus book he would prefer to have had written by now, and he could not deny a churlish resentment of the distraction, but – as hackwork – Cracked Jack's eulogy was satisfactorily stylish.

The Old Writer had approached this filial duty as he might the production of a blurb for an acquaintance's bad novel. He had sifted his father's unremarkable life-story, extracted rare sympathetic nuggets, polished and spun them professional; he offset the degree of hypocrisy inherent in the task through satirical observation of his subject's many foibles.

Glancing up from his script to scan the sparse audience huddled beneath the crematorium-chapel lectern, The Old Writer was gratified by an occasional wry smile evoked by his 'affectionate' humour. Belly laughs were rarer, but that may have been down to his delivery, impeded now and then by an involuntary constriction of the throat that forced him to pause and swallow emotion.

The Old Writer quit the stage and reviewed his performance from a pew, while Helen read Kahlil Gibran, and then Viola, Christina Rossetti. John was excused participation on grounds of 'shyness', Jude, through illiteracy.

Motorised plush curtains stuttered closed around the catafalque and coffin and – to the accompaniment on the reedy crematorium organ of second-son Ollie's rendition of 'Scarborough Fair', an interminably shrill-whistled favourite of their father's that had haunted The Old Writer's childhood – Cracked Jack trundled off unseen to the inferno.

As they shuffled out past solemn ushers the maestro changed his tune, let rip with a virtuoso recital of something awesome by Mozart. Grandstanding prick, The Old Writer snarled inward as Viola moved to turn sheet music timely in her uncle's dazzling limelight and Helen sopped tears with a hankie.

Outside, The Old Writer swallowed irrational bile, smiled grave and exchanged funereal platitudes with the scattering of mourners gathered on the forecourt in a thin shiver of winter sun. A helicopter circled overhead. The harsh percussion of its rotors disrupted the fond reminiscences of Phillip and Mo Abercrombie – who were, they proudly reminded him, the last good neighbours of lovely Jack and Doris in the dear old Chalfont Crescent days – and, as a pleasing bonus, brutalised Ollie's transcendent arpeggios long before they could rise to inspire tears in the eyes of the angels awaiting the fumes of Cracked Jack above.

Respects received and invitations issued to refreshment at the local pub, flowers perused and pallbearers tipped, The Old Writer – attracted by a sympathetic plume of spliff-smoke – sloped off to join John, and Jude and Natalya undercover of an arbour bedraggled with winter-faded vines of climbing rose.

'That's the boring shit done with,' said Rude Jude, as his father intercepted the joint he passed to Jilted John. 'Hope the wake's more fucking fun.'

'Please to accept my condolence.'

Natalya bowed stiff-necked.

'Thank you.'

The Old Writer shook her offered hand; it was cool and dry in his grip.

'Good of you to come.'

'Yes. I am sorry for the disrespect of late arriving.'

Natalya turned a skin-tight black-jeaned leg, displayed the broken high-heel of her knee-boot.

'Jude makes me climb over some walls. I am slow.'

'Walls?'

'Clocked a Task Force wagon in a lay-by near the gate,' said Jude, frowning up through foliage at the sky. 'Thought we might need to make a swift exit. Parked in a lane round the back.'

'Guilty conscience?'

The Old Writer coughed smoke.

Jude spoke again.

'Better safe than sorry, man. That white Volvo v70 with the tinted windows in the car park is kind of spooky, too. And the fucking chopper hanging around.'

'I'd give the skunk a rest, bro',' said John. 'You're fucking paranoid.'

'Perhaps some local crime-boss popped his clogs and his cop-pals are waiting to pay their respects,' The Old Writer mused, stubbed the roach and stepped out of the arbour. 'See you all in the backroom at the Railway Inn. Don't hang around. I put fifty-quid behind the bar—after that you're buying your own.'

'Okay.'

John moved to follow.

'Anyone need a lift?'

'I've got Helen and Irene. Angie's got the kids in her van.'

The Old Writer eyed his daughter arm-in-arm with his brother.

'Your sister will go with them, I guess, when she's done schmoozing her favourite fat uncle.'

'You can run me and Natalya back round to the 'cruiser,' Jude said and fumbled at his fly. 'Go on and fire-up your shitty old nail—I just need to grab a slash.'

The Old Writer walked towards Helen and Irene where they stooped to collect cards from funeral flowers, but his eyes were on Vile Viola and Evil Ollie; they walked and talked together, relaxed, almost intimate. Perhaps it was just some kind of empathy of the elephantine that they shared: a conspiracy of corpulence, gravitational mass-attraction? He was bothered that it bothered him, but he could not deny it did.

His brother had flown in the day before. Helen had answered the door and welcomed him with a hug, or at least attempted to; the length of her arms was inadequate to circumscribe his bulk.

Although under heavy manners, The Old Writer's fraternal greeting was strained; it had cost him two-hundred quid for the taxi from the airport because absent-minded Ollie had 'neglected to change any dollars'.

Left together in the sitting room while Helen summoned family members and put the kettle on for tea, The Old Writer and his brother had renegotiated their precarious 'state of relationship'.

'So, you're looking very American.'

'Fat, you mean.'

'You get health-care with the new job? We're not getting any younger, kid.'

'Yes. I heard you had a stroke.'

'Not as bad as Dad's.'

'And someone stabbed you, too.'

'My fame is truly international.'

'How is your professional life? It seems a while since you had a book out—unless one sneaked by under my radar.'

'Just a brief hiatus. I'm back in the saddle now.'

'Glad to hear it. Middle-age is a sod.'

'Yeah. Your cathedral gig turned up just in time.'

'New York was weird to adjust to—but, after Michael left me, I just needed to get away.'

'Makes sense. New career in a new town. It must have been awkward teaching music at a public school where your ex-partner was still headmaster.'

'I loved that job.'

'I bet. All those rosy-cheeked posh young choristers singing from your hymn sheet.'

'Fuck off.'

'And the money problems are sorted out?'

'Call me Croesus. Why? Do you need a loan?'

'Not yet. Capitalism could implode any day now, of course—but so far Leepus residuals are still trickling in nice and steady.'

'And letting you laze about on your fading laurels year after idle year?'

'A big family is an impediment to creativity. It occupies the mind.'

'I wouldn't know.'

'Someone had to maintain the bloodline.'

'Yes.'

Ollie paused; his eyes darted evasive.

'By the way,' he picked up. 'Thanks for taking the weight with Dad these last few years.'

'Five.'

'It couldn't have been easy. He was always hard work—even before the dementia.'

'If it wasn't for Helen I'd have stuck him in a home.'

'You're lucky to have her.'

'Yes.'

'And your children.'

'I know.'

'How's Viola? Do you remember when she was born and—?'

'Let's not.'

'Hard to believe she's half-way through her thirties now, with children of her own.'

'Yeah. And still growing, too. She's nearly as big as you.'

Helen had returned then with Obscene Irene in tow. Her eyes flickered between the two brothers, searched for traces of bad blood and blurred with sudden moistness when Viola bustled the kids in and cheek-kissed her uncle, shy and flushed.

Helen and Viola busy in the kitchen, Ollie had indulged the little ones for an hour as they clambered his mountainous body; this rambunctiousness, The Old Writer observed, studied surreptitious by Angie.

Although breathless by then, Ollie had not resisted when Cormac dragged him outside to the paddock to admire his prowess with bow and arrow. Despite his baser instinct, The Old Writer was touched by his brother's patient attention to the youngsters. He had to be knackered, after all, from flying transatlantic wedged into a tiny seat.

Impending solemn occasion notwithstanding, dinner had been convivial. Later, Ollie sipped wine at the piano and performed a moving repertoire of funeral warm-up tunes.

The gathering had listened respectful: Obscene Irene waltzing the room alone, decorous but distracted; The Old Writer holding teary Helen's hand, swallowing resentment with his Rioja and wishing, not for the first time, that he could tickle emotion from his own keyboard with as much accomplished subtlety as his fucking musical little brother.

'Nice flowers—but not that many of them,' Irene said as The Old Writer came alongside. 'I hope I get a better show.'

'Bound to.'

The Old Writer nudged her arm.

'With all those bereft old beaus competing to pay their respects it'll be like the Death of bloody Diana.'

Irene cackled obscene.

'I've got some nice black lingerie put aside for my big day. Do you think I should go open-casket—give those dirty buggers one last sly eyeful to remember me by?'

'For God's sake, Mum,' Helen said and stalked off to join Ollie and Viola who still lingered arm-in-arm.

'Like Tweedledum and Tweedledee, those two, aren't they dear?' said Irene. 'If I didn't know better I'd swear they were fath—'

The rest of her sentence was lost as, sudden and low, the helicopter howled round the crematorium chimney, thrashed the air and reared to a halt a hundred feet over the car park. Shocked and awed by the unfolding incongruous Hollywood action-scene, The Old Writer stared, his subconscious sifting potential final clauses automatic.

The options were limited; it did not take long.

By the time the doors of the big white Volvo had gaped open, and bellowing body-armoured-cops-with-guns had surrounded Jilted John now spread prone on the car park asphalt, he had glimpsed the long-hidden truth.

The Old Writer looked at his wife, appalled. Ashen, she stared back. Together they turned again to their son. One cop had his foot on the boy's neck, another forced his arms hard behind his back and yanked a cable-tie tight round his wrists.

A white van – blue-flashing, with meshed windscreen – revved low-geared down the drive from the gate; it lurched to a stop, spewed paramilitary riot-cops from sliding-doors slammed open. With Roman drilled efficiency, the cohort spread to form a shield wall between stunned mourners and rough-handled detainee. Their helmeted centurion was a woman, or so The Old Writer deduced as – megaphone raised to semi-visored face – a high-pitched voice commanded them to, 'Stay calm and stay fucking back!'

His instinct was to rush them, the rational reticence of self-preservation subsumed by paternal rage, but he hesitated for a second and his moment slipped away. Turning in a blizzard of downdraft-driven leaves and car park grit The Old Writer saw his hoped-for backup, not stepping up to bellow loyal berserker-bloodlust at his father's side, but lumbering across the last few yards of the crematorium gardens instead to employ his awesome might, first to toss Natalya over the boundary wall, then to vault after her out of sight. As The Old Writer turned back disappointed to reassess his options, his mother-in-law slipped the leash of Helen's arm, launched forward to steal his thunder.

'Get your hands off that innocent boy, you dirty vicious bastards,' the old lady screeched and flew at the centurion.

'Stop! Keep your dist—' was all the amplified cop had time to say before, megaphone flailed from her grip, she staggered back, lip burst and welling blood.

'Serve you right for abusing decent folk and spoiling an old man's funeral,' said Irene, a little uncertain now as legionaries shuffled robotic to surround her. 'You should all be ashamed of yourselves.'

Her defiance was heartening but futile. She went down hard between clashed shields. They dragged her by her thin arms to the van and dumped her inside on the floor.

'For fuck's sake,' The Old Writer heard himself say. 'She's only a crazy old lady. What the fuck do you think you're doing?'

'Taking her to the local nick and charging her with assault.'

The centurion spat snotty blood at his feet.

'Turn up there in three or four hours if you want the silly cow back.'

'What about John?'

Helen sounded calm but her chest was heaving.

'Who the fuck is John?'

'My son. The boy those other thugs just assaulted and arrested.'

'Sorry, missus. Not my business. Anti-terrorist boys have ownership. I can't tell you where they'll take him.'

The centurion sneered bloody, smeared mouth with gauntleted hand.

'We're just here for crowd control—and to secure the suspect's vehicle until the bomb squad get on-scene.'

The Old Writer stared at the cop.

'Bomb squad? You're fucking mad. This is some kind of sick fucking joke.'

'Laugh yourself to death, mate. I'm just doing my bleeding job.'

Capacity for one-to-one communication exhausted, the officer turned away, stooped and grabbed up the fallen megaphone, addressed the small huddle of stunned mourners.

'Your attention,' she demanded, voice shrilled with a touch of feedback. 'Vehicles inside the police cordon may be retrieved on production of valid photo ID. Please assist by leaving the scene in a prompt and orderly manner. Your co-operation is appreciated by the dedicated officers of your overstretched local police service.'

Cracked Jack's wake passed with the deceased unmentioned and barely remembered. Most mourners – unsurprisingly – failed to make it. The fifty pounds The Old Writer had put behind the bar turned out to be more than ample; it was dented only by ASBO Angie's routine requirement for strong lager and the brace of large whiskies with which The Old Writer settled his stomach. Of the sandwiches – 'Cold meats with a vegetarian option, appetisingly presented to cheer your guests on this sad occasion.' – not even a crust was nibbled. The Abercrombies were the last to leave, after less than half-an-hour. Mo comforted their host with a sympathetic squeeze of his arm, while Phillip expressed the sincere but understated wish that, 'The day's unfortunate little misunderstanding' be quickly sorted out.'

Duty of hospitality fulfilled then, The Old Writer went in urgent search of ASBO Angie and tobacco.

She was not in the pub car park – where a glimpse of Helen and his brother sequestered behind the steamed windows of his car caused him to clench his jaw and jolt his sensitive tooth – so he fled to check the front.

'I said, no fuckin' comment,' Angie snarled with chilling vehemence as The Old Writer rounded the building. She was toe-to-toe with a pretty microphone-thrusting boy accompanied by a camera crew from their regional TV station.

'But is it true that the man arrested by anti-terror police this afternoon is the son of a well-known local author of outlandish fict—'

The boy's sentence was clipped short as Angie nutted him, with hard precision, on the bridge of his pretty nose.

'Fuck's sake,' she said with exasperated scorn as her rebuffed interrogator knelt stunned at her feet and snivelled. 'Learn to fuckin' listen, cunt—and save us all the aggro.'

'You do know this is being recorded,' said a nervous girl with a clipboard. 'To be broadcast on 'The News from Where You Live' tonight at six o'clock?'

'That right?'

ASBO Angie's grin was ugly.

'Well if that bastard camera's not out of my face in five fuckin' seconds or less, it'll be recording future outtakes of the inside of your tight little arsehole that'll probably end up on YouTube.'

'Nice one, Angie,' The Old Writer said, as the newshounds slunk off to their van to whine and file their story. 'Two family members incarcerated already today—you want to make it a goddamn hat-trick?'

'Cunts'll never take me alive, man.'

Angie turned to recover her drink from a nearby rustic table.

'Ciggie—now,' The Old Writer demanded, not convinced that she was joking.

She obeyed with a steady hand; he failed to exhibit a similar *sang-froid* as he lit it with her lighter.

'Jack's send-off's gone a bit tits-up then?' said Angie and drained her glass. 'The fuck were those cop pricks talking about? Cunts wouldn't know a terrorist if one cut their fuckin' heads off.'

'I don't know.'

The Old Writer relished smoke.

'John's been a bit bloody strange for a while but this is a strike from space.'

Angie chuckled and relit her ciggie.

'Glad you can see a funny side,' he said.

'Helen's mum's got some bottle, giving that cop a fat fuckin' lip.'

'Yeah. She beat me to it by about two seconds—or it'd be me banged-up now instead.'

Angie's lip twitched a hint of doubt which she did not vocalise.

'What happened to Jude and his shady Russian shag?'

'She's Latvian.'

'I never saw them bail.'

'Tactical withdrawal. The boy's always leery of the law. Between you and me I think he sails a bit close to the wind'

'Cool. And I thought getting it on with a middle-class writer's daughter would be my pass to the civilised Easy Street I suffered and killed to defend.'

Angie hawked and spat.

'Turns out I'm embedded in bleedin' Storyville with a shambles of fucked-up crims.'

'Sorry. No way out now.'

The Old Writer hoped that she believed him.

'Screwing with fantasy worlds is risky—lose your grip and they fuck you over.'

'Angie!'

Cormac slouched from the pub's front door.

'Mum wants you to help her get the kids strapped in the van. Says it's time to get them home.'

'You okay?' asked The Old Writer as Angie went inside.

'I s'pose,' said Cormac, grateful to be considered. 'It's been a mad scary day though. I don't get what's going on.'

'Yeah, things are a bit of a mess, mate. But don't worry.'

He steered his grandson back round the pub, arm rested along thin shoulder.

'Let's scare-up your grandma and Great-uncle Ollie, and get started on sorting shit out.'

The lawyer's name was Anthony Mine-By-Fucking-Birthright; at least that was how The Old Writer heard it as his brother introduced them in the bar of the overpriced boutique hotel where they had reserved him a private suite.

Anthony – The Old Writer had discovered on interrupting Helen and Ollie's car park tryst to drive them home from the wake – was another of his brother's former fucks. Summoned by Ollie's urgent plea for assistance, the alacrity of the brief's response to the call suggested a degree of devotion had survived the demise of their manly passion. Anthony – his diary of lucrative appointments summarily abandoned – was already entrained from London to Dismal while The Old Writer and ASBO Angie still brawled in the street with the press.

Four hours later, with a wink and a kiss for Ollie and dry handshakes for The Old Writer and Helen, the lawyer folded his long pinstriped body luxuriant into a chair. He combed a shock of white hair from high forehead with elegant manicured fingers, stirred the ice in his tall gin-and-tonic and studied his anxious clients with eyes as blue as his blood.

'It has been a long and distressing day for you, I'm certain. Let me update you without further delay.'

Anthony straightened his silk tie.

'First, the good news. I have spoken with an Inspector of the local force in respect of the arrest of the elderly lady.'

He looked at Helen.

'Your mother, I believe?'

'Is she alright?'

'I understand her vigour is little diminished.'

Anthony smiled minute amusement.

'In fact, the prisoner's release to your custody would be welcomed, I believe—given her acceptance of a simple caution.'

'Understood,' The Old Writer said and took a breath. 'So what's the score with John?'

'Ah.'

The lawyer moistened his thin lip with gin.

'Your son's position, I'm sorry to say, is a little more concerning.'

'Concerning?'

'Yes. Acquiring access to suspects detained by SO15 Counter Terrorism Command is sometimes less than straightforward.'

'Our son is not a terrorist,' said Helen with conviction. 'He's not even bloody religious.'

'No. Far from it, it would seem,' Anthony said dry and sipped a little more gin.

Helen frowned.

'I'm sorry if I'm stupid, but I really don't understand.'

'Let's cut to the chase, Tony, there's a love,' advocated Ollie. 'Have you seen the lad, or not?'

'Fortunately my network of acquaintances in the Crown Prosecution Service includes some whose position is influential. Through their intercession I was able to establish my credential as the legal representative of the suspect, ascertain the charges laid against him and ensure due respect for *habeas corpus*.'

Anthony paused to grimace discrete distaste.

'Unfortunately, the Officer Commanding of the anti-terrorism task-force with custody of your son was professionally obstructive. My access to his arrest interview was impeded, thus preventing my advising that he refrain absolutely from signing his statement of confession to offences under section fifty-seven of the Terrorism Act, Two-thousand.'

'Shit,' said The Old Writer.

'Not a legal term.'

Ice-cubes clattered on perfect teeth as Anthony drained his glass.

'But nonetheless expressive of the situation.'

'But how could he confess? He is *not* a *terrorist*.'

Helen was stubbornly emphatic.

The lawyer signalled for a second drink, turned back to offer explication, not entirely without compassion.

'While your son may not be a 'terrorist' as the term is commonly understood – a jihadist or other religiopolitical extremist intent on the mass-murder of innocents – he has admitted the planning and perpetration of potentially lethal incendiary attacks in a number of UK locations—namely various church buildings and similar venues with a specific evangelical connection.'

'What?' said Helen. 'Why the hell would he want to do that?'

'Shy Skye.'

The Old Writer took his wife's cold hand in his.

'The boy's been waging some kind of mad holy war of vengeance on the Army of bastard Light. I should've known it was serious. I should've fucking stopped him.'

'I want to see him.'

Helen pulled free and stood.

'I want to see him now.'

'I'm afraid that won't be possible.'

Anthony paused as The Old Writer signed for his drink.

'Remanded in custody for pre-trial review, your son is currently *en route* to an unspecified HMP.'

'When can we arrange to visit?'

'That is uncertain.'

The lawyer was discomfited by The Old Writer's question.

'Your son has instructed me to convey his heartfelt regret for the pain and grief he has undoubtedly caused, to both you and the rest of your family. In addition, he asks your forgiveness in advance for his insistence – for reasons unspecified – that you not attempt to visit him in prison.'

'I don't understand.'

Helen chewed at her lip.

'He won't even let us see him?'

'His position may change.'

Anthony attempted reassurance.

'I will certainly – should you be content to retain my service – attempt to soften his resistance when next I meet with him.'

'Oh,' said Helen, flat.

'Thank you,' said The Old Writer, sick inside. 'For your efforts today and ongoing in what, I'm sure, is the best interest of our misguided boy.'

'I am only too glad to be of service,' the lawyer said, graciously overlooking The Old Writer's unconscious mimicry of his syntax.

'Oliver has always spoken with affection of his family. Your well-being is of importance to him, and therefore also to me.'

The Old Writer stood, fumbled to help Helen on with her coat.

'Is there, perhaps, some message I can communicate on my next consultation with your son?'

'Just—just tell him that, whatever stupid thing he's done, we love him and we're here to help him whatever it takes,' Helen said and blinked against her tears.

'Tell him I'm sorry.'

The Old Writer faced his own hard time.

'I'm sorry I let him down.'

'Best go home and get some rest now,' prompted Ollie from his seat.

'What? You're not coming with us?'

Helen was surprised.

'Oliver and I have some catching-up to do.'

The lawyer patted his ex's plump hand.

'Perhaps you'll let me hang onto him for just a little while longer?'

'Oh. Okay. When will we see you?' asked Helen.

'I'll cab over in the morning to say goodbye to Viola and the kids.'

Ollie smiled shy.

'My flight doesn't leave until late.'

"Bye then, kid,' The Old Writer said, surprised by the warmth of his tone. 'And thanks for going the extra mile for us both today.'

'You're welcome. What are families for?'

Ollie winked sly as they turned for the door.

'Take care of each other, now. And don't forget to spring poor old Irene from the nick.'

twenty-one

'It's not going to be cheap.'

Sat at the kitchen table with Helen, The Old Writer reviewed the letter from the lawyer's office outlining his terms and conditions.

'Good. Why would we risk our son's liberty with some cut-price off-the-shelf shyster? Anthony's bespoke. He's bound to be expensive.'

'Just like the raft of shrink 'expert witnesses' he wants to hire-in to prove the balance of John's mind is disturbed. You'd think the evidence spoke for itself.'

'Oliver says he's the best. You'll just have to hold your nose and swallow.'

'There goes the trip to Machu Picchu.'

'Trip? What trip?'

'Never mind. Just one more fucking paving slab to smooth my road to Hell.'

The Old Writer scrawled his signature on the Memorandum of Understanding.

Helen shook her head, baffled by his Peruvian excursion. 'I still can't believe John's really guilty,' she said. 'How can we not have known?'

The Old Writer studied her for a moment and answered, 'It's easy to miss even massive shit sometimes—especially when it's hidden right under your goddamn nose.'

Helen's glance was edged as she tried to decipher his tone.

'I don't get it. You're weird with me just lately. Everything you say seems to have a subtext.'

'Sorry,' he said. 'Weird fucking times, I guess.'

'I wasn't trying to put the blame on you.'

'I know. How is Ollie, by the way?'

'He emailed to say he'd got back safely, sent his love to all of us—and attached some sound-files of his music that I think Viola must have asked for.'

'Right. That's nice.'

'Do you want something to eat? I'm going to make Mum some lunch. She said she'd cash-in her ISAs, bless her, if we needed money for the case.'

'Irene's a stand-up gal.'

'So, ham or cheese?'

'Thanks—but I'm not that hungry. I think I'll go for a walk.'

'Oh.'

She looked hurt.

'See you later then.'

He was halfway out the door. He had not planned to say it; it just overflowed his brain.

'All these years together, Helen. I can't believe you never told me.'

'Told you what?' he heard her ask behind him as he fled for forest refuge.

The Old Writer trudged 'The Green Woodpecker Trail' heedless of the risk of casual human encounter this way-marked route implied.

Trapped by dense woods, the air hung wet and cold. It tasted sweet and sour. He breathed shallow. His chest was weak, vulnerable to infection by the clouds of invisible winter leaf-rot spores that doubtless swirled malevolent around him.

It was eleven in the morning but it was barely light.

He peered gloomy, scanned the path-side scrub and leafless trees for life. Nothing flitted flew or scurried.

Snagged on a twig, a child's orange knitted mitten tuned his eye for random colour. Silver: a flash of crisp-bag in the ditch. Purple: a ruined-umbrella fruit bat hung-up in a birch. Virulent red: a double helix of bryony berries coiled around a hazel branch, toxic DNA.

The genetic connotation did not improve his mood. The Old Writer trudged on. A puddle, still frozen in a frost-prone hollow, snatched his foot. His violent reflex restored his stolen balance but electrified his hip with a sudden thrill of pain.

'Bastard.'

He hobbled forward. Each step generated a shocking new jolt of volts.

'Bastard. Bastard. Bastard.'

He cursed for fifty paces; the object of his venomous disgust evolved through several mutations.

Jilted John: deranged bastard; lost his perspective on life and got caught with a van full of fucking firebombs.

Rude Jude: callous bastard; habitual goddamned criminality a catalyst for his father's inherent paranoia.

Vile Viola: baffling bastard of gigantic proportion.

Obscene Irene: borderline bastard only; a crazy liability, like ASBO bastard Angie.

Helen: a bastard mystery; filled his life with both love and a frustrating distraction of children.

Cracked Jack: misanthropic bastard; it seemed that, just as the old man had predicted, the inherited gene of embittered resentment was now pathologically active in his son.

Evil Ollie: smug bastard whose deft response to emergency had shown his brother inadequate by contrast, and the legacy of whose bastard betrayal now undermined The Old Writer's bastard world.

'Bastards. Fucking bastard bastards.'

The Old Writer rounded a hawthorn-screened corner of the path into the Teddy Bear's Picnic Field. Distracted by his roll call of resentment he had failed to detect the gabble of excited voices in time to avoid the shrill ambuscade of infant nature-explorers into which he now blundered dismayed.

Alarmed child-care professionals rallied to stout defence of precious charges, gathered and enfolded the bright-coloured milling of screeching tots as he lurched – a dark, ungainly predator – into their innocent midst.

The Old Ogre grimaced disarming, signalled reassurance with a friendly wave of his talons. Responsible young-adults glared back with cold suspicion. Cut off from the flock, an anxious straggler wailed. A plump woman lunged heroic, recovered this potential morsel, nestled it safe inside the circled-wagon sanctuary of rustic picnic-tables. Her companions watched alert, bared teeth, lashed tails, hardened the protective perimeter around their cubs, yellow eyes unblinking.

Chastened, all thought of child-depredation banished, The Old Writer loped on his way, nape scorched by a silent blast of righteous accusation. Relieved of threat, the children resumed their twitter.

Eager for solitude he left the path. He slalomed through a dark stand of larch, continued off-piste through the overgrown old stone pits, came to a stop, sweaty and breathless, at a point beyond the range of even the most piercing juvenile squeal.

The Old Writer felt an urgent need to chill. He had a nice lump of powdery Moroccan hash in his pocket. He had salvaged it from John's place, diverted – *en route* home with Helen and Irene post the boy's arrest – by a spontaneous urge to pre-empt the inevitable police search of the suspect's dwelling and forestall the additional misery of vindictive supplementary charges. He was equipped with papers and tobacco, too; he just needed a sheltered spot to roll a joint and smoke it.

It was sleeting now: soft grey slanting down to whisper on black trees.

It was a while since he had been in this neck of the woods but – if his memory could be relied on, which he suspected was not a given – somewhere nearby there was a saltlick, maintained by forest-rangers to entice supernumerary deer into range of their hidden guns.

Ten minutes later, The Old Writer paused cautious at the edge of a clear-cut avenue. At one end, pinkish, tongue-smoothed and tempting, a rock-salt iceberg on a larch-stump. At the other, back-dropped by dark conifers, a tower-hide. He scrutinised the camouflaged structure. It was late in the day for culling, but getting himself mistaken for a roebuck and heart-shot by an over-eager marksman would be a stupid way to die. Icy rain dripped down his neck, spurred him to break cover. Walking upright and manly, he hoped, he made it to the tower's base unshot. No Public Access, insisted a sign nailed to a rough-hewn support. He hauled himself up the ladder to the shooting-platform, grateful to be under cover.

The Old Writer sat on the bench, looked out through the gun-slot at the killing-ground while he rolled and smoked a joint. Its effect was beneficial; he coughed only once or twice. He felt secure as the ice-rain curtained past his eerie, snug and detached from the calamitous world outside. He decided to smoke another.

Boats, hobby workshops, allotment sheds: every man needed his hermitage, his bunker of solitude; every man needed a place in which to smoke, to think, to write; a place to launch sudden violence from when the opportunity presented.

Two deer stepped from cover: doe, ears flicking, her fawn dancing at her heel. They high-stepped delicate over tussocks to the saltlick. The Old Writer sucked in smoke and held it, sighted his imaginary rifle. The doe's life: his finger-twitch. Armed, would he refrain from pointless slaughter or succumb to the primal instinct hard-wired into his evil human brain? The doe lifted her head and swivelled radar-ears. Beside her, the fragile fawn tensed and quivered. They were gone before the ringtone of the phone vibrating sudden in his pocket could travel as far as his ear.

The caller was unrecognised; he answered anyway.

'Alright then? What you up to?' Jude's digitised voice stuttered weak-signalled.

'Huh?'

The Old Writer was unprepared.

'Just smoking-up a bit of hash and playing sniper in the woods.'

'Playing what? Some fucking Xbox game is it? You hanging out with Cormac?'

'Good of you to get back,' The Old Writer said sarcastic. 'I've called at least a dozen times since you abandoned ship at Cracked Jack's funeral and left your brother to drown in cops.'

'Yeah. Sorry. No clue what was happening with that shit. Gear in the car. Couldn't risk getting sucked in.'

'You could have called to find out the score.'

'Distracted. Stuff going on. Got the gist from the TV news.'

'Bet they cut Angie's head-butt scene.'

'Yeah. Must've.'

Jude chuckled.

'Anyway, the number you were calling on is dead. So's this one—soon as we've done talking.'

'What are you telling me?'

'Bit of a problem. Me and Natalya might need to go travelling for a while.'

'Police?'

'Latvians. Or maybe they're Lithuanians. I can never fucking remember.'

'This problem? How bad?'

'Uh, worst case? Potentially fatal, I suppose.'

'Jesus fucking Christ, Jude. What the sweet fuck is going on? What can I do to help?'

'Help? You?'

Jude found the suggestion amusing.

'Forget it. This isn't some stupid story, man. This shit is fucking real.'

'But—'

'There is one thing.'

'Yes.'

'You know mum's old beehive?'

'You mean the one with the automatic pistol in it—and a locked memory-stick?'

Despite the situation, The Old Writer took satisfaction from Jude's ten-second baffled silence.

'Yeah. That's the one. How the fuck did you find it?'

'There were bee-wings on the carpet—like confetti.'

'What?'

'I put two and two together. You never had a clue.'

'Whatever. No time for mind-fucks now. This phone's about out of credit. Listen. Keep the nine and the flash-drive safe. I'm going to send you instructions what to do with them. Meantime, watch your back—for real.'

'Jude, I—'

'Love to Mum and everyone. Just do what I say and the chances are we'll see you all, live and kicking, when our position gets un-fucked.'

'Hang on. What about—?'

'Later, Dad. Thanks. Sorry for being a troublesome prick all my life and for bringing this shit to your door. Love you. Keep safe now, you feel me?'

The call was over. The Old Writer relit his joint with a shaking hand and remembered the callback function.

'The phone you are calling is not switched on. Please hang up and try later.'

He listened to a couple more robotic repetitions. The sleet had stopped; pale tree-shadowed sunlight now dappled the killing-ground. The Old Writer closed the phone and lit his joint for a final toke. He sucked a fleck of tobacco through the roach. It stuck bitter to his tonsils. He retched and puked at his feet.

Although extensive, the gamut of catastrophe contemplated by The Old Writer slouching home through sleeted woods did not include the possibility of his encountering Vile Viola in a mud bath.

Water-buffalo, was his first thought when – attracted by a plaintive bellow and flash of high-visibility chartreuse – he came upon her wallowing in the deep ooze of a path-side ditch. His second, no more charitable, was hippopotamus.

'God,' she said as he stared down amazed. 'Why did it have to be you?'

The Old Writer had no answer.

'Don't you dare even think of laughing? One smirk and I'll fucking kill you.'

Impassive, The Old Writer gathered brushwood, arranged it on the slick slope of the ditch-side to offer a chance of traction. Resolutely straight-faced still, he searched-out and recovered a stout fallen branch suitable for use as a tow-bar. Three strenuous cursing attempts at extrication failed; the fourth, while evoking serious aneurism-terror, was successful. Sprawled on his arse in a chilly puddle – Viola panting and tearful on hands and knees, filthy tracksuit pants dragged down to her ankles by the friction of the struggle – The Old Writer refrained from redundant comment. Considerate of her dignity he averted his eyes as he clambered to his feet. When he summoned the nerve to look again, Viola was still distraught but decent.

'You okay?' The Old Writer enquired sincere.

'Yes. Thanks.'

She sniffed.

'But my ankle hurts—and my knee.'

She was shivering, he noticed, shocked pale-faced beneath smeared slime. He took off his heavy jacket, draped it around her shoulders.

'My leg just gave way when I was running and pitched me into the ditch.'

He leaned her against a tree-trunk, crouched and felt her knee. He thought it was probably swollen, although it was difficult to be sure.

'Running?'

It wasn't really a question, more an expression of amazement.

'Oliver says his doctor told him his weight could kill him within five years.'

'Right. Can you walk?'

She tried; it was obvious that it hurt her.

'I couldn't get out. I just couldn't. I felt so huge and stupid and useless. I was scared I'd freeze to death in there.'

She sobbed; her shoulders shook. The Old Writer rehearsed a comforting cuddle, concluded that was overambitious, took her huge hand in his instead.

'Get your breath back while I call for transport.'

He fumbled his phone cold-fingered.

'Can you hobble half-a-mile to the car park—or do we need the air ambulance?'

The Old Writer allowed the ghost of a smile to haunt his lips; Vile Viola forgave it.

'If I can't, just call the vet to shoot me where I fall.'

Helen was incommunicado; it was Irene's Senior Singalong Morning, Viola suggested.

ASBO Angie was fitting new brake pads to her van. 'Give us twenty minutes to finish the job and I'm under-fuckin'-way,' she said.

They limped off together. With Viola's arm laid across his shoulder The Old Writer felt like a butcher's porter hauling a side of beef. Progress was slow and painful but at least the sleet had turned to rain. They made it to the rendezvous with time to spare. Viola groaned relief as he helped her transfer her weight to a bench in a corner of the car park by the vandalised ticket machine. It had been thoughtfully provided, a plastic tag informed, In Memory of 'Captain' - our beloved little Yorkie.

Viola sat and massaged her leg. The Old Writer rolled a ciggie.
'Thanks, Dad,' she said.
'Don't thank me. Thank 'beloved little Captain'.'
Viola frowned.
'I thought you'd given up smoking.'
'I have.'
He frowned back.
'You called me 'Dad'.'
'Yes. So?'
'You haven't called me Dad for years.'
'Oh? Really?'
'Not since you were nine or ten, I'm pretty sure.'
'Okay. Right.'
She was flustered.
'Sorry. I hadn't noticed.'
The Old Writer was cold, tired, stoned and a little bit emotional or he would probably have dropped it.
'I guess that must be around the time you first found out.'
'Found out what? I'm not sure I know what you're talking about.'
'I think you do.'
She did; he could see it in her eyes, in the flush that mottled her neck. Last doubt, or hope, removed, The Old Writer led her on.
'Sorry if I'm prodding an old sore—but it never seemed that relevant until the bloody funeral.'
'I suppose seeing Oliver stirred things up?'
'Bound to, really.'

'I really didn't think you knew.'

'No reason you should,' he said and sucked in smoke. 'So how did you find out?'

'I don't know. I just kind of guessed.'

Viola took the ciggie from his hand, studied its tip with heavy-lidded eyes as she inhaled.

'Early-onset feminine intuition, I suppose. I was always a bit precocious.'

He smiled recognition. She breathed smoke out down her nose.

'It was after my ninth birthday-party. Uncle Oliver came. His present was money to pay for piano lessons. I remember he had a strange look in his eye when he gave me the envelope—called me his 'little music-girl', or something just as daft, and blushed when he thought you'd noticed.'

'He was never good at lying. Cracked Jack always picked on him to find out all the bad shit us kids had been getting up to.'

'After that, the more I thought about it the more it just had to be. Little things, you know? The shape of his ear lobes in a photo, the angle of my nose? In the end I just came out with it, asked Mum straight if she'd ever had sex with my uncle.'

'She said 'yes'?'

'She didn't have to. I could tell by the way she chewed her lip and twisted the tea towel round her hands.'

The Old Writer pictured the scene.

'Mum told me she knew as soon as she saw me when I was born,' Viola continued. 'But she thought it wouldn't matter because she loved you and you loved her—and both of you loved me more than anything in the world.'

'She was right about that.'

The Old Writer remembered the endless hospital day-of-terror and eventual slither and squeal of bloody relief; he remembered the surge of pride, and the chill of fear returning as he held her life in his hands.'

'Really?'

Viola examined him, moon-face upturned muddy.

'Yes,' he said, relieved that it was true.

'Mum said it was up to me in the end, but she thought it would be best if I kept what I knew to myself. She said you'd be uncomfortable if you knew that I knew the truth—and that Uncle Oliver didn't know, though she thought he might have guessed, because gay men are more in tune with stuff like that.'

'What do you think now?'

'It was massive for a little girl to have to keep that to herself. You always felt hard to reach when I was growing up—distant and bad-tempered, shut away working on your books. Sometimes I thought you avoided me because you blamed me for not being yours. I suppose it made me insecure—and I punished you for that.'

Viola smiled a hint of remembered vileness.

'I was a nasty little cow to you sometimes, I think.'

'Oh, only now and then.'

The Old Writer smiled back.

'I hardly even noticed.'

'Precisely—all I ever wanted was a reaction. Now roll me another of your nasty ciggies.'

He complied and lit it for her, rolled one for himself.

'How's the leg? Are you warm enough?'

'Throbbing. And no. I wish Angie would hurry up.'

'I'm glad we talked. It's good it's finally out in the open—even if I did have to exploit an opportune rare moment of vulnerability to crack your fucking shell of silence.'

Viola frowned, stared at him hard; her eyes widened as she understood. Fear darkened them first, then anger. 'You bastard,' she said. 'You sly evil bastard. You never knew at all.'

'I was always a little bit slow—but I got there in the end. I just needed confirmation. Sorry.'

'Now what? Shit. You and Mum—is this going to make a difference? You need to be together for John. Oh God, you rotten bastard—what have you made me do?'

'Viola.'

He took her hand.

'It's cool. It's not going to make a difference.'

'Are you sure?'

It surprised him just a little that he was.

'Absolutely. All life is accidental, isn't it? Just because it wasn't my sperm that sparked you, doesn't mean you haven't been my daughter for the last fucking forty years.'

'Thirty-six.'

'Anyway, Ollie's my goddamn brother. The genetic link's still there.'

'What about Cormac? You're not going to go cold on him—because he relies on you, you know?'

'Cormac is—'

The emotion that strangled his words took The Old Writer unawares.

'Cormac is my grandchild—just like the rest of your troublesome rabble. You don't really think that I could drop him? Not after all those centuries of endless war and bonding in ancient fucking Rome?'

Viola clamped his neck with a massive arm, smeared his cheek with a cold muddy kiss. 'I love you, Dad, you arsehole,' she whispered and made The Old Writer happy.

They parted, further embarrassing sentimentality avoided by the interruption of ASBO Angie's brake-testing skid-to-a-halt in a rattle of gravel behind them. 'Someone here shout 'medic'?' she said as she slid from the van, dead cigarette in corner of mouth, open Tennants can in hand.

On tiptoe, with the fanlight open, The Old Writer could achieve just enough perspective from his Tower of Babble window to see the old black Mercedes pull away. Parked-up in the field-gate across the lane from the house when they had got home in the van from the forest, it had been there another hour. He probably would not have noticed it if he had not spoken with Jude. He turned from the window to the safe, inspired to look at the gun.

'Hello?'

Helen's brief knock and entrance caught him with hand closing around cold steel. He snatched back guilty and shut the heavy door. Damn her cat-paw sneaking, he thought as she handed him one of two cups of coffee she carried.

'Thanks,' he said, curious; she never climbed the tower.

Helen scanned the room, swivelled his chair away from the idle computer, sat and sipped from her cup. 'What are you doing?' she asked with an undertone of tension.

'Nothing useful. How's Viola now?'

'She had a hot bath. I put a support bandage on her knee. I think she'll be okay if she keeps her weight off it for a while.'

'Her weight is the problem.'

'Yes. It was lucky you were out there and found her. She shouldn't have gone on her own.'

'It was embarrassing for her, I think. But it gave us a chance to talk.'

'How did that go?'

'Good, actually—a worthwhile communication.'

'That's nice. I know it's not always easy. Anything I need to know?'

'Like what?'

'I don't know—how things are with her and Angie?'

'We didn't talk about Angie.'

'Okay.'

Helen stood and gathered the empty cups. The tiny tremor of her hand chattered china on china.

'It was good, though,' he said. 'I think we talked ourselves closer.'

Helen moved for the door, paused and looked back at him. A ray of setting-sunlight from the window tinted her face with red. She lifted her free hand to shade her eyes.

'What did you mean when you went out earlier? About something I'd never told you?'

'Nothing really,' he said. 'I was just a bit confused. I meant to tell you how much I loved you—but it came out sort of wrong.'

'That's nice,' Helen said and left the room. 'I love you, too. See you for dinner in an hour.'

twenty-two

There was no denying, The Old Writer acknowledged – hand squeezed between stacked plastic storage-solutions and rough barn wall in quest of a vaguely remembered light switch – that he felt considerably strung-out and weird.

But then there was nothing new in that.

He had always been edgy, unsettled by a kind of vertigo when – an overflying predator – he circled the herd of a story, assessed its shifting shape, identified his best angle of attack. It was always strange and disturbing to negotiate the tipping-point between observation and imagination, to commit to that opening sentence, take the plunge into the maelstrom of possibility, extrude talons over the keyboard and snatch significance from a panic of incoherence.

The difference was that this time his timing was screwed. The story had advanced under his lax radar, gathered momentum ignored, surprised him out of position. Now he was caught flapping clumsy on the ground – objectivity compromised, in urgent need of perspective – as, already spooked into wild stampede, the surging drama of events threatened to run him down.

Stay calm, get a grip, he told himself, cheek jammed claustrophobic against cold plastic, overstretched shoulder cramping, fingernails clawing flaky plaster.

The primitive Old Writer was troubled by his seeming phlegmatic acceptance of the biological reality of Vile Viola's origination. His partner of a lifetime – Helen, The Unseen Hand from whom no secret could be kept – had, if only by omission, lied to him for thirty-five years. Surely that was a dire betrayal of his trust; surely he should be resentful, if not downright enraged.

But her lie had been altruistic; it had served the greater good. Disclosed before the slow accretion of their love had built the reef that for decades had safe-harboured them against life's oceanic storm-tides, the truth would have fatally corroded their nascent emotional alliance.

The Old Writer shuddered, considered the ramifications. Outraged, he might have abandoned putative domesticity for the wilderness of imagination. Helen and Ollie might have given it a whirl for the sake of the innocent babe, but even Helen's undoubted charms could not have straightened out his brother's predominant gayness. There would have been pain; there would have been grief. Jilted John and Rude Jude would never even have been born. Given the current state-of-play, that may have been a circumstance not wholly undesirable; The Old Writer entertained the fleeting thought but dismissed it as glib delusion. With the benefit of a higher selfishness – painfully evolved through years of naturally selective experience and fortuitous mutation – he recognised the wisdom inherent in Helen's deception. Without the anchor of family to ground his life and give purpose to his work, The Young Writer would have taken it far too seriously, let the Evil Word consume him, drive him into addled sociopathy and a probable early grave.

Of course Helen had known all that instinctive. The Old Writer was grateful for her foresight; it had assured life's load was shared. Their romance may sometimes have rambled erratic in search of a common destination but the journey had been hopeful. It was true he had got complacent in the latter stages – delegated responsibility to mindless cruise control, nodded off at the wheel – but there was nothing like an unplanned off-road excursion to refocus a driver's attention. And the error need not be fatal; a light touch on the steering wheel, some precision heel-and-toe applied to throttle and brake and another runaway mixed metaphor could be reined in at the brink of disaster.

So that was all good then, The Old Writer decided, relieved finally to feel fingertip trip the elusive light switch. Now he just had to locate whichever random item he had set out to recover from the confusion of domestic detritus that filled his once spacious barn.

A low-energy light bulb glowed its slow progress to incandescence. It was some kind of tool that he had come for; there was some kind of task outstanding that the tool was needed for.

Waiting for full illumination, The Old Writer plotted a three-dimensional route across the crazy platform-game of boxes, bin-bags, furniture and white goods he and ASBO Angie had constructed several months before.

CDs avalanching from a toppled cardboard box; a ruptured bin-bag herniating baby-clothes; another spewing a frustration of tangled wire clothes hangers: he was not the first to blaze a trail here.

He scrambled, lurched, slithered breathless to his remote workbench destination.

Which tool?

There were plenty to choose from scattered around the rusty old ammunition case that usually contained them: Stanley knife, with blade left dangerously extruded; tenon saw; gaffer-tape, rejected off-cuts crumpled, stuck to wall and bench; hacksaw, blade snapped; a set of rusted needle files, faces scraped by someone's recent use. He narrowed it down to Cormac or Angie. An ex-soldier would be tidier, he decided. That placed Cormac in the frame.

A hammer, that was his mission objective; tacks too, to fasten Irene's rug down. A fractured hip might finish the old girl off. 'And you don't want that on your bloody conscience,' Helen had suggested. 'Just because you can't be arsed to fetch a few tools from the barn.'

The Old Writer found tacks in an old tobacco tin; he stuffed it into a pocket, rummaged the ammunition case tool-tangle for the hammer. He extracted it by its handle; snarled precarious on its clawed head, a pair of tin-snips came too. He winced as they wobbled free, anticipated their inevitable impact on his toe.

'Stop it now. That's enough.'

Obscene Irene cowered in her chair, cushions hand-clamped to the sides of her head: oversized tapestry earmuffs.

'Feels like I'm in my coffin and you're nailing down the lid.'

'Just one more.'

The Old Writer spat out a tack, pounded it into the floor.

'And it'd be screws I'd use for your coffin-lid, Irene. Nails are far too easy for the un-dead to push out from inside.'

'What did you say? Something about a screw?'

The old lady lowered her earmuffs and cackled.

'I'm up for it if you are, boy. Just push the door to first.'

'Okay.'

The Old Writer leered close as he gripped her chair-arm, hauled himself up to his feet.

'But none of your filthy fellatio, huh? I'm not in any hurry to catch up with Cracked Jack.'

'Piss off,' Obscene Irene said and hit him with a cushion. 'You shouldn't have reminded me. Now you've gone and killed the passion.'

'Oh well—another time.'

The Old Writer flipped and caught the hammer by its handle. Hobbled by his bruised foot, he limped towards the door.

'Dinner's in twenty minutes—Helen said to tell you about twenty minutes ago. Are you coming down?'

'About bloody time.'

Irene was a scrawny greyhound out of a trap.

'I'm starved—I could eat a scabby-kid's head.'

'Save a few flakes for me,' The Old Writer called as she scurried past, cut him off on the threshold, left him in her dust.

'Skye phoned.'

Helen's words surprised The Old Writer with soupspoon wobbling between bowl and lip. Some new quirk of physiology made the simple precision of the task unachievable without tremor. The first four inches of lift was smooth enough, but then things started to get messy.

'Shy Skye?'

'Yes,' said Helen. 'It was a bit of a shock to hear her voice, out of the blue like that.'

'I bet.'

The Old Writer chuckled. Helen frowned; she had not intended the joke.

'She wanted to know what was happening with John—asked how we were doing and if there was any way she could help.'

'What—like remember us in her fucking prayers?'

The Old Writer dipped his head to meet his spoon.

'Pick the bowl up and drink from it, dear,' Irene intervened. 'I always find that's the best way when I've got a dose of the shakes.'

'I got the impression she's not doing so much praying lately,' continued Helen. 'Seems the rock-star Rasputin's excommunicated her—got cross when she refused to cooperate with the police and prosecution—accused her of being Satan's temptress and debasing his holy mission.'

'Right.'

The Old Writer abandoned the rebellious spoon to bread-sponge his soup instead.

'Glad the boy's campaign of fiery vengeance wasn't totally fucking futile.'

'She wondered if she should write to John in prison,' Helen said and gathered empty bowls. 'I said it couldn't hurt—and I gave her Anthony's number, too, in case he can use her as a witness for the defence.'

'No trial date yet?'

The Old Writer watched his oven-gloved wife extract a sizzling pie-dish from the Aga.

'Anthony says it'll be a couple more weeks until the preliminary hearing. Pre-trial review has to be completed first, or something.'

Helen spooned steaming mush onto plates, set one in front of Irene. 'Be careful, Mum,' she said. 'It's hot and there may be bones.'

'Fish pie is it?'

Irene sniffed and sniggered.

'That's a relief. I was worried that whiff was me.'

'Still no word from Jude?' Helen ignored her mother to ask.

The Old Writer speared a prawn, studied its tiny vibration at the end of his upraised fork. 'No,' he lied. 'Bastard must've forgotten our bloody number.'

'Oh.'

Helen was disappointed.

'The postmark on that letter that came for you this morning looked familiar. I thought it might have been from him.'

'Letter? I didn't see it.'

The Old Writer choked down the rubbery crustacean.

'Can't imagine it was from Jude, though—the oaf can barely scratch his name.'

'He's got a fancy big car, though,' Irene said sharp. 'And his girlfriend's a stunner too. Just because the boy doesn't like books doesn't mean he isn't clever.'

'No, but—'

'But nothing. It gets on my bloody nerves sometimes when you come on all pompous Great Man of Letters—as if stupid words and how you spell them is all that matters in the world.'

'Eat your pie before it gets cold, Mum,' interceded Helen.

Irene was undeflected.

'And it's not as if you've even put pen to paper for ten bloody years or more.'

She jabbed her fork emphatic, Jackson Pollocked the table with a ribbon of cheese sauce.

'Call yourself a writer? How much longer do I have to stay alive to find out what the hell happens in that last wretched Leepus book?'

'What?'

The Old Writer stared surprised.

'You mean you've actually read my stuff?'

'Of course I have. All of them—some of them more than once. My favourite's "Viking Funeral"—with "Badger Boys" a close second. I peed myself laughing at the fishing-trip bit—where Shady Sean spikes Mike the Mope's flask with Viagra—then films him trying to shag the bag of slimy live bloody eels.'

'Shit,' The Old writer said. 'How come you never let on you were such a massive fan?'

'Because your head was already as big as a blimp.'

'Right.'

The Old Writer watched his mother-in-law fiddle with a fishbone that had lodged between plate and gum; he was flattered by her compliment but wary of a sting.

'But you enjoyed them? They made you laugh?'

'Well,' Irene said and narrowed her eye. 'I don't suppose you'll ever be up for a Booker—but, as filthy slapstick trash, I have to admit they poked this old tart in the G-spot.'

'We're eating, Mum,' Helen said with an eye on The Old Writer, as he stood sudden and loomed towards Irene.

'Sorry, dear.'

Irene shrugged.

'But the miserable sod's had a face like an old man's ball-bag on him for bloody months—thought he needed goosing up a bit.'

'Thanks, Irene. Consider me goosed.'

The Old Writer bent, kissed the old woman's powdery cheek.

'And that G-spot line is a perfect quote. Mind if I steal it as a blurb for "Book Thirteen"?'

'Chuffed to bits, I'm sure.'

Irene winked.

'But if you do ever get your finger out and write the thing, you might want to give it a luckier title.'

The Old Writer took his after-dinner coffee to the tower. He wavered between joint and electronic ciggie as he studied the thin envelope addressed to him in a neat faintly Cyrillic script that hinted at Natalya. Still undecided he slit it open. His first examination found nothing inside; but then a king-size Rizla slipped out, fluttered down in a falling-leaf spin to vanish between wall and printer. He took a breath and a mouthful of coffee, grovelled, recovered it to the bright light of his desk-lamp, peered at a faint pencil-scrawl.

Greekforintellectuallyboneidle@cloudmail.co.uk - say hi to me to get in..., he read

Joint, he decided; a fat one. He rolled it while the computer booted, smoked most of it and finished his coffee as he contemplated the riddle. Leepus would have solved it in half the time but eventually he narrowed it down to 'bibliophobic'. Or, he thought again, more likely 'bibblephobic'. He decided to try Jude-speak first, typed the latter option into the mail-account login box.

It took another joint to crack the password. The Old Writer realised only as he entered it that he had been humming it for five minutes. 'hey_jude' was the typographical variation that finally got him in.

Don't be afraid, the song entreated plaintive in his head as he clicked the inbox icon. The words failed to reassure him. He rolled himself another spliff before he opened the solitary email.

Okay. Well done. At least your brain's not totally dope-fucked yet.

So—no time to chat. This is what I need you to do. Bit of a long-shot—but if you do it right it could just take the heat off, or cool things down enough for us to get our arses out of reach.

The flash-drive first—you need to post it (from a random mailbox at least 20 miles away) to D.I. Colin Small at Paddington Green nick, W2. He knows it's coming but not where from—so give it a wipe-down and wear gloves to wrap it. You can't trust a cop not to try to get fucking clever.

Send a separate letter with the password in it— 'bangtofuckinrights'

I know the Leepus inside you is going to make you open the drive, even though there's some fucked-up shit on there it would be best you didn't see. So just so you don't get the wrong idea—the guy on the shitty end of the deal is N's big brother (a piece of shit I have very much shame for - N). The other two are uncles. N and her bro' had a private game running to scam the family business. But bro' fucked up on a side bet and everything went bang. N managed to slide with a pretty good chip-stack and the stuff on the flash-drive for insurance. But the insurance bit didn't work out. Ho fucking hum. So we had to make a sharp exit.

The other thing is a work-tool of Bro's. You need to make it disappear. Bro' may have used it for a couple of dirty jobs it wouldn't be good to get tied to.

So—there it is. A true story of low-life criminal fuck-ups. Right up your bloody street. Stick it in a book if you want to—just change the fucking names, huh?

Love to all, again (N sends her love too—she's typing this in case you hadn't guessed). I feel like a dick for dumping this on you on top of the shit with John. But hey, no choice—and what are fathers for?

Take care

'J the prodigal arse'

PS: Don't reply to this mail. I'll check in a couple of days to see if you got it and then the account is closed. I'll find ways to give you the nod from time to time just to let you know we're cool—so watch out for carrier pigeons and messages in bottles.

PPS: I figured out the bee-wing deal. Nice work, you sly old fuck.

The Old Writer memorised his instructions, logged off, rolled another joint with the riddle-scribbled Rizla. He spilled the tobacco a couple of times before he got it right. The lighter flame was a candle in an anxious wind as he steadied one hand with the other, brought fire to twisted paper, inhaled the evidence.

twenty-three

Bangtofuckinrights was right. Rude Jude had been spot on the money when he predicted that Leepus would insist that his father know the worst; and that once he did, The Old Writer would wish that he did not.

It was still early in the morning. He had not intended to drive so far but the motorway had sucked him into perpetual motion. The Old Writer felt sick and clammy; while workers raced each other to their jobs, his pulse raced blood to his head. He wondered how many of his fellow high-speed travellers had also spent their nights stoned stupid, chilled to their sleepless marrows by a soul-corroding episode of My Big Fat Psychopathic Outrage. In consideration of general road safety, The Old Writer hoped not many.

Cars hissed by. He hissed by cars.

On the radio, babble: the Today Programme's erudite icons of rational reportage cataloguing the mundane global evils that consumed the lives of strangers and their children. Compared to the personalised black horror radiated by the double-bagged isotope of savagery on the seat beside The Old Writer, their schtick was light relief.

He drove another twenty minutes, forced himself to swerve up a random exit ramp. He wished he had another joint to smoke as he prowled a gloomy conurbation in search of a suitable repository for the burdensome responsibility that curdled his anxious bowel.

A flash of familiar red: a hooded scarlet mailbox-owl perched on a suburban-junction post. The Old Writer braked, reversed clumsy into Coppice Close, ground wheel-rims on kerb as he parked opposite the gated drive to what was, a couple of prominent signs suggested, the home of a dedicated neighbourhood watcher. He killed the engine, turned up his collar, pulled on the surgical gloves pillaged from Helen's eldercare hygiene kit, reached for one of the two envelopes next to him on the seat. The file on the flash-drive inside it was CCTV footage; it had been recorded three months earlier if the time-stamp was accurate.

The movie started slow and grainy: silent atmospheric tension anticipating horror.

A split screen: exterior camera shows a shabby brick-constructed shutter-doored industrial unit, a litter-strewn puddled-asphalt forecourt; interior camera shows a dim-lit warehouse, walls lined with stacked boxes stencilled 'Viktory Vodka'.

A sweep of headlights; a white van on the forecourt; its driver – thirty-ish in jeans and bomber jacket – climbs out, crouches to remove a padlock, rolls up the shutter-door, drives the van inside.

Cut: one camera inside the warehouse now; The Driver rolls down the shutter-door; he moves to the off-camera rear doors of the van. A new figure stumbles onscreen, roughly pushed from off: a girl with long dark hair, hoodie and ripped jeans; she huddles, lost in warehouse space.

The Driver lights a cigarette, laughs harsh in the flare of the match; he takes a drag and hands it to her; she smokes with trembling hands.

The Driver rips a vodka bottle from a box, chugs a third of it down; he wipes his mouth with the back of his hand, offers the rest to the girl. She shakes her head, grinds cigarette butt between concrete floor and thin-soled trainer.

The Driver lunges, grabs her nape with one hand; he mauls her crotch with the other. The girl struggles, slaps him; he punches her twice, hard in the face, drags her by the hair to the open door of a breezeblock corner cubicle. He shoves her inside, reaches for a light switch; a bare bulb glares, illuminates a plastic bucket at the end of a stained mattress on the floor.

The Driver holds the girl against the cubicle wall, hand around her throat. She kicks and spits; he punches her in the belly, rips the hoodie off over her head. The Driver claws at the waistband of her jeans, exposes bony hips, tears at thin pants, pushes the girl back onto the mattress, follows her down.

The rape happens mostly out of sight, obscured by the cubicle wall. The Driver kicks for purchase as he thrusts; his foot hits the bucket; it spills a lake of shitty piss across the floor.

The image blanks, restarts, time-stamp advanced fifteen minutes.

The Driver exits the darkened cubicle, zips his fly; he locks the door, locates the vodka bottle, drinks from it again. He sits on a couple of stacked boxes, checks his watch, lights and smokes a cigarette.

A minute or two later he glances up sharp, moves to the shutter door, opens it. A flare of headlights outside; they dim.

Two men duck in under the shutter. One older, not tall but a brick shithouse, as wide as he is high; the other is probably nicknamed Horse-head. The three joke and smoke together, finish off the vodka.

The Driver grins, cuts his head towards the cubicle, hikes his balls with his hand. Horse-head slaps him on the back, pantomimes cunnilingus. Everyone laughs; they chat on convivial for another five minutes or so.

The mood changes sudden. There is fear on The Driver's face; Shithouse jabs a thick accusing finger. Horse-head encircles The Driver from behind, clamps his arms to his sides. Shithouse hits him hard in the gut; The Driver doubles, pukes. Horse-head drops him, flips out an extendable baton, beats him hard on the knees and lower legs. From the silent screaming agony that contorts The Driver's face, it seems likely bones are broken.

Shithouse leans in close, sneers a thin-lipped interrogation. The Driver's blood-snot snivelled answers fail to satisfy; Horse-head shatters his arms.

More questions; more wrong answers. Shithouse nods to Horse-head. Horse-head kneels behind The Driver; he lifts the broken man's head by the hair, puts knee to spine, lays baton across throat, applies crushing pressure to windpipe. The Driver's eyes roll; his heels drum; the paradiddle lasts no longer than five seconds.

Shithouse and Horse-head enjoy post-execution cigarettes and vodka. Refreshment break over, Horse-head fetches plastic sheeting.

The Driver's corpse is bundled, tied, hauled to the van. Horse-head rolls up the shutter door. Shithouse drives the van out into the night.

The camera watches the shutter come down. The screen fades to noise-flecked black. No credits roll; there is no emotional buffer zone, no reassuring interlude between nightmare and cool reason.

The Old Writer screwed his mind's-eye shut, hoped fervent that the film would not loop back and run yet again as he clambered from his car. A curtain twitched in the neighbourhood watcher's window. The Old Writer's rubbery fingers slipped envelope into mailbox. He turned up guilty collar, ducked back into car.

It was personalised action-replays only with which he was afflicted as he cruised in search of another town and mailbox: Rude Jude screaming and thrashing as Horse-head breaks his arms and legs, chokes off his breath, throws his plastic-wrapped corpse into the van over and over again.

By the time the second envelope was consigned to a heritage pillar-box – outside a cottage Post Office, on the with-duck-pond green of a chocolate-box village that might have been in the Cotswolds – The Old Writer was sweating cold and breathing shallow.

Think positive, man, he urged himself – 'No Massive Wind Factory Here' sign mud-spattered as he wheel-span from the verge, scattered a waddle of raucous ducks, hauled his arse for home – that Bad Evil shit must never consume his son. He had to get a hold on this plot. Jude had to survive the story.

'Where have you been?'

Helen's ambush trapped him in the car.

'Why didn't you come to bed last night? Why don't you answer your bloody phone?'

'Forgot to take it with me. Fell asleep in the tower. Woke early—decided to go for a drive,' The Old Writer answered his wife's questions in random order. 'Why?' he asked in return.

'I was worried. You're so bloody erratic lately.'

'Sorry. Didn't mean to be thoughtless. Put it down to stress.'

'You look like shit and you stink of smoke.'

'Stress again.'

'Why are you scrunching your eyes? Have you got another headache?'

'I'm tired,' said The Old Writer. 'Can we go inside now? I need a cup of coffee.'

They sat at the kitchen table. Helen's eyes accused him of crimes unspecified.

'Good coffee,' said The Old Writer. 'Thanks.'

'What's going on?'

Helen had poured one for herself but made no move to drink it.

'There's something you're not saying.'

'It's Jude.'

'I knew it.'

In his head, The Old Writer approved a version of Rude Jude's story redacted for general release. Helen lowered her head and sighed, harrowed her hair with her fingers. 'I tried to phone him this morning,' she looked up and said. 'But his number's not recognised.'

'No. He emailed last night—said something's come up and Natalya and him are going abroad for a while, and they'll be in touch as soon as they're able.'

'Able? Something? What the hell is that supposed to mean?'

'Trouble—knowing Jude.'

The Old writer reached for her hand.

'But there's really nothing we can do. He'll have to play his cards himself, the best way that he can.'

'Christ,' said Helen forceful. 'What's wrong with all our children? They're driving me fucking mental.'

'Defective gene, most likely,' said Vile Viola from the door. 'Probably all that drinking and drugging you feckless hippies indulged in back in the day.'

'Yeah—good times,' The Old Writer said and winked at his daughter. 'But with the benefit of hindsight, we should've balanced all that careless love with a little more contraception.'

Viola winked back, resplendent in laundered chartreuse. 'No use crying over spilt semen,' she said, and then turned to address her mother. 'I thought you'd be ready by now.'

'Ready?'

Helen's disconnection was uncharacteristic.

'You said you'd come with me to that Pilates session at the village hall. I've been psyching myself up for it all morning. Don't tell me you'd forgotten.'

'No—no of course not.'

Helen got up flustered, hurried for the door.

'Just give me a minute to get my tracksuit on. I didn't realise the time.'

'Everything okay with you and Mum, Dad?' Viola asked suspicious. 'She seems a bit distracted.'

'Yeah—she's fine,' The Old Writer reassured her. 'We were just talking about John and Jude.'

'Okay. Good.'

Viola was not certain.

'What about you? You look sort of drained—like you spent the night with a couple of vampires.'

'Thanks. A shower and a nap will sort me out.'

'No more headaches?'

'Not yet.' The Old Writer stood, shepherded Viola to the door. The movement provoked a sudden temple-twinge. 'But make yourself scarce now,' he said. 'Before your fetching DayGlo sportswear induces a terminal migraine.'

He was using the handgun as a hammer to nail down Jude's coffin-lid. Jude stared up at him through a glass panel, rolled his dead eyes in despair. Bang: he hit a nail; the gun went off in his hand. Bang: he hit another; bang; bang; bang. Bullets bounced around the room. One hit him in the head...

The Old Writer lurched awake. He lay for a moment in the half-light, touched fingertips to temple. His skull felt tender but intact; he detected no presence of blood.

A fusillade of dull reports outside started him from the bed. Another Chamber of Commerce stress-relief afternoon hosted at Grange Farm: expensive countryman's apparel donned by middle managers, a thousand pointless shotgun cartridges purchased and consumed to shatter sylvan quietude and coveys of clay pigeons.

The Old Writer was reminded he had his own gun business outstanding. He took a breath to settle the flutter in his stomach, trudged up the tower stair.

Cormac was in the paddock at the archery butts. Perhaps he could sneak past the distracted boy unnoticed, The Old Writer thought as he left the house, big iron heavy against his thigh in cargo-trouser pocket.

'Hey, Granddad,' Cormac called. 'Bet you a tenner I can put three out of five in the bull.'

'Four out of five and you're on.'

The Old Writer swung across the grass with the gait of a stealth gunfighter.

"Kay.'

Cormac nocked his first arrow.

'Start reaching for your wallet.'

The bow was bent and shafts were loosed, five times in less than a minute. Triumphant, Cormac turned with palm extended. 'Pay me,' he demanded.

The Old Writer stared down the range. Three arrows were planted firm in the target's yellow centre, one, a clear miss, in the red. The other one looked borderline; it required closer adjudication. 'Not so fast, lad,' he said. 'You might be paying me.'

'In your dreams,' sneered Cormac. 'Come and bloody see.'

There was a millimetre of doubt. The Old Writer grudged his grandson its benefit, paid up with gruff good grace.

'See, I told you I was good,' said Cormac. 'I reckon I need better kit now. You can get a really cool traditional recurve hunting bow from China for about a hundred quid on eBay—what do you think, Granddad?'

'I think you need to get nine more sucker bets paid off and then you'll be able to buy one.'

'Damn.'

Cormac smirked.

'You're the only rich sucker I know.'

The Old Writer watched him recover his arrows from the target, noticed a sixth one buried half a shaft-length deep in a backstop hay bale, reached to tug it free.

'It's alright—I'll get that one later,' Cormac said hasty but too late, his grandfather already frowning at the evidence of perfidy that tipped the extracted arrow.

'That explains the needle files and broken hacksaw blade, I guess.'

The Old Writer looked down his nose, ran a finger along the edge of the bronze Carthaginian arrowhead the boy had secured to the shaft of an adapted practice arrow, found it razor-sharp. 'Neat job, you devious little bugger,' he said. 'But totally out of order.'

Cormac shuffled guilty.

'I saw a muntjac out here a couple of mornings. I thought I'd practice hunting—in case I had to go outlaw again.'

'Right.'

The Old Writer's own inner-renegade appreciated the temptation.

'But it was too quick for you, I bet.'

'No.'

Cormac rejected the accusation.

'I could've dropped it cold if I'd wanted too—but it seemed cruel if I wasn't hungry, so I decided to let it off.'

'Good decision. Gratuitous slaughter should be left to aristocratic inbreeds and cynical politicians. Killing things is wrong.'

'But it's okay to do it if you're hungry—or if something's trying to kill you?'

'It probably makes the decision easier—but I suspect there're always personal ramifications,' The Old Writer said pompous as, across the fields, shotguns resumed their percussion.

'Rami-what?' asked Cormac.

'Consequences, you ignorant brat,' The Old Writer growled. 'You know what they are, don't you?'

'Yeah.'

Cormac looked glum.

'What I get from my bloody mum if you tell her about that arrow.'

'Right.'

The Old Writer handed the modified projectile to its owner.

'So you might want to consider unilateral disarmament and avoid unpleasant sanctions.'

'Okay.'

Cormac sniffed hope.

'What's 'unilateral', Granddad?'

'Google it,' The Old Writer called back as, hand on lethal weight in pocket, he headed for the gate. 'What's the point of paying for broadband and answering your damn stupid questions myself?'

The Old Writer paused on the motorway bridge, watched the constant vehicular coming and going below: a twin triple-lane parallax of overtaking traffic. Tyre-noise overwhelmed his inner ear. He swayed vertiginous, stepped on for the forest. The gun disturbed his balance; it needed to be gone.

The Old Writer imagined tossing the weapon: its squat weight airborne; a resonant liquid clap as the bottomless black water of Old Razor Mouth's pool absorbed it; a diminishing complexity of ripples lapping leaf-moulded shores as it sank, made safe beyond the reach of light and human mischief.

When the car passed him, The Old Writer was still ten yards short of the hidden start of the path by which he planned to enter the wood. He was already undercover of the trees before he understood why it made his nerves jangle cold and electric. By the time he had fast-walked back to the bridge – adrenaline-tanned scalp shrunk tight to his skull – the old black Mercedes was swinging into his gate. A few yards behind the car, Helen and hi-vis Viola, home from the village hall, with Callum, Carmen and little Christy in tow, collected *en route* from school and playgroup.

The fear; everything he was scared of closing in.

The Old Writer groaned, put on a spurt. It was not quite a full-tilt run but it was as near as he could manage.

His heart galloped across the bridge. Stereophonic traffic-noise phased around his head. His feet slapped the ground. The gun pounded his thigh. Cold sweat trickled from his hairline, prickled into his eyes. A ragged clap of shotguns from across the field applauded the athletic effort that – half a nauseous gasping lifetime later – brought him to the threat-penetrated perimeter of his home.

The Old Writer lurked outside his castle gate. Concealed behind its stone pillar, he sucked air into inadequate lungs. Only when the amoeba-swarm of exhaustion had receded to the periphery of his vision did he risk a snatched glance towards the house.

Shithouse was face to face with Helen. He was too close for Helen's comfort. Helen scowled. Helen wanted Shithouse to leave.

Horse-head squatted and smiled at Carmen. Carmen did not like Horse-head; his smile was not child-friendly.

Viola held Christy on her shoulder. She reached her free hand to recover Carmen, looked towards the caravan for Angie.

Wary, Callum peered around his mother's buttress leg.

Cormac's whereabouts was not apparent.

Dizzy, The Old Writer closed his eyes, leaned back against the solidity of the pillar; the minute abrasions of its stone surface tugged at the hairs of his head. He imagined he was Leepus; how the fuck would his avatar play this one?

Leepus slid sly hand into deep thigh-pocket. He pulled out the loaded pistol, worked the slide and cocked it. Leepus' hand was steady as he re-concealed the weapon, finger on trigger, safety-catch located under thumb.

The Old Writer followed Leepus' cue, took a deep breath, stepped out into the story.

'I don't know where he is—and if I did I wouldn't tell you.'

Helen shoved Shithouse, stiff-arm to solid shoulder.

'So you can just get back in your fucking car and off our prop—'

Shithouse slapped Helen hard. Helen staggered, shocked silent.

'Angie!' Viola yelled, grabbed Carmen and tugged. Horse-head held onto the little girl's arm. His smile widened. He tugged back.

Still unnoticed, The Old Writer edged closer.

Callum snarled his mother's legs. Viola staggered, lumbered into Horse-head with the force of a charging bison. Horse-head cannoned into the side of the car; when he got up he was not smiling.   Horse-head flicked his wrist, snapped-out his extendable baton.

'You fuckin' shits—you're fuckin' dead.'

A voice of raucous fury from the direction of the caravan. All heads turned towards ASBO Angie. She was moving fast in a crouching run, carving knife held low and jutted ugly.

Horse-head stamped on sprawled Viola's arm, re-established his hold on Carmen.

Helen – flushed and wailing incoherent – clawed two-handed at the breezeblock head of Shithouse. Shithouse punched her in the face. Helen went down to her knees. Nose-blood squirted between her clamped fingers.

'No, Irene.' Leepus heard The Old Writer say, as the old lady came around the corner of the house, garden-broom crooked under her arm mediaeval lance-like. She surprised Shithouse as he turned. Her jab came close to taking his eye out; but then his hand was clamped around her neck and her airborne feet kicked helpless.

'Everybody stops still now!' Shithouse said as if he meant it. 'Or I squeeze the head from this old bitch.'

'And the little girl suffers also,' chipped-in smiley Horse-head.

Angie was twenty feet short of her target. She aborted her attack but kept hold of the carving knife.

'And you cunts want fuckin' what, exactly?'

Her chest heaved; her eyes were stab-wounds in her face.

'The thief-bastard called Jude and the money he steals.'

Shithouse lowered Irene, relaxed his grip just enough to allow her to spit on his shirt.

'You tell us where he hides now—or we take the child to help you remember.'

'Shit, man,' Angie hissed tense, as Leepus pulled pistol from pocket, flipped off the safety, levelled it – a little unsteady – at the frowning face of Shithouse.

'You punched my wife, you arsehole.'

Leepus put words in The Old Writer's mouth.

'I may have to kill you for that.'

Shithouse cocked his head, squinted curious at The Old Writer. 'No,' he said. 'You won't do it. Weak men don't kill strong ones.

Put down your stupid gun. Do you think I don't say the truth about how I will kill this old woman?'

The gun was heavy in his outstretched hand. His vision blurred. The Old Writer felt pressure behind his eye. He wanted to capitulate but Leepus was on a roll. 'Kill her, for all I fucking care,' he said. 'She's had her life—she's old and useless now. And we don't even like her.'

A shadow of doubt on the face of Shithouse; his hand tugging at jacket pocket, pulling out a gun.

A stab of pain in The Old Writer's head; a spasm in his arm.

A flash.

A detonation, too loud and close to hear.

Shithouse staggering, blood pissing thick from his leg.

In the corner of The Old Writer's eye: Horse-head, eyes darting, now with knife to Carmen's throat.

Shithead lifting his arm then, saying, 'I kill you, fucker.' His gun-barrel winking black at The Old Writer.

Shoot him again, urged Leepus in The Old Writer's pulsing head. Shoot the bastard now.

But the pistol's weight was planetary; The Old Writer could not lift it.

Time stopped.

He heard Helen scream through gargled blood.

He saw Viola wrestling Horse-head for his knife and for her life.

He saw Angie lunging forward; and Cormac, fifty feet behind her with longbow held outstretched, his other arm bent double, fingers beneath his ear.

An arc of motion in the air: a drone of flying feathers in a burning desert sky.

Shithouse gurgling on his knees, Cormac's arrow through his throat.

The Old Writer felt Angie move beside him. She twisted the gun from his numb hand, moved swift to stand by Shithouse. She fired twice in quick succession, once into his head and once into his heart; and then she stepped over to Horse-head, did the same fucking thing to him.

'Put your dirty hands on *my* little girl—you ugly fuckhead cunt?'

ASBO Angie hawked up phlegm. She ejected a round, slipped magazine from gun and, sphincter-lipped, gobbed thick into the mess of brain that oozed from Horse-head's shattered skull. 'So now you're fuckin' dead,' she said then. 'How do you fuckin' like that?'

twenty-four

The Old Writer and ASBO Angie had left the corpses to cool untouched for an hour. The Old Writer used some of the time to catch her up with the story so far.

'Fuckin' shitbags deserve to be fuckin' dead,' was Angie's succinct comment. 'But that prick Jude is getting his arse well-fuckin'-spanked the next time I fuckin' clock him.'

A shared half-ounce of Angie's tobacco had ameliorated the remainder of the tense hiatus. No police helicopter had appeared above the scene of their domestic violence; no armed-response units had cordoned their OK Corral. No remote negotiators demanded prostrated surrender; no snipers squinted telescopic. Most likely, they decided, the clay pigeon shoot had inoculated concerned-citizen neighbours against alarm at local gunfire; and so the need to engage with law enforcement – and all the complex misery inevitably entailed – was, at least in the short-term, conveniently negated.

It was dark now; Angie wore a hands-free work-light on her forehead. Foot to the face of Shithouse, she pulled Cormac's arrow from his throat, frowned at its dark-glistening Carthaginian head, stuffed it into a crumpled Tesco bag, tossed it to one side. The man's leg-wound was through and through; they would look for the round in daylight, Angie said.

The Old Writer was queasy. His head throbbed dull and his weakened arm tingled; but he took a weird grim pleasure in the poetry of the justice – evoked by CCTV flashback – as he and Angie rolled the corpses onto rough-cut plastic sheeting.

'Hang about,' said Angie as he started on wrapping Horse-head. 'We need to deal with the cunt's fuckin' damp patch.'

She fetched Helen's garden-trowel from the barn, used it to scrape up blood-soaked turf and gravel, dumped this on the sheet with Horse-head, peered and sifted through it.

The Old Writer watched and learned.

'Okay,' said Angie after a few moments probing. She showed him two misshapen slugs of lead on her palm, wrapped them in a tissue, stuffed them in a pocket.

The Old Writer re-engaged his inner Leepus. Possessed of a weird forensic detachment, he scraped up Shithouse's damp patch. With the aid of Angie's headlight he found the bullet that had knocked the back out of the man's skull, but the second one was elusive.

He shrugged, invited expert opinion.

'Let's have a fuckin' butcher's,' Angie said.

She heaved the corpse onto its stomach, and then snapped open a lock-knife, sliced jacket and shirt vertical, spread the cloth agape. Her light illuminated wire-haired shoulders. A naked tattoo-redhead pole-danced Shithouse's spine; a snake writhed up from his arse-crack.

'No exit-wound,' said Angie. 'Let's get the fuckers wrapped-up and in the van. Then we'll have a couple of cans and a sarnie—suss out body-dump tactics.'

The Old Writer left Angie to cover the Merc discrete with a tarpaulin, headed for the house. He puked once on the patio, again on the back doorstep.

Helen and Viola were in the sitting room with Irene and the children. They were all staring at – though not, he suspected, watching – 'In the Night Garden' on CBeebies. The surrealistic HD landscape and wordless squeak of Igglepiggle further unsettled The Old Writer's stomach. He hurried through to the kitchen, threw-up in the sink. He was not the first who had done so, he noticed. There were carrot-chunks in the plughole; he had not eaten carrots.

'What the fuck? said Helen behind him. 'What the fuck have you done?'

'I'm sorry, love.'

The Old Writer reached out gentle to touch his wife's battered face. Helen flinched, slapped his hand away.

'You had a gun. You shot it at that vicious pig while he was holding my mum—and the children were all watching.'

'I'm sorry,' he said weak. 'It just went off in my hand.'

'But you had a fucking *gun*.'

There were tears on Helen's cheeks; they were tears of baffled rage.

'Jude left it in your old beehive. I was going to the forest to throw it in a pond.'

'AAAAAAH!'

Helen swept crocks from counter, collapsed shattered to the floor.

'Leave her, you bloody psychopath.'

Vile Viola shouldered him aside as he stooped to offer comfort.

'If it wasn't for Angie we'd all be dead. And you've made Cormac into a killer.'

The Old Writer turned away in dismayed confusion, walked straight into the tight-fisted blow aimed by Obscene Irene at his balls.

'You said I was too old and useless to live, you prick. You told him none of you liked me.'

'I'm sorry.'

The Old Writer dry-heaved on his knees.

'I—I was just trying to play a bluff.'

'Come on, Granddad.'

Cormac helped him to his feet, led him into the sitting room, sat him in his chair. Huddled on the sofa, the little ones snivelled, eyed him wary.

'Thanks, boy,' The Old Writer said. 'Your arrow saved my stupid arse. Hell of a bloody shot.'

'It was pretty jammy, really—but I couldn't stand there and let that bad-guy shoot you. I didn't really aim it—I just let go of the string and wished.'

Cormac's lips writhed; he trapped the bottom one between his teeth. His shoulders shook. He choked a sob. 'I'm suh-scared, Granddad,' he spluttered as The Old Writer arm-wrapped him tight. 'I killed somebody, didn't I? Now the cops are going to get me—and put me in jail for ever.'

'No, son.'

Angie stepped into the room.

'Your arrow took that bastard down. Just in time, thank fuck. Top shooting, kid—but it was me that put the kill-shot in his brain-box and then did his sick pal too. So if anyone's going to jail for ever, it's going to be fuckin' me.'

'But I don't want you to go to jail,' Cormac moaned. 'What are we going to do?'

'First thing—stop crying and blaming each other for the shit-tank of fucked-up bollocks we all just got fuckin' dunked in. Second—close ranks, stay schtum and cover up, in the best fuckin' army tradition.'

ASBO Angie paused to glare round the circle of stunned faces. With varying degrees of shock and awe, the family stared back.

'And let's get our fuckin' heads up, girls. Those two arse-rags came onto our ground with enemy-intent. We took 'em on and shut 'em down—we should be fuckin' proud of that.'

It was around midnight. The Old Writer sat and smoked behind the wheel of ASBO Angie's Transit. He was parked – unostentatiously, he hoped – amongst fly-tipped household waste, on the unlit redundant access road of the derelict Cheep Chicks Poultry Products site on the eastern boundary of Dismal.

A sick smell permeated the van. Although he knew it was from the adjacent sewage treatment works – the wrapped bodies in the back still too fresh to stink – The Old Writer wound down the window. The night air was cool but it didn't stop him sweating. He opened the ragged road-atlas again, distracted himself with a torch-lit review of their proposed 'scenic' route to the hinterlands of East Anglia. There was less chance of a random traffic-stop if they stayed away from trunk roads, or of number-plate recognition cameras recording their passage in a police database that might be mined for future evidence.

Fuck, The Old Writer cursed inward. How could the average casual murderer get a fair go at avoiding detection oppressed by the illiberal asymmetry of the twenty-first century surveillance state?

A car-alarm wailed sudden. Behind the disused-railway embankment – where a traveller township sprawled, banished beyond the spiteful gaze of citizen taxpayers – gypsy dog's barked and stretched their chains.

A rustle in the undergrowth, a doubled-shadow weaving across the scabbed tarmac between abandoned fridges and sofas, a hand scrabbling at the door: ASBO Angie was in the van before The Old Writer had time to panic.

'Okay, mate. Let's do one.'

She had a can from under the passenger seat, ring pulled and foam-spurt supped, before he had fumbled into reverse.

'And no fuckin' lights, remember—not 'til we're out of the badlands.'

The Old Writer followed her instructions. 'Anyone see you?' he asked.

'Nah—I sparked the alarm from cover with a brick. Those pikey boys'll have that Merc stripped and sold by the time the fuckin' sun's up. I left their phones in the glove box too. Anyone who traces them will likely wish they hadn't.'

'What about the guns?'

'I broke them down. We'll toss the parts off bridges as we go— and the knife and baton too.'

'Just the two corpses to get shot of then—shame they don't have the same scrap-value.'

'Don't worry.'

Angie's eyes flashed sharp in the hand-cupped flare of her lighter.

'They won't go to fuckin' waste.'

'Right.'

The Old Writer took the cigarette she passed him, raised a curious eyebrow.

'So, you ready to unseal the orders now—share our mission objective?'

Angie lit another ciggie for herself.

'Thought you'd appreciate the suspense—as an expert storyteller.'

'Wrong. Writers are control freaks. We get off on omniscience—not having our emotional strings pulled, like simple bloody punters.'

'Tamworths.'

'What?'

'My brother, Frank—he's got a fuckin' farm-full of the hungry bastards. He owes me—so I gave the old boy a yell.'

'You're talking about pigs?'

- 250 -

'The penny teeters on the edge.'

'You're talking about feeding pigs?'

'Ker-ching! The penny drops.'

'You want to feed those two dead men to your brother's fucking pigs?'

'Why not? They're used to eating shit. Besides, it's standard practice, innit—in the body-disposal business?'

'They did it in "Deadwood", and that bullshit London gangster thing—but I always assumed it was just a movie trope. Are you sure they'll really eat a human? What about the bones?'

'Well.'

Angie paused to pop another can.

'We can always put the fucks through the chipper first—but when Frank and me did our bastard dad, they choked down every fuckin' scrap.'

The Old Writer stared at ASBO Angie.

ASBO Angie grinned. 'Steady, mate,' she said as the van-wheels clipped the verge.

The Old Writer gave it going on for thirty dark back-road miles before he followed up. He was already far outside the pale of his experience; how much wilder could it get?

'You told me your father went walkabout—that afternoon of Cormac's birthday, when we were shifting bales.'

'I lied, man. That's what we told anyone who missed him—and that wasn't fuckin' many.'

The Old Writer bit his tongue and drove on. The headlights spread across flat roadside fields of fetid wet cow-bean. He wanted her to tell him; he did not want to ask.

'Felt good to get out of this wilderness of brain-dead fuckin' peasants. Swore I'd never come back.'

ASBO Angie defenestrated an empty can, reached under the seat for another.

'They say it's shit for women and gays in fuckin' Afghan—well they're not short of Taliban round here either, man. Our dad was a fuckin' mullah.'

'He was religious?'

'Not so you'd notice—just naturally repressive and full of ugly hate.'

'What about your mother.'

'Mam never had a chance. She was married to him at seventeen—thirty-two when he killed her. Bastard smacked her when she was pregnant, knocked her down the stairs. She went into spontaneous labour, miscarried and bled-out on the fuckin' kitchen floor.'

'So you and your brother were still just kids.'

'Frank was sixteen. I'd just turned twelve—just old enough to pick up where she left off. At least that was how the old man saw it.'

'Pick up?'

'I wasn't cut out for domestic slavery. I did my best for the sake of Mam, but the fucker always wanted more.'

Angie drained her can.

The Old Writer focused his attention on the road. A steep-banked drain flanked their nearside; mist-skeins fucked with his spatial awareness. 'You don't have to tell me if you don't want to,' he said. 'I think I get the picture.'

'It's all good.'

Angie shrugged.

'The shame's not fuckin' mine.'

'No, it's not.'

'He only got me the first time. Cunt took me by surprise. The next time I had the castrating-knife handy—showed him I was ready to use it and he suddenly wasn't so keen. After that when he got randy, he took it to the sows.'

'But you stayed there on the farm? There was no one you could tell?'

'Nowhere else to go, mate. And I couldn't leave Frank there on his own—not with him being barely sharp enough to fuckin' feed himself. The Old Man would've worked the poor sod to death.'

Angie's reflection in the windscreen grinned as she cocked her head and lit a ciggie.

'Anyhow, if I'd legged it I'd have had to leave school—and the gorgeous student-teacher tart I had the mad fuckin' hots for.'

'Right.'

The Old Writer reached out a hand for the ciggie. The landscape was cold-dawn monochrome now: stunted black trees cowering against a dead grey sky.

'So how long before you killed him?'

'About three years. I was bangin' the teacher by then. Someone fuckin' dobbed us. Cops couldn't get me to confirm it, so there were never any charges—but Maggie got her career trashed, and I got my arse kicked out of school without any fuckin' levels.'

'Your father didn't take it well?'

'It double-fucked the sick bastard's head. He drunk himself into a frenzy one night, dragged me out of the shower and into the fuckin' barn. Frank was already out there, three parts cut as well. The old man told him I was a dirty little sow who needed seeing to—told Frank to get on and do it. Frank said he fuckin' wouldn't. The old man went ballistic—said Frank must be fuckin' queer as well and set about kickin' his brains out. I ran back to the house and fetched the rabbit gun—slotted the evil piece of shit, right in his fuckin' ear-hole.'

'Fuck,' was all The Old Writer could say. Her story was deeply disturbing. He wished he had made it up.

'By morning, the fucker's mortal remains were disappeared-by-pig. It was tense for a couple of months—but there wasn't any comeback. Frank liked pigs. He sorted out the farm. I stuck it out for a few more years until I was sure he was cool—then I met a couple of dyke squaddies out on a bender in a club in Lincoln.

Next thing I'm signed up for five years queen and country, happy as a pig in shit, up to my tits in army fanny.'

The Old Writer was tired. The image Angie planted in his head was literal, not metaphoric. He tried not to but he giggled.

'So, all's well that ends well,' he rallied lame.

Angie leaned forward and pointed. 'Next gate on the fuckin' right,' she said. 'We can talk about endings later.'

The Old Writer breathed acrid smoke. He shivered and leaned on the fence of a field of corrugated-iron pig-huts that reminded him of miniature aircraft hangars. The field was nude of grass. Hot pigs as big as submarines steamed in the chilly air, ploughed black-earth waves with conning-tower snouts.

Close-by in the clapboard shed, a motor growled alive, revved high, and then screamed harsh under sudden load.

The Old Writer had kept it together while Angie and her silent brother dragged the wrapped bodies from van to shed. He had offered Frank his hand to shake; the man had just frowned baffled.

'He's a bit of a shy one,' Angie had said and winked. 'Doesn't mix all that much with humans.'

Angie had cut off the dead men's clothing while Frank donned rubberised work-gloves and a tattered plastic raincoat. Angie had taken the shredded garments outside then, while Frank sharpened a butcher's cleaver. The Old Writer had reached his limit as Angie fuelled the chipper from a can and Frank dragged a corpse over a drain in the concrete floor, went back to fetch the cleaver.

'Here,' Angie had said and passed him the can. 'Take this, mate, and burn their fuckin' clothes and shit.'

Grateful of her consideration, he had done as he was asked. His mind had wandered as he watched the flames take hold. He had thought of military conquest represented filmic: leather-earth scorched, cloth-continents consumed by armies of spreading fire, pocket-trash civilisations ravaged and erased. He had thought about young lovers in some chilly Cold-war Baltic state, of sons conceived in passion, born in love and raised through childish hope. They would be corrupted in adolescence, brutalised as men, and then die depraved in some bleak foreign land, flesh used to fatten pork.

An epic tragedy for sure, The Old Writer had admitted as he retreated to the fence to escape the sound of chopping. But the dead men were dead enemies, and some killer-gene deep within his DNA relished the totality of their destruction.

The chipper revved and screamed and revved and screamed, and so on for another five minutes. And then it was quiet in the shed. The Old Writer risked a quick squint. Frank poured a lumpy pink mush from a plastic fertiliser-sack into the hatch of a trailer-tank; Angie mixed in pig-meal with a shovel. The Old Writer returned to his fence. The pigs' behaviour was different now; their heads were up, their black eyes shone, they snuffled the air and grinned.

The Old Writer lit a cigarette, watched a pair of buzzards circle a copse across the field. A mole of deep discomfort burrowed through his brain.

Another engine fired up in the shed. Frank towed the trailer-tank out with a quad bike. He manoeuvred adjacent to a row of troughs that lined the pig-field fence. The grunting herd came galloping as he hand-pumped human hogwash. The Old Writer turned back to the shed.

'Just a bit of tidying and we're done,' said ASBO Angie.

The Old Writer looked on as she connected jet-washer to power supply, hosed down chipper and concrete. Clouds of water-spray rose and drifted, misted the skin of his face. He flashed on a childhood butcher's shop: cold blood, the sweet sick reek of dead meat thickening in his throat. He was tired and he was lonely; he wanted to talk to Helen but he did not have his phone.

'Cell-phone's are personal trackers,' Angie had said. 'Leave the thing at home, man. We don't want our electronic footprints all over the fuckin' map.'

Home; that was where The Old Writer wished he was right now, waking sweaty and confused, another sordid black-iceberg nightmare melting away in the daylight.

But things were all arse-backwards. His bed was lost in another world. The Old Writer curled up in the van instead, huddled tight and closed his eyes. He counted mental pigs for a while, and then drifted into black.

'Fuck me—it lives.' said ASBO Angie. 'Shift your bloody arse, mate. I need to get at the handbrake.'

The Old Writer forced an eye open; he would have opened the other as well but pain had collapsed his eyeball. His fingernails clawed dashboard vinyl as he hauled his spastic body upright in the seat. 'Uh-unngweh?' he vocalised, mouth stuffed with fattened tongue.

'Truck-stop,' Angie answered intuitive. 'Fancy a bacon sarnie?'

'No thanks.'

The Old Writer ignored the wind-up.

'But I could probably choke down a coffee.'

Diesel exhaust gusted in as Angie climbed from the van. A generator rattled.

The Old Writer prised open his reluctant eye, peered out through the windscreen. Even three-dimensional, the view was not inspiring. They were parked in a cut-off curve of disused road, adapted for use as a lay-by, and then co-opted as a dumpsite for the ubiquitous jetsam of shoddy consumer durables deemed surplus to their requirements by the filthy and fuckwitted natives of England's green and pleasant land. To his left: a discarded condom dangling from a hawthorn; ahead: an artic tailgate, random obscenities scrawled in road dirt.

Presumably there was, obscured from view, a mobile café, too. It would be called Heart-attack Hut or Cholesterol Cabin and be owned by a couple of chubby entrepreneurs sympathetic to the English Defence League.

The Old Writer felt seriously jaded. He spotted Angie's tobacco on the dash, rolled himself a cigarette with the aim of improving his outlook.

The coffee was better than nothing but only just. The Old Writer's hands shook as he drank it.

'Got a touch of the wobbles, mate?' Angie asked rhetorical. 'Combat rush come-down, that is.'

'I guess I'm not cut out for war.'

'I dunno—you didn't do too bad, for a geriatric civilian.'

'Thanks. That means a lot, coming from a stone-cold psychopath like you.'

'Nice.'

Angie fired up the van.

'Shit is easier with practice—but there's always a fuckin' price.'

The van lurched as Angie popped the clutch, bit her lower lip, steered out onto the road. The Old Writer let her get settled into the traffic flow before he spoke again.

'Sorry if I was out of order. I'm a bit beyond my depth. Writing scary stories is different to being in them.'

'Yeah—real life happens on the fly. It's made up by other people. Like being fuckin' army. Shit gets fucked up around you day on day. You keep your head down, deal with it—until it's your turn in the spotlight and it all goes tits-up fuckin' big-time. Boom. Game over—written out of the fuckin' movie.'

'You managed to make it to the credits.'

'Yeah—not so much face-to-face enemy engagement when you're a fuckin' Provost.'

'I still struggle to see you as a cop—even in the army.'

'I signed up to REME—thought they'd teach me to be a mechanic. Didn't work out—got sick of taking crap from thick-as-shit fuckin' squaddies. Got myself transferred to the Provost Branch so I could get my own back. Did good—after a couple of years I was qualified for Special Investigations and Close Protection.'

'And they sent you to Afghanistan.'

'Fuckin' Afghan. That's where it all goes bad.'

'Bad?'

'Yeah—soldiers aren't all heroes. The army's a sociopath-attractor. You take a vicious fuck to a foreign land, give him a gun and tell him it's okay to throw his weight around he thinks it's fuckin' Christmas.'

The Old Writer rolled a cigarette, lit it and passed it to Angie. She took a drag, held it in for twenty seconds before she spoke again.

'Like, a hypothetical—some lads on night patrol might get Taliban sniper contact, take cover in a compound. Next day we get a complaint from the head turban—some farmer and his wife and kid are dead and the word is the kid was raped.'

'Not the best strategy for winning hearts and minds.'

'Ammunition for the anti-war mob too. So brass sends us up to the FOB to make a show of investigation—interrogate the boys involved, do a half-arsed scene-of-crime. We leave it a couple of day's though—give the bad-lads a chance to come up with some justified-force jackanory.'

'I don't suppose they waste the opportunity?'

''Course not—unless they're total fuckin' Muppets. Default army response is 'no further action recommended'. Victims get paid-off with a couple of grand in compo, and it's tea-break over, back on your heads, say no fuckin' more. Burns your fuckin' arsehole, man—but that's how war fuckin' goes.'

'Shit—no wonder you have nightmares.'

'Who told you I had nightmares?'

'Uh—no one. I just assumed you would.'

'Right. Cormac.'

'Kind of pressure you were under is going to fuck up your head, I guess. But you can't blame yourself for shit you can't control.'

'You don't know the whole fuckin' story yet.'

'There's worse?'

'It was the kid that finished me off.'

'The one that was raped? You knew what that was like and—'

'No, mate. Not that one. The one I fuckin' shot.'

The Old Writer glanced at Angie, caught her blinking a tear. He turned back and stared ahead at the road; they were rolling past a deserted village-playground. It had a climbing frame in one corner that reminded him of a scaffold.

'Picture it,' Angie picked up. 'You're on your way back to camp for rations and a shower, rolling past another bunch of mud buildings with no name. The IED detonates a couple of seconds late—blows you into the bastard ditch instead of pink fuckin' mist. The movie goes fuckin' slo-mo HD. Your driver with his leg in tatters trying to reach the radio. You dragging the LMG up the ditch-side, looking for black turbans. You see a shadow in a doorway and everything flashes red—whirls and turns fuckin' black. You wake up in the ambo. There's a hijab outside wailing with a limp kid in her arms. There's a medic standing with her, he's telling the interpreter to tell her sorry but there's nothing he can do, the kid's already dead.'

The Old Writer stared ahead out through the windscreen, tried to think of words appropriate to the situation. None came to mind, so he just stared on in silence until Angie spoke again.

'Last fuckin' nasty straw or something, man. I hear that hijab wailing most times I close my eyes. That's why I finished with the army. That's why I'm a mad hair-trigger bitch and why I like to drink. If I hadn't found Vi and the kids to hang onto, I'd have fuckin' topped myself by now. We're good together, me and your girl—even when we're not.'

'Yeah—Cormac says you fight a lot,' The Old Writer thought aloud. 'It bothers him. He likes you but he's scared you might piss off any day—just like his other useless dads.'

'He's wrong about that. I'm not his other dads. Vi and the kids bring out the best in me—and I like the way that feels.'

'He's wrong about the fighting too?'

'It's not the way he reads it.'

'No?'

'Vi's got her own dark side—says she runs on high-octane emotion. She needs to pick a fight sometimes—provoke a strong reaction. She's a big girl and hard to handle. But it all turns out good in the end.'

'What?'

'Use your imagin—' Angie began but reconsidered. 'But fuck it—you're her dad, man. Fuckin' cancel that.'

'Ah.'

The Old Writer was embarrassed. The sexual peculiarities of others often left him baffled.

'I get it now. Forget I mentioned it.'

They drove an hour in silence. The Old Writer dozed between pokes from his nagging headache. They were fifteen miles from Dismal, a road-sign pointed out, when Angie spoke again.

'It must be weird to spend your life making up stuff about what happens to other people.'

'You think?'

'It's like keeping the world at arm's-length.'

'Maybe. Writer's will tell you they're just trying to make sense of the chaos of human existence—wrestling the mad shit into a frame, making it manageable. But you could say they're just sly shy bastards showing off to make a living.'

'Sounds like a mug's game to me. Like I say, life's not a fuckin' story, is it? It's more like fuckin' war. Just a bunch of random shit that happens. It doesn't have a meaning.'

'Maybe you have to read to the end to get it?'

ASBO Angie coughed and sniffed, rolled down her window and spat. 'There isn't a fuckin' end,' she said. 'The road rolls on forever. You're just on it, and then you're not.'

'But you need to travel hopefully. You need a destination.'

The Old Writer shivered as they came over the hill, looked down on The Village of Idiots.

'There was this old Spanish cartoonist, years ago. We were getting drunk and shooting the shit in a bar in Asturias. I can't remember just what brought it up, but he said that, although when he was young he was happy to live for the moment and take the world as he found it, the older he got the more badly he wanted to stick around to see how it all turned out. Kind of struck a chord with me, you know?'

'Fair enough, mate. One drunk's meaningful insight is another's sentimental old bollocks.'

ASBO Angie swung the Transit through their gate.

'But what the fuck do I know? I'm just fuckin' cannon fodder. You're the general.'

twenty-five

It was all kind of anticlimactic. He almost felt post-coital.

The horror was spent. Life had picked itself up and wobbled on. Everyone had their good days and their dark ones. They were all closer to each other now, and somehow more distant, too.

Violence had bombed their castle, shaken their defences, scorched them with its heat. They had dodged incineration but the world that they inhabited was not a safe one anymore. This vulnerability made them both mutually protective and resentful; at least that was how The Old Writer read the situation.

But no one seemed to blame him – as he certainly blamed himself – for letting coarse Bad Evil come bellowing into their lives. If they did, they kept it hidden. No shrouds were waved, no cold shoulders turned, no accusations muttered. But then he had been holed-up for two weeks in his Tower of Babble: hammering out his angry guilt, dumping the shit on Leepus, trying to make amends.

It was not quite the PokerTart outline he had ad libbed wild onstage – "Book Thirteen" had been mutated by events – but he had the first three chapters of the new story first-drafted now. Spared the nagging numbness of his arm that forced him to type single-handed, he might have managed four.

The Old Writer had been doing okay catching up with the runaway plot, but he had dropped a massive bollock letting Rude Jude and Leepus collude to plunge his family drama into a slapstick fucking bloodbath. Without ASBO Angie's cool hand to pluck it from the carnage, the finale would have been classically tragic. There was no way to re-edit the damage done. He just had to bash on and get ahead; and make damn sure his amoral bastard of a son was banished safe beyond effective range and muzzled from now on.

'So write, damn you,' The Old Writer exhorted Joycean. 'What the hell else are you good for?'

'Give me a minute,' said Helen behind him. 'I need to think about that.'

'Thanks,' said The Old Writer as she put down *maté* and a sandwich. 'Sit for a bit and tell me what's happening out there in the world.'

Helen pulled up a chair; she seemed glad of the invitation. 'Well, since you ask,' she said. 'I had a letter back from John.'

'How's the prisoner holding up?'

'Okay—as far as I can tell. He only managed a couple of lines. Anthony's told him the CPS won't try to prove intent to endanger life if he pleads guilty—but he should expect at least five years.'

'Jesus—the money we're paying that bastard and that's the best he can do?'

'The maximum tariff for aggravated arson is life.'

'Okay—that puts it into perspective.'

'John still won't let us visit, though. Says first he's got to come to terms with letting the family down.'

'Silly sod. Compared to the rest of his male relatives, the boy's a paragon.'

'No comment.'

Helen's lip curled reflexive.

'Any word from Jude?'

'Nothing,' The Old Writer said. 'He's probably making the most of his fugitive life, living it large with the gorgeous Natalya in a beach resort in Tahiti.'

'At least he's not being hunted by her psychotic Lithuanian uncles.'

'Latvian. But it would be nice if he knew what we'd done for him—had a chance to say fucking thanks.'

'No—better he stays away a while. I might bloody kill him myself.'

The Old Writer stood to stretch, ambled to the window. Energetic in the paddock below, Vile Viola engaged in what he imagined must be step aerobics, while ASBO Angie dawdled on the children's swing, offered loyal encouragement intermittent with swigs of lager. 'By the way,' he said.

Helen looked up at him from her chair.

'I talked a bit to Angie—while we were doing what we did.'

'Oh?' Helen said, moved to stand beside him.

'That thing with the bruises that worried you—seems it was more passion than abuse.'

'Really? Okay. I never thought of that.'

She cocked her head wry.

'But I'd have thought you'd be too squeamish to get into that kind of private business.'

'Nothing like a douche of cold blood to wash away inhibition.'

'I suppose not,' Helen said and shivered.

The Old Writer watched his daughter try to touch her toes. 'Is it just my imagination or is Viola losing weight?' he asked by way of distraction.

'She's trying.'

Helen tiptoed to look too. He felt the warmth of her body on his flank.

'She wants to get in shape before they all move to France.'

'France?'

'Apparently a couple of well-off lesbians they know have bought a women-only campsite on the Loire. They were looking for someone to manage it for them and thought of Viola and Angie.'

'An obvious choice.'

'It could be really good for them all—although Cormac's not that thrilled.'

'You can see his point.'

'Viola thinks he's the one who needs to get away the most. He's taken a bit of a turn for the worse since... Well, it preys on his mind, I think. A bit of distance might help him get perspective.'

'Yeah. It'll be weird, though—without them all around. Just you and me and Obscene Irene. At least for a little while.'

'You'll miss Cormac, I know. But you'll have more peace and quiet to concentrate on working—and that'll be good for us all.'

'I know. Sorry. It all went a bit weird and dark for a while there, didn't it? I think perhaps I might have gone just a little bit barmy.'

'Yeah. So what's new?'

Helen smiled tight.

'It's always a nightmare when you can't write. Things get all out of proportion in your head, or something. Stuff eats you up when you can't blurt it out on a page.'

'Yeah. But it'll be okay—now I've got "Book Thirteen" to download the sickness to.'

A buzzard circled low over the field beyond the paddock. It turned sharp over some invisible carrion, wing-flared and dropped out of sight. A hard cold beak hooked behind The Old Writer's eye and tugged. He winced, turned away.

'A letter came for you,' Helen said soft and held his arm. 'It's from the hospital—your follow-up appointment with the neurology consultant, I expect.'

'Right.'

The Old Writer smiled weak, stooped, dry-kissed his wife on her cheek.'

'Perhaps I'll ring them later—when I've finished this next chapter.'

'Okay. I'll leave you to it for now.'

Helen bit her lip, turned to gather crocks.

'Dinner's at six, remember. There's no need to overdo it.'

'Irene?'

The Old Writer nudged open the door of the granny flat.

'It's getting on for seven, love. Are you coming down to eat?'

She was sprawled back in her chair: eyes closed, jaw slack, teeth exposed askew. A photo album lay open across her lap. He stepped in for a closer look. Perhaps she was really gone this time.

'Irene. Wake up.'

He touched a bony knee.

'Leave me,' the old woman gurgled. 'Can't you see I'm trying to die.'

'Plenty of time for that later. Your dinner's getting cold.'

The Old Writer glanced at the album as he slid it from her knees: a nineteen-fifties office Christmas party; Irene, face shining under paper hat, leading a black-and-white conga line, flashing plump-thigh stocking-tops. He laid it closed on her coffee table, reached and took her arm.

'Please,' Irene said plaintive. 'I really am too tired. I shouldn't have hit you in the balls for telling that gangster the truth. I am too old and useless to live—it would've been better if he'd choked me.'

The Old Writer flashed back and sniggered.

Irene prickled. 'What's bleeding funny about that?' she said and shrugged him off.

'Just remembering you galloping into battle, trying to take his eye out with that broom.'

'If I'd had a gun like you did I'd have shot his bollocks off—not just winged him and then stood there with my stupid mouth wide open catching flies.'

'Yeah, well,' The Old Writer defended, stung. 'We can't all be natural-born killers.'

'No. Men aren't what they used to be, that's for bleeding sure. The girls have kicked your arses.'

Irene gritted her teeth, swayed up from her chair.

'Give me your arm to lean on—if you think you can take the strain.'

'You've decided against dying, then?' The Old Writer said as they promenaded to the door.'

'Dying? Who the hell mentioned dying?'

Obscene Irene nail-gouged his arm, hurried him beside her along the evening-shadowed passage.

'Dying's for the weak, boy—and, judging by your pasty face, you'll be mouldering cold in your lonely grave long before I'm even halfway close to giving up my ghost.'

twenty-six

The Old Writer fed the envelope into the slot of the shredder unopened. The shredder stuttered and ate it. The sound recalled Frank's chipper eating bones.

'What are you doing?' Helen asked as she entered the kitchen behind him.

'Just recycling redundant paper.'

'Very conscientious.'

Helen narrowed her eyes.

'Where's that letter from the hospital? I left it on the table.'

'You look different today.'

The Old Writer reached out an arm. His fingers felt fat. They tingled as he touched her hair.

'Is that a new colour you've put on?'

'Must be the grey showing through. I haven't dyed it for weeks.'

Helen turned, stooped to primp in the mirror. Her eyes reflected undeflected.

'So what about the letter?'

'Oh well,' said The Old Writer. 'It's looking nice, whatever.'

'You really are a stupid arse.'

'I know,' he said and held onto her, prevented her from leaving. 'I'm sorry.'

Helen's eyes were moist. She hooked his neck with a sudden arm, pulled his face down to hers, kissed him hard on the lips. 'Bastard,' she said as she let him go, turned and hurried out. 'Sometimes I could fucking kill you.'

Another day in the tower: another chapter of "Book Thirteen". Leepus was co-operative; he showed The Old Writer which threads to pull to unravel the knot in his head. The Old Writer was grateful. He crept to bed in the small hours, calm, content, pain-free.

A cymbal-clash in his head. The Old Writer opened an eye. Ten seconds later, the cymbal clashed again. It was someone outside, he decided after three more metallic percussions. Angie, most likely, loading shit in her van. Now she was shouting, too. 'Bloody selfish bastard,' he cursed and rolled over, dived back down into sleep.

'Get up!'

Helen flung the curtains wide.

'It's ten o'clock in the morning—and there's another problem.'

The caravan looked as if it had been punched by giant fists. Dents pocked its aluminium skin. The glass of its picture window was starred jagged and concaved. Misshapen severed heads of clay littered the ground around it.

'Cormac,' said ASBO Angie, in answer to The Old Writer's raised eyebrow. 'He doesn't want to move to France. Woke us up with an artillery barrage—from that fuckin' old catapult thing.'

The Old Writer followed the cut of her head. 'Trebuchet,' he corrected. 'Good job we didn't build the bloody thing full-size.'

Superseded by longbow and arrow after the frozen-turnip attack, the quarter-scale mediaeval siege-engine – their misguided experimental archaeology project – had been abandoned forgotten to the weeds for getting on for a year. Now it stood proud in the high corner of the paddock, effectively re-commissioned.

'The lad's been a bit weird and arsey since he neck-shot that fuck with his arrow,' said Angie. 'The French deal fuckin' topped it. We had a bit of a row last night. He says no way he's leaving all his mates at school to go and live with a bunch of foreign dykes. Says he'd rather go to jail.'

'Roll me a ciggie,' The Old Writer said. 'Where is he? I'll have a word.'

'No idea. He had it away on his fuckin' toes when I came out after him in my skivvies.'

'Really?'

The Old Writer ran the image through his head.

'There's plenty would pay for a thrill like that.'

'Fuck off.'

Angie smiled, passed him a stiff-finger roll-up.

'So this campsite thing's all sorted? When are you going to leave?'

'He's got a month or two to get his head around it. A job and somewhere for the kids to run wild—opportunity like that's too good for us to pass on, man. Way me and Vi see it, if civilisation's going to go tits-up we might as well be somewhere warm.'

'Sounds good to me. Don't suppose a fucked-up old writer would be welcome with his tent?'

'Not without a fuckin' sex-change.'

The Old Writer and ASBO Angie sat together on the caravan step and smoked. The sun came out but its light was cool, the colour of weak piss.

'Be good if you could fetch him back before I get Vi home with the kids.'

Angie flicked her dog-end.

'You think he's holed-up in those fuckin' woods again?'

'Probably,' said The Old Writer with his eye on the door of the barn. It was open a couple of inches now. He was sure it was shut before.

'By the way,' he added as they stood. 'What happened to that arrow? I remember you wrapping it in that bag—but I lost track of it after that.'

Angie frowned.

'I looked for it the next morning. It wasn't where I'd chucked it—figured you'd tidied it up.'

'Not me.'

The Old Writer stood by as she climbed into the van.

'But don't worry—I think I can probably track it down.'

''Kay,' said ASBO Angie. 'I'll leave it with you and get rolling. I'll get shit if I'm fuckin' late.'

The Old Writer watched the old Transit rattle out through the gate. He gave it a couple of minutes, and then headed for the barn.

'I don't want to come out,' said Cormac. 'I like it here in the dark. Don't try to make me, Granddad. The Evilness might hurt you—and that would be too sick.'

'What Evilness, boy?' The Old Writer said to the igloo of black bin-bags heaped in the far corner of the barn. 'What are you talking about?'

'The Evilness from ancient Carthage—that lives in my bad arrow.'

'Okay.'

The Old Writer sat down awkward on a squashed cardboard box of shoes. The effort required to conquer the assault-course of stored possessions had started his head-throb again. Relocating the light switch had been too much of a challenge, but piss-sunlight seeped through a tiny cobwebbed window. He watched gossamer-snared insect-wings waft delicate in the draughts that crept through its warped frame.

'Are you still out there, Granddad?' said Cormac after a while. 'Sorry about the caravan. I didn't mean to smash it up so much—but I got really angry and once I started I couldn't stop.'

'Yeah—I'm still out here, boy. But it's chilly and uncomfortable. I'd rather be in there with you.'

Cormac thought about it for a while. 'Alright,' he said then. 'The Evilness says that's okay—as long as you come in on your own and we don't have to come out.'

It was snug inside the bin-bag igloo. Of the outrageous world beyond its insulation, only a glimmer intruded. Cormac reclined in the gloom, stared narrow-eyed at the arrowhead, shaft gripped vertical, tight-fisted.

'No!'

The boy twitched it out of reach of his grandfather's fingers.

'Don't touch it, Granddad—or The Evilness will get inside you, too.'

'You think that's what it does?'

'Uncle John had it first. And he went mental, didn't he? And had to go to jail.'

'Yes, but—'

'Soon as I had it more bad stuff started happening around here. Great-granddad Jack died. You got a stroke and got stabbed.'

'True—but it doesn't mean the arrowhead caused it.'

'No one knows how many centuries it was waiting for another chance to kill—lying there buried in the parched desert sands of Zama.'

Cormac turned the arrow in his hands; its bronze head gleamed dull in the glimmer. The boy's dark eyes glittered sympathetic.

'It was thirsty. It made me sharpen it and fit it on a shaft. It made me want to kill things with it—like the muntjac in the paddock.'

The arrowhead trembled as Cormac's hands tensed on its shaft. His tongue-tip flicked over his lip.

'And then The Enemies came. And all that killing happened. And now The Evilness has tasted blood again and it feels like it's trying to tell me it wants to taste some more.'

'Okay, I understand the problem.'

The Old Writer knew enough to recognise a mind in thrall to its story. Cormac's imagination had constructed a deluded but convincing rationale for the dark disturbance of his world, a supernatural caricature of a complexity of emotion. The boy had picked a tough fight. He needed an effective strategy to survive his interior forces; his grandfather would have to suspend his own disbelief, dip into his grandson's story, influence his quest.

'I'm scared, Granddad. The Evilness has got me in its power. It's putting bad thoughts in my head. I keep having really weird dreams. I don't know what to do. I think I'm bloody doomed.'

'Hey—I don't blame you for being freaked,' said The Old Writer. 'Bad spirits are hard to handle. But you're strong enough to stand up to them—and I know a few tricks for lifting curses.'

'Do you? How?'

Hope flickered Cormac's pale face but his voice was doubtful. The Old Writer summoned his most cunning aspect.

'You can't spend your life writing horror stories without learning a bit of magic.'

'Really? Magic—like in Harry Potter?'

'No, boy. Not that bullshit fantasy bollocks.'

'I'm talking about real magic—the kind of magic that works.'

'Okay.'

Cormac swallowed hard.

'Is it going to hurt?'

'There's always a risk,' The Old writer said solemn. But as long as you're brave, and do what I say, I reckon you'll get away with it.'

'Alright, then. I don't suppose I've got much choice.' Cormac pushed aside bin-bags and stood in the gloom of the barn. 'I'll do whatever you say I have to, Granddad,' he said and smiled weak. 'As long as there's none of that pervy naked moonlit-graveyard mad bloody witchy stuff.'

'Damn.'

The Old Writer nudged him towards the door.

'We'll have to go with Plan B.'

twenty-seven

It was an hour before dawn, and wintry. The Old Writer had left Helen in bed, fortified his inner magus with coffee, and then rendezvoused with Cormac outside the kitchen door.

'Okay, mate. You've got your bow and the arrow. Did you write down the stuff like I told you?'

'Yes.'

'All the things that bother you—the bad thoughts The Evilness put in your head?'

'I tried to make it all into a kind of a poem like you said—only I'm not that good at poems.'

Cormac fished folded paper from pocket.

'Perhaps you'd better read it—see if I did it right.'

'No—it's your magic. It'll be stronger if it stays a secret, just between you and the arrow.'

'Okay.'

Cormac tucked the paper away, nibbled nervous at his lip, waited for instruction.

'Let's do it, then,' The Old Writer said and led off for the forest.

They walked to the motorway bridge side by side in silence. Below them as they crossed it: three rumbling lanes of stationary northbound traffic, exhaust-smoke drifting shot with lights; the southbound carriageway vehicle-less, emptily expectant.

'Accident.'

Cormac pointed north to a distant sapphire sparkle.

'Yeah,' The Old Writer concurred. 'Someone's day's gone wrong.'

Cormac leaned over the balustrade, dropped a spit-bomb onto vacant tarmac. The Old Writer turned, looked back at his house for no apparent reason. The sky was lightening cloudless behind it: an eggshell sea of tranquillity sailed across by a flotilla of black gables. A light flicked on in an upstairs window as he watched. Helen getting up, he thought. She would wonder where he was.

'Come on. Let's keep moving, mate—and we'll be back in time for our breakfast.'

'Granddad?' said Cormac a few minutes later, as they ducked through dark trees, intersected cycle path.

'Yes,' The Old Writer replied wary. The boy's tone prefigured supplication.

'You know this thing about moving to France to live on a bloody campsite?'

'I did hear a rumour.'

'Yeah—well I don't want to do it. I want to stay here and live with you and Nan.'

'It's always strange and a bit scary to move on into the unknown—but we don't always have a choice, mate. Some things just have to be done. Maybe you'll feel different when The Evilness is out of your head—decide a change could be cool.'

'You don't want me here. You think I'd just be a nuisance.'
'That's bollocks.'
The Old Writer punched the lad's shoulder.
'You've always been a bloody nuisance—never stopped us wanting you around before though, did it?'
'S'pose not.'
'And it's good your mum and Angie have got a plan for you all—and they're trying to make stuff happen together. You're not still worried she's just going to do one?'
'Not so much. She called me 'son', didn't she—after she'd shot those two men dead? It sounded as if she meant it.'
'Right.'
'But I don't know French. And you won't be there. And—'
'Shut up, now,' The Old Writer said and steered the boy from the path. 'We're coming up to Old Razor Mouth's pool. You need to get your poem out.'
Light crept between bulbous beech trunks, delineated vegetation. The black pool lapped it up without reflection.
'Screw it up and put on there.'
The Old Writer pointed to a waterside rotten log, pulled out his lighter with clumsy fingers.
'It's like an altar, right? Cormac said and crouched. 'And this is a magic place?'
'Yeah.'
The Old Writer folded down stiff beside the boy.
'That's why Old Razor Mouth lives here.'
He tried to flick a flame from the lighter but his thumb had stiffened awkward. The signal required to move it was jammed by the dead-zone in his arm. 'Burn it,' he said, fumbled the lighter to Cormac.
'Shit. It took me ages to write that,' Cormac said but did it.
Flame flared, faded, died; paper writhed and became ash.
'Now get some water from the pool.'
'What in?'
Cormac eyed the deep darkness, doubtful.

'Use your hand,' The Old Writer said. 'Old Razor Mouth won't get you—as long as you move sharpish.'

Cormac stooped and scooped.

'Now drip it on the ashes. That's right.'

The boy dried his hand on his jeans.

'Now what?'

He frowned.

'Is something supposed to happen?'

'Only in the magic realm,' The Old Writer said solemn. 'Now get your arrow out and rub the head in the paste of ashes.'

Cormac did as he was told. The Old Writer felt his leg begin to cramp. He stood, swayed, looked down. There was something wrong with his perspective; the boy crouched tiny on the ground several miles below.

A crackle ripped the air, then. The Old Writer spun around. He expected falling timber but the sound was in his head. 'Ah,' he said, surprised.

'What?'

Cormac loomed up sudden with ash-daubed arrow.

'Okay,' The Old Writer said and refocused on their mission. 'You have to fly solo for the rest.'

'Why?'

'Because some things you can only do on your own. That's just the way it is.'

His temple-throb was much deeper now, colder and more distracting. He gripped Cormac's shoulder for support, pointed a route through the trees.

'You need to find another magic spot. Somewhere you feel comfortable. Somewhere fairly high.'

'Like the old Sanctuary Tree?'

'That's it. When you get there, string up your bow and wait for the sun to rise high enough to get a clear shot—then fire that bloody arrow right at it.'

'Shoot the sun? That's bonkers, Granddad. It's ninety-three million miles away—my best shot's only two-hundred and fifty metres.'

'It's nearer in the magic realm—and you can shoot a lot further too, boy. Just imagine that arrowhead is loaded with every last bad thing and scary thought. Then bend your bow as far as you can and let it go—say goodbye to The Evilness as it disappears forever into that blazing eye of fire.'

Cormac swallowed hard as The Old Writer shoved him off.

'Then you can come home sorted and strong—head up, ready to push on into a future that can be any damn way you want it. And we'll eat Bovril bagels for breakfast, and fix up the caravan.'

'Deal,' Cormac said over his shoulder and went.

There was something weirdly English about the image of the boy – longbow over shoulder, stepping stoic through sun-shafted woods – that evoked surprising emotion.

The Old Writer gulped sudden pride, and then sat down abrupt on the altar log, blinked at the black water. It felt as if something strange had just happened, as if somehow he had slipped sideways, relocated his consciousness in a most peculiar place.

The pool was a mirror of darkness. Its surface was impenetrable. Scattered thoughts skittered across it. He blinked again and saw himself sitting lonely there.

And then there was another: standing tall at his shoulder, smoking insouciant, elegant, composed.

'I suppose you think you're fucking clever,' said Leepus and passed him the joint. 'But what if it all goes wrong—some early-morning hacker knocked off her horse by young Robin's freedom-arrow?'

'Bastard—I'm doing my fucking best.'

'Yeah. And you did such a great job with the rest of "Book Thirteen".'

'Fuck off. You're the one who went AWOL and left me in the shit.'

'I was tired of living your life for you—thought I'd see how you did on your own,' Leepus said and took back the joint.

'I'm doing okay. It could have been worse. There's still time to bring it all together before The End.'

'Is there? Okay, let's run it down. What happens to Jilted John?'

'He gets his head together doing his time in jail. Comes out inspired with a new artistic vision and gets it on with Shy Skye again. In a couple of years he's got enough new work for an exhibition that knocks the art-world's fucking eyes out.'

'Oh.'

Leepus discarded the roach with a flick of his wrist.

'That's nice. I had visions of the poor sod being raped in his cell by a big ugly mental deficient—then getting all weird and dark about it, torching the fuck with a hooch firebomb and pulling another ten years.'

Leepus slid another joint from his top pocket, smoothed it between his long fingers, sparked it into life.

'What about Rude fucking Jude? I suppose him and his *femme fatale* from Riga don't make a dubious fortune and a couple of kids in their South Sea paradise—get dangerously relaxed and decide to go home to show them off to her family? And if they do, her sick cousins will have forgotten all about her dead fucking uncles, of course. They're not going to take savage revenge on your boy—cut his fucking head off, sell his kidneys to a sick rich Russian?'

'Give me that joint.'

'And Vile Viola's heart doesn't give out trying to save happy campers from drowning in a flood when the Loire bursts its banks in a storm? And ASBO Angie can cut it just fine on her own—doesn't drink herself fucking yellow, then lose it one day, bottle a couple of gendarmes and get shot resisting arrest?'

'None of that mad bollocks is going to happen?'

'Okay. It's your story,' said Leepus. 'As far as it fucking goes.'

'Yes,' he said and tried to stand. 'So shut the fuck up now and leave me alone. I need to get home to meet Cormac.'

'Sorry, mate.'

Leepus smiled, kind of sad, plucked the joint from his numb fingers.

'That's not going to happen.'

'Are you sure?'

Shadows of doubt across the ground, now.

'Helen will be waiting for me. I said I'd help her move the old beehive. She wants to extend the rockery, or something.'

'She'll have to manage on her own.'

Leepus' hand rested weightless on his shoulder, cold but not unkind.

'Thing is, you silly arse, your brain-vein burst about three-and-a-half seconds ago—and now you're already dead.'

Leepus waited, blew a smoke-ring, watched him try to take it in.

'What—just like that? You sure?'

'Yeah. Just like that. ASBO Angie was right.'

'Shit.'

'I know. It hardly seems fair. All that desperate creativity. The crazed vicarious shit you put me through, grasping for immortality, fighting your fugue of oblivion-terror. Turns out it was all pointless. It didn't fucking work. The End was always inevitable. And now it's fucking here.'

Leepus in the black water smiling *fait accompli.*

'But...' he groped for effective comeback. 'Fuck you, you smug prick,' was the best that he could manage.

Leepus taking a toke.

'Can't blame you for being bitter, mate.'

Leepus relishing smoke.

'Pretty damn sick headfuck, huh? I go on forever, but you still disappear.'

The Old Writer blinked.

A smoke-snake slithering off.

Fucking Leepus had made himself scarce; and the bastard had taken the joint.

The Old Writer blinked again.

The water rolling black. Something darker beneath its surface.

The Old Writer blinked for the last time.

Beech trees looming curious around him. The wind whispering dead-leaf rumours in their tops.

He looked up. Buzzards circled overhead.

Above them, blue infinity.

For one final dizzy moment everything turned about his axis.

And then The Old Writer lost the plot again, fell backwards off his log.

It was easy.

Dying.

Everything just stopped.

A. William James is the novel writing incarnation of comic book scriptwriter **Jamie Delano**.

Delano admits responsibility for contributing to the development, among others, of such titles as:

CAPTAIN BRITAIN - *Marvel Comics*
NIGHT RAVEN - *Marvel Comics*
HELLBLAZER - *DC Comics*
ANIMAL MAN - *DC Comics*
CROSSED - *Avatar Press*

His original comics work includes:

WORLD WITHOUT END - *DC Comics*
2020 VISIONS - *DC Comics Vertigo*
THE TERRITORY - *Dark Horse Comics*
GHOSTDANCING - *DC Comics Vertigo*
CRUEL AND UNUSUAL (co-written with Tom Peyer) – *DC Comics Vertigo*
OUTLAW NATION - *DC Comics Vertigo*

Cover design: A. William James ©2012